I0778676

THE VAULTS OF LEPANTO

First published London: A. K. Newman and Co., 1814
First Valancourt Books edition 2015

Published by Valancourt Books, Richmond, Virginia
Publisher & Editor: James D. Jenkins
http://www.valancourtbooks.com

All Valancourt Books publications are printed on acid free
paper that meets all ANSI standards for archival quality paper.

ISBN 978-1-934555-10-1 (hardcover)
ISBN 978-1-939140-07-4 (trade paperback)

Set in Dante MT 11/13

PUBLISHER'S NOTE

FROM the 1790s to the 1820s, the Minerva Press, founded by William Lane and later continued by his business partner, Anthony King Newman, was one of the most prolific purveyors of popular fiction in Britain, much of it—but by no means all—in the Gothic mode. Many of the most popular novelists of the day appeared under the Minerva imprint, including Regina Maria Roche, author of the major bestseller *The Children of the Abbey* (1796), Mary Meeke, and Francis Lathom; Minerva also published reprints of earlier 18th-century classics and imports from foreign authors such as Charles Brockden Brown and Pigault-Lebrun. But, perusing the list of Minerva publications today, one finds that the vast majority of them were published anonymously, or may as well have been: many of the authors' names on the title pages, whether actual or pseudonyms, convey nothing to us. They belong to long-forgotten individuals, men and women who have sunk so completely into the mists of time that we often can discover nothing about them— in many cases, even determining a year of birth or death can be an impossible endeavor.

T. R. Tuckett, the author of *The Vaults of Lepanto* (1814)—who never wrote another book, and whose sole Gothic effort survives in only one known copy worldwide, at Germany's Corvey Castle— would have shared the same fate of total oblivion but for the happy fact that Richard Ford, a London bookseller, has listed for sale an item he calls *The MS. Notebook of a Gothic Novelist*. This manuscript book, inscribed by Thomas R. Tuckett, and with entries dating from 1805 to 1822, provides us with at least a few clues concerning this elusive author.

Most significantly, of course, the notebook includes a reference to the present novel: "Sent my Novel entitled 'Urbino', or the 'Vaults of Lepanto', to Newman Minerva Press Leadenhall Street, the fifteenth of February 1813 – and I am to receive an answer in six weeks from the above date." The answer, of course, was that the novel was accepted for publication. Publication notices appeared, somewhat confusingly, in October 1813 and April 1814 in the *Morning Chronicle* and the *Star*, in both cases stating that *The Vaults of Lepanto* "this day was published". The print run must have been a small one: besides the fact that only one copy survives today, we know from the *British Fiction, 1800-1829* website that the book was only stocked at the time by seven of the 22 largest circulating and subscription libraries in the British Isles, and it received only one review, in the *Critical Review* for December 1813, which reads in full:

> We believe that the rage for reading the improbables and the *horrid* and the *horribles* is not yet quite gone by. We therefore felicitate T. R. Tuckett, Esq. on the production of the present performance and conjecture that he has a reasonable chance of paying his printer and publisher and having something over and to spare. For in the work before us there is as much of the *improbables* and the *impossibles* as a romance reader can desire for his heart's content. Most favourable is the taste of the present times for this species of rhodomontade; and if T. R. Tuckett, Esq. finds this to be the case, he may well exclaim 'All's well that ends well.'*

Ford states that Tuckett's notebook concerns itself primarily with two subjects: military records and literary endeavors. With respect to the military entries, we find that Tuckett served in the Buffs during the Peninsular Wars, at one point achieving the rank of Captain. A number of entries also refer to Guernsey, leading Ford to speculate that Tuckett was either a native or was serving there. The literary entries are slightly more interesting, including both Tuckett's own poetry and handwritten copies of his favorite poems by others. Tuckett's verse sometimes touches on Irish subjects ("Green Erin") or American ("Madison's Lamentation"); a note indicates the latter was published in the *Guernsey Star* on Nov. 22, 1814. Regrettably, beyond the few details in Ford's catalogue, I have been unable to unearth any more facts of Tuckett's life. Given that the entries in the journal end in 1822, could he be the Thomas

---

* The review lists the original price of the three volume novel at fifteen shillings and states, oddly, that it was published by Sherwood instead of Newman; the mention of paying his printer is curious too, since the novel's title page does not indicate it to have been self-published (in such cases, it would ordinarily read 'Printed for the Author by A. K. Newman at the Minerva Press' or something similar.

Tuckett of Chudleigh, Devon, who died in 1829 and whose will is held at the Devon Heritage Center? Ultimately, perhaps, the assorted scribblings in Tuckett's journal, like the crumbling manuscripts found in the dank vaults of Lepanto in his novel, will some day lead to more information on his life and ultimate fate.

The text of this edition of *The Vaults of Lepanto* is that of the original three volume edition published at the Minerva Press by A.K. Newman in 1814 (the date given on the title page, though the book was more probably, given the Oct. 1813 advertisements and Dec. 1813 review, issued in late 1813). Regarding the preparation of the text for this edition, a few remarks are necessary. The original text contains many errors; some are attributable no doubt to the typesetter at the Minerva Press, but many are probably the fault of Tuckett, an inexperienced writer. The overuse of commas—common in texts of this period—reaches a level of near absurdity in this novel, particularly in the first volume, with commas appearing virtually everywhere they should not. Words are often misspelled; sometimes these were common variant spellings at the time (pannel, choaked, journied, encrease, etc.), and they pose no barrier to comprehension of the story. Tuckett seems to have had considerable difficulty with the spelling of French and Italian words, and errors like "madmoiselle", "palazza", and "signiora" appear with regularity (though it's worth noting that these mistakes, too, were common in Gothic novels of the period, since it's likely neither the authors nor the compositors working for the printer were particularly proficient in foreign languages), and his spelling in English often isn't much better: "neice", "seige", "lightening", etc. appear throughout. Conjugation of verbs can also be problematic, particularly in the archaic second person singular, so we encounter repeated instances of "thou shall" and "thou will", etc. Curiously, too, Tuckett usually employs what we would consider American spellings of words like honor, labor, and ardor, though even this is not uniform throughout.

Other than a very small number of obvious typesetter's errors, such as a missing opening or closing quotation mark, and an instance of "were" where "where" was clearly intended, the text here presented is the same that was originally published, with the first edition's errors preserved. Why? Why not correct the obvious misspellings like "neice" and clean up some of the punctuation and gramm ar? For several reasons, really: first, it's part of the experience of reading 200-year-old popular fiction—it's also the text readers in 1814 would have read, and the experience they would have had; also, because of the rarity and inaccessibility of the original edition, we preferred to reprint the text as close to verbatim as possible to obviate the need for scholars to go to considerable expense to access the Corvey copy. Finally, there's the question of, when an editor starts making "corrections" or "improvements" to a text, where does it end, and what different impressions does a reader take away? If we correct Tuckett's misspellings of English words, why not his use of foreign words as well? While we're at it, we might as well clean up his punctuation and grammar—and for that matter, a little judicious editing might improve the story in places. But the fact is, Tuckett was a young man, probably of moderate education, writing his first novel, perhaps partly for his own amusement to while away free time while on military service; he was neither a linguist nor an accomplished prose stylist, and it would be dishonest to rewrite the text to turn him into one.

This isn't the place for an extended discussion of the literary merits or faults of the novel. If you're holding this book, you've likely already read Horace Walpole's *The Castle of Otranto* and the novels of Ann Radcliffe, and probably some or many of their imitators, and you know that minor Gothic novels of the period could be silly, awkward, clumsy, imitative, and that this is part of their charm. One final note: though the original title page (reproduced here) gives the title as *The Vaults of Lepanto*, the drop-title at the head of each of the three volumes gives the title as *Urbino; or, The Vaults of Lepanto*. This has been retained in the present edition.

And now I leave you to make your way down into the gloomy subterranean vaults of Lepanto. Turn out the electric lights, light a candle, preferably a flickering taper, and begin your descent . . .

James D. Jenkins
Richmond, Virginia
August 11, 2015

THE
VAULTS OF LEPANTO.

A Romance.

—⁓⊙⁓—

IN THREE VOLUMES.

—⁓⊙⁓—

BY

T. R. TUCKETT, Esq.

Murder most foul, as in the best it is;
But this most foul, strange, and unnatural.
    My hour is almost come,
When I to sulph'rous and tormenting flames
Must render up myself.   SHAKESPEARE.

. . . .

Oh! then at last relent; is there no place
Left for repentance, none for pardon left?
    MILTON.

—▸⊙◂—

VOL. I.

LONDON:

PRINTED AT THE

Minerva-Press,

FOR A. K. NEWMAN AND CO.

LEADENHALL-STREET.

1814.

URBINO;

OR,

The Vaults of Lepanto.

CHAPTER I.

Chill blew the wind as Fernando passed through the winding galleries of the deserted Castello, cautiously feeling his way—no cheering voice was heard, or ray of light seen, to guide his weary steps; the forest was dreary in the extreme; and at that hour of the night not even a star illumined the vast expanse of the Heavens; and fearful of being entangled in the intricacies of the wood, he determined to pass the night within one of the apartments of this lonely place.

However it was necessary for him to return to the court-yard, where he had left, in charge of the horses, his faithful Gaspardo, who breathless with anxiety, waited his beloved master.

Gaspardo was in every respect an honest faithful adherent to Fernando; he was brave and temperate; fearless of danger, but too prudent wantonly to tempt it; nothing could ever sap the invincible attachment he felt towards his master, by whom he was treated more as a friend than a servant:—Fernando, who knew thy amiable qualities—esteemed thee, and revered thy virtues! The youth retraced his steps with as much celerity as the darkness would permit, and found Gaspardo where he had parted from him; to whom he briefly mentioned his determination of remaining in the Castello during the night: some difficulty occurred where their horses could be placed, and after a fruitless search, they were compelled to let them graze in the court at their will, on whatever chance happened to throw in their way.

"This Castello appears," said Fernando, breaking silence, "by its dilapidated state to have been deserted for many years."

"No one," answered Gaspardo, "would conceive it now to be any thing else but the abode of birds of night, banditti, or assassins—Heaven knows! I heartily wish for morning, that we may take our departure; for independant of the badness of our accommodation, we have not any provisions to cheer ourselves with."

Fernando and Gaspardo soon gained an apartment, and being much fatigued by a long day's journey, they stretched themselves on the floor to court the refreshing influence of Somnus; but for some time Fernando could not compose himself, so much was he occupied with the idea of his journey, and the pleasure that awaited him on his arrival at the Conde di Vincenti's: at length however wearied nature overcame the anxiety of his mind, and he sunk into a sound sleep. The faithful Gaspardo had rolled himself in his large cloak, and taken his station close to the door of the apartment, determined to watch over Fernando, lest in this lonely situation they should fall a prey to any designing villains, who might have taken up their residence in this dreary habitation. Some time had elapsed, when Gaspardo thought he heard the sound of voices through the corridor—he listened—it was nothing but the wind—he tried to calm his mind, but in vain—it was no longer supportable—he raised himself up to ascertain the fact, resolved to sell his life dearly in defence of a master, who he loved; when the noise he made in moving, awoke Fernando, who, springing from the floor, enquired eagerly of Gaspardo, if he had occasioned it?

"Be silent I pray you Signior," said Gaspardo, "or we may be lost—for some time I thought I heard footsteps and the sound of voices; therefore feeling anxious to know from what cause it proceeded, I was on the point of going to the door, but the unguarded noise I made has disturbed your rest, which you so much stood in need of."

Scarcely had Gaspardo concluded, when his fears were confirmed, by the heavy tread of persons advancing down the corridor.

"This place, Bernardo, suits our purpose well," said one of the party—"when the business is concluded, you shall further feel the effects of my liberality."

"Rely upon my discretion," answered the person who had been addressed—"all shall be as silent as the grave!—and you freed from your enemies.—"

Nothing more could be distinctly heard, as they moved on, but the dying echoes of their steps.

"Let us," said Fernando, "pursue these ruffians, and extort from them a confession of the guilt, their words import they mean to commit; or let us assist in averting the danger which seems to hover over some unhappy being—alas! even at this moment perhaps some wretched victim is falling beneath their murderous daggers!"

Impelled with the generous desire of staying the assassin's arm, the noble youth, followed by his trusty servant, hastened in the direction the persons were supposed to pass; when his attention was attracted by the loud shutting of a door, within one of the rooms leading from the corridor; Fernando hurried into it, expecting to meet the objects of his pursuit, when beneath the doorway, a warrior, completely clad in armour, with a taper in his hand, struck his astonished sight:—for a moment Fernando remained silent, at a meeting so unexpected, but collecting himself, he demanded, in a firm commanding tone of the warrior; who he was, and what his purpose, in that dreary Castello?

"Seek no further," said the warrior, "depart!—for danger dwells beneath this roof!—pursue thy journey.—"

The figure waved his hand, and instantly disappeared from the view of Fernando.

"Stay one little moment longer!" cried the youth, "O! stranger, and explain, what dreadful mystery remains concealed beneath these mutilated walls?—or teach me rather how to lend my ready aid, in succouring virtue in distress; for even though my arm be vigorously opposed; I have a shield of adamant within my breast—a feeling heart, and mind untainted.—"

"No more delay!"—replied the now invisible stranger, "I am thy friend—we soon shall meet again!"

"Even let the threatened danger come," exclaimed the youth passionately, "I will brave it all!—Fernando will never, like a coward, fly from whence his honour bids him stay!—"

"Signior," said Gaspardo, who had remained silent, near Fernando, "remember we have not to deal openly and fairly with an honorable foe, but with nothing else than a set of rogues and assassins, who would cut our throats in the dark in preference to any other mode, as being the most secure way of saving their own; therefore had we not better take the advice of this strange acquaintance, and go directly."

At the conclusion of this, the stranger's voice echoed back—"*go directly!*"

"Ah!" continued Gaspardo, "we are again directed to depart—do, my dear master, let me lead the way to the court-yard, and seek for our horses, for the sun begins to peep above the lofty wood!"

With slow and measured, but reluctant steps, Fernando suffered his servant to conduct him through the corridor into the court-yard, where their horses were grazing on the grass and weeds, which grew between the pavement.

"Poor animals," said Fernando, "you have passed a miserable night, without food or covering."

"I hope Signior," said Gaspardo, "that we shall soon reach some cottage to refresh them as well as ourselves—but this forest seems to be of a most dreary length, for in passing through the corridor, nothing struck my eye but the branches of trees, casting a gloomy shade around."

"Be quick," said Fernando, with an unusual degree of petulance, "be quick and let us mount—no doubt some cottage or village must be near this."

Gaspardo held his master's horse as he vaulted into his seat, and following his example they proceeded at a brisk rate through the wood; onward they journied for a considerable time, each wrapt in his own disturbed thoughts, respecting the occurrences of the night, when they discovered an humble cottage in the vale beneath, nearly hid by a thick grove of trees which surrounded it; thither they bent their course, and with some difficulty succeeded in reaching the lowly roof. Fernando knocked at the door, when he was answered, by a female voice, requesting to know who was there and what their business?

"One Signiora," replied Fernando, "who wishes to be permitted to rest a few hours, having lost his road, and been obliged to pass the night in the forest, therefore prays you would allow him to enter, that he might seek repose."

"Yes, Heaven bless you Signior, and welcome!" answered the voice which had before been heard.

An old woman opened the door to the strangers, and directed them to take their horses round to the back of the cottage, where they would find stabling and fodder for them.

"Gratefully I thank you," replied Fernando, (with that graceful and winning air, which conciliates and gains the respect and esteem of every one) as he moved off with Gaspardo to put up their wearied horses in a place of quiet and security. Having done every thing for the fatigued animals that was necessary, they returned to the cottage, where they found Theresa, which was the name of the old woman, who had spoken to them, busily employed in laying out the table to the best advantage—fruit, milk, bread and light wine covered the hospitable board.

"Lord bless you, Signior!" said the garrulous Theresa, "you must have passed a dreadful night in the forest—I am sure I would not have stayed there for the world."

Fernando seated himself, and at the entreaty of the old woman partook of some of the food placed before him.

"Who does this romantic cottage belong to?" enquired Fernando, after a long silence.

"Sanguinario lives here Signior," replied Theresa, "when the Duca di Urbino does not require him at the Castello; he went from hence yesterday morning, and I have not seen him since; but that is not at all extraordinary, as he is sometimes away for weeks together—God knows where! for he never informs me where he is going,—and seldom speaks, and then but to use gross language to me."

"Know you," said Fernando, "the name of the old Castello, that stands in the forest, some distance from hence?"

"Yes, Signior, it is the Castello di Lepanto—many years have passed since it was inhabited—the Duca di Urbino owns it, but it has entirely gone to decay.—Ah! there have been sad doings—but it is not right for me to speak, and before strangers—if Sanguinario knew I had said so much I should lead a terrible life."

"Why do you remain with him, since he is so morose as you represent him?" said Fernando.

"What can a poor woman do, Signior?—I was a vassal to the Marchese di Lepanto, and when he died (God rest his soul in peace!) the Castello came to the Duca di Urbino, and he sent me here to take charge of this place, and all my friends are gone to a better world!"

"How long has the Duca di Urbino been in possession of these domains?" enquired Fernando.

"It is now one and twenty years since the Marchese di Lepanto was brought home, covered with wounds, and quite insensible, no one could find out how he came by them—and all that ever was made known respecting the business, was, that some people passing through the forest, picked him up in that state—he had been to visit a Marchese, whose Castello is some day's journey from hence, and I believe something of a relation—it is supposed he was waylaid by banditti, but resisting them, they were induced to slay him—he had only one servant with him, who has never been heard of.—The present Duca at first wished to throw all the odium on him, but the character of Rhinaldo was too good to be blackened, and no one believed a word of it. The late Marchese had only one son, and a daughter, who was stolen from the Castello when a baby in arms.— The young Marchese was about three years old when his father was killed in the forest—the Marchesa doated on him—but poor sweet lady she took her husband's death so much to heart, that in a week after she followed him to an untimely grave, leaving her helpless babe to the mercy of an unfeeling relative!—Oh! Signior, indeed it is a piteous tale. The Duca di Urbino took the young Marchese to his Castello, and about a year after he disappeared—from that day to this he has never been heard of—the report was, that Sanguinario, who always attended on him, had walked out with him and his nurse, when he was attacked and wounded; report further says, the child suffered in the fray, and Jacquelina hardly escaped with her life.—O, Jesu!—God only knows the truth! But, Signior, had you not better take some rest?"

Fernando had for some time finished his meal, he therefore accepted Theresa's offer, though he hardly knew how to quit his seat, so strongly did he feel himself interested in the tale Theresa had been relating; yet he did not think it just to take advantage of the old woman's loquacity, and pry too much into her secrets.

Fernando was shewn into a comfortable apartment, and without undressing, threw himself upon the bed, and soon sunk into repose.

CHAPTER II.

Fernando, after having slept a few hours, awoke perfectly refreshed, and descended to the apartment, where he had partaken of Theresa's hospitality:—to his enquiries after Gaspardo, he was informed, that he was in the stable attending the horses.

"Bless me, Signior," said Theresa suddenly, "here comes Sanguinario; I declare he looks more ferocious than ever!—I tremble for you, Signior.—"

"Do not alarm yourself on my account," replied Fernando, "but I am sorry, lest you might meet with ill treatment through your kindness in admitting me within the cottage."

"No, Signior," answered Theresa, "let the consequence be what it will, the weary traveller, shall never be turned from the door, whilst I can offer him shelter, or lend a helping hand to administer to his wants."

"Thy sentiments," replied Fernando, "my worthy Theresa, are the spontaneous flowings of a generous heart unhackneyed in the vices of the world, and happy would it be, if many in a superior station of life possessed such virtuous principles and humanity."

Scarcely had he ceased speaking, when Sanguinario entered; at seeing a stranger in the cottage, he started back, throwing his large cloak around him, even so as partly to conceal his face with the hood; this was not so rapidly done, but that Fernando perceived he was armed—casting a penetrating look around, he seated himself, without taking any notice of Fernando, and desired Theresa to bring him refreshment, of which he began to eat heartily; but Gaspardo, at that instant making his appearance, he quickly sprang up and placed his hand under his cloak as if to grasp his sword—Fernando, who had never taken his eyes off the figure of Sanguinario, observed the action, and interposing, told him it was his domestic, who, with himself, had sought a refuge in the cottage for a few hours, having spent the night in an old Castello, not far from thence.

"The Castello in the forest, Signior?" enquired Sanguinario.

"The same," answered Fernando.

"It is a gloomy pile," said Sanguinario, "and, as report says, infested with a cruel and savage banditti—you are one of Fortune's favorites, Signior, to have escaped; many have not been so lucky as yourself—felt you not terrified at the lonely situation you were placed in?"

"A good conscience need not fear," replied Fernando, "and being confident in the courage and fidelity of my domestic, who would never desert me, I therefore dreaded not any attack that might have been made on me."

"Whilst I have breath, my honored master," said Gaspardo, "never will I leave you in the hour of danger, and whilst our consciences are clear, we need not care for the savage banditti who inhabit the Castello, and infest the surrounding forest." At the concluding part, Gaspardo cast a sharp and penetrating glance at Sanguinario.

"You are bold," said Sanguinario in a harsh discordant voice, and with a tone full of significant meaning, added, "and perhaps may rue this bravado 'ere long."

"Whenever the period arrives that is to prove my fidelity and courage," answered Gaspardo; "if you or any one should tempt it, it will be found that I am no braggart."

Fernando, fearing his servant might encrease the tempest, which he saw gathering on Sanguinario's brow, desired him to prepare the horses, that they might depart.

Gaspardo left the room to obey the orders of his master.

"What rout do you take, Signior?" demanded Sanguinario.

"That which leads to Ravenna," answered Fernando.

A mutual silence then ensued, each busied with his thoughts, until the horses coming to the door, roused Fernando from his revery, when kindly bidding the hospitable Theresa farewell, he mounted his horse, without taking notice of Sanguinario, and gently moved off from the door.

"We shall meet again," muttered Sanguinario to Gaspardo, as he was preparing to follow, "when you least expect it—beware, when the hour arrives!"

"I know thy calling well," replied Gaspardo—"until we meet again farewell;" and spurring his horse, was close up with Fernando in a few minutes.

The last words of Gaspardo sunk deep in the mind of Sanguinario; he had not been in the habit of being treated thus cavalierly,
which rousing the passions of his depraved mind, were ready to
burst forth: it was with difficulty he restrained himself from plunging his murderous steel into the breast of Gaspardo, whilst in the
cottage, but the presence of Fernando restrained him. For though
Sanguinario was bold and cruel, yet he possessed all the caution
and cunning so necessary to complete the formation of an accomplished villain; and saw from the fine manly form of Fernando, that
he was not an antagonist to be despised—no, in his mind's eye he
planned a surer mode of vengeance.—It was not ten minutes' ride
to Bernardo: they were both acquainted with all the intricate paths
of the forest, therefore there would be no difficulty in overtaking
the travellers, and with little assistance to overcome them. "By
Heavens!" exclaimed he, vehemently, "it shall be done!—ye reach
not Ravenna this night!—your doom is fixed—ye die within these
two hours!"—His dark eyes scowled beneath his long bushy eye-
brows; his features were convulsed with all the various contending
passions of a vicious mind: and his tall muscular figure gave him the
appearance of a dæmon, more than a human being.

Whenever Sanguinario formed a resolution, no earthly power
could turn him from his purpose—Gaspardo had offended him and
treated him with contempt; it was impossible to brook the insolence of a menial.—What! could that Sanguinario, who had made
many tremble before him, be obliged to submit without revenge?—
The countenance of Fernando had brought back gloomy reflections to his memory; and his firm resolve was, that he and Gaspardo
should die!—He, Sanguinario, would destroy them, even though
he sought them to the extremity of the earth, his hate and vengeance should pursue them!

Fernando journeyed at a quiet pace, ruminating on the different
occurrences, which had taken place in so short a period.—The mysterious expressions he had heard from the unknown persons, passing down the corridor, whilst at the ruined Castello—the warning
he received from the warrior; and the extraordinary tale, that Theresa related respecting the total extinction of the Lepanto family; all
tended to raise doubts and unpleasant reflections in his mind.

That Sanguinario, was in some way implicated in all these horrid transactions, he almost felt convinced; yet, it was unjust to attach the stigma of guilt on a man, because he possessed a rugged exterior and uncourtly manner: but that the Castello had been the scene of some dark and bloody deed, that was never meant to meet the prying eye of mortal, was in his mind beyond a doubt. The more he thought the more he was lost in a labyrinth of vague conjecture.

Fernando had suddenly altered his plan, with respect to the rout he intended taking: it had been his original intention to have travelled slowly, that he might have enjoyed the beautiful scenery, with which the country every where abounded; but from the harrassed state he found himself in, he resolved to proceed directly to Ravenna, and from thence embark for Venice, whither he was going to pass some time with his friend Alberto.

Fernando calculated, that he could with ease, reach Ravenna that evening, and intended not to lose one moment in embarking, and ending his journey as speedily as possible.

"Gaspardo," said Fernando, motioning to him to approach nearer, "what think you of our late host, Sanguinario?"

"Why, Signior," replied Gaspardo, "I must confess, I do not much like his appearance; he seems ferocious, and I am much mistaken if he be not a deep villain."

"I agree with you, Gaspardo," said Fernando; "his features, at least the little I could see of them, were not very prepossessing; and much I dread, that he is leagued with the banditti, through whose merciless hands it appears we have escaped."

"Be not, Signior, too secure on that head," replied Gaspardo; "we have not yet passed the whole of the forest, and it is impossible to foresee what may happen."

"What mean you?" quickly enquired Fernando—"know you any thing of Sanguinario—or what do your words imply?"

"Nothing more, Signior," answered Gaspardo, "than that I have formed a bad opinion of him, and until we get beyond the precincts of this wood, I cannot think we are safe from his wiles."

Hardly had Gaspardo ended his remark, when their attention was roused by the clattering of horses' hoofs near them, and on suddenly turning an angle of the road, they perceived four horsemen emerge from among the trees, who, wheeling, rode rapidly towards our travellers; Fernando, with his faithful Gaspardo, immediately placed themselves in a posture of defence, which they had scarcely time to effect, before the horsemen, who were evidently banditti, from the menacing attitude in which they placed themselves, attacked them without speaking a word. Vigourously were these lawless depredators opposed by our hero and his domestic, though contending against superior numbers.—Fierce indeed was the conflict; the light breast plate Fernando wore, was pierced in several places, and his helmet nearly cut asunder, but his native courage, herculean strength, and great science in the art of defence, triumphed over every disadvantage, which he laboured under in fighting with such odds against him; but just as he had laid one of the villains low, and was himself most desperately pressed, an unknown rushed from the thicket, and placing himself by the side of Fernando, the banditti were soon compelled to seek their safety in a precipitate flight.

Fernando, full of gratitude, turned to the stranger to thank him for his timely aid, request his name, and seek his friendship, for having rendered him so essential a service, as the preservation of his life.

But 'ere the words could pass his lips, the unknown waved his hand, as if to demand silence, and with a firm impressive voice, thus spoke—"Hasten quickly! hasten from this place of danger, and join your friend Alberto!"—then spurring his fleet courser, was soon lost among the intervening trees.

Mute with astonishment, Fernando, remained the picture of surprise, straining his eyes to catch another glimpse of the person of the stranger.

"This is most wonderous!" at length exclaimed he, "it can be no other than the warrior, who so strongly urged me to quit the ruined Castello—he seems to take a lively interest in my fate—I will follow his advice, and leave this place, which seems replete with villany and danger."

Gaspardo cast a scrutinizing look on the corpse of the miserable ruffian, who had fallen beneath the sword of Fernando; but his master putting his horse into a gallop, prevented him from making any remark; and they soon had the satisfaction of finding themselves in Ravenna. As soon as Fernando had taken some refreshment, he engaged a vessel to convey him the next morning to Venice; therefore he retired early to rest, where we will permit him to enjoy that tranquillity, which his agitated spirits so much required.

CHAPTER III.

THE Condi di Vincenti, to whose Palazza, at Venice, Fernando was now journeying, had been brought up from his infancy, on terms of the most social intercourse and friendship with the Marchese Durazzo: he was a man of the world, and fond of mixing in the gay circles, which his rank and fortune entitled him to; the better therefore to enjoy the pleasures of society, he chiefly resided at Venice, where he had a splendid Palazza.

The Condi married, while a young man, a lovely and accomplished woman, who, three years after their union, left him a widower, with two children, one a boy, called Alberto, the other a girl, named Rosara. Severely was the loss of this amiable young woman felt by her adoring husband, who, awfully impressed with the situation of his helpless children, clasped them to his sorrowing bosom, and vowed never to withdraw from them the fostering care of a fond parent. He formed the pleasing idea of rearing his children in the paths of virtue, and of moulding their tender minds, to emulate the worthy actions of their forefathers: to the accomplishment of this purpose, he placed the young Rosara in one of the most respectable convents in Venice; and procured every master, that was necessary to assist in the education of his son. His intention was, to take Rosara from the convent at the age of sixteen, that she might, early, have the advantage of polishing her manners, which the gloom and seclusion of a convent too frequently cause to be reserved and repulsive.

As Alberto and his sister grew up, their friendship became cemented by the strongest ties of mutual affection and esteem; scarcely a day passed, that Alberto did not fly to the convent as soon as his studies were over, to see his dear sister, Rosara—their minds were congenial, and each was the pride of the other, and both the admiration and idol of their father, who most scrupulously fulfilled the duties of a parent.

At the time proposed, the Condi took Rosara from the convent, in which she had been educated, to reside with him at the Palazza; and shortly after introduced her to all his numerous and fashionable acquaintances, Signiora Luzia, being her chaperon. This lady was related to the Condi, and consented to take up her abode at the Palazza, that she might offer her assistance in presenting to the world the lovely Rosara; all the graces were united in this amiable girl; all the attractions that beauty and virtue could bestow, ornamented the young Rosara—her fine black hair waved in ringlets over her polished forehead, and her soft blue eyes, beaming benificence, gave to her expressive countenance a dignity, combined with timid modesty;—such was the lovely daughter of the Condi di Vincenti.

About a year after the introduction of Rosara to the world, the Condi received a pressing invitation from his old friend, the Marchese Durazzo, to pass a few months with him at his Castello, and requested that his son, Alberto, might accompany him, as he had not seen him for several years: to this the Condi readily acquiesced, leaving his daughter with the Signiora Luzia, who tenderly loved her, and on whose discretion he could safely rely.

Alberto had entered his twentieth year, and his father deemed it necessary to dismiss his masters. Never had Venice known a more accomplished cavaliero; Nature had given Alberto every advantage that could be wished for; his figure, robust, but graceful; his hair, dark; and his fine black eyes gave to the contour of his countenance an expressive intelligence; in disposition, lively, gay and volatile; an enthusiast in his friendship, and ardent in every thing he undertook. His society was universally sought after, and all were happy in ranking themselves of the number of this amiable young nobleman's acquaintance.

The Condi and his son, after taking an affectionate farewell of Rosara, set off on their intended journey, which they performed much to their satisfaction, and had the heart-felt gratification of being greeted with every testimony of friendship and hospitality by the Marchese Durazzo, who immediately after the first salutation, introduced Fernando to the Condi and Alberto.

On the Marchese retiring with the Condi, Fernando conducted Alberto to his apartment, and offered all those little attentions which spring from a generous and noble mind. The two youths in a few days began to appreciate the merits of each other, and the basis of a lasting friendship was soon formed, which ripened with their maturer years.

The young men amused themselves with reading, sporting and fencing; or occasionally rambling to admire the beauties of the surrounding country. In these excursions, Alberto always dwelt on the virtues and excellent qualifications of his amiable sister; his tongue never appeared wearied in dwelling on this delightful theme, and Fernando listening with mute attention, would often wish that he knew the bewitching object.

At length the time drew near when the two friends were to separate; but in consequence of letters, which the Condi received, requiring his presence in Venice, he was obliged to hurry his departure sooner than he intended from the Castello of Durazzo.

Alberto requested the Marchese to permit Fernando, shortly to visit him, which being strongly seconded by the Condi, who was extremely partial to Fernando, it was agreed he should join them in Venice, in the space of a few months; after many promises of strictly corresponding, the Condi and Alberto took their leave, and arrived in safety at the Palazza, where he had the supreme happiness of clasping his child again to his bosom, who had in his partial eye improved equally in beauty as in accomplishments. The good Signiora, shared the warm embraces of the Condi, who showered down thanks on her for the attention she had bestowed on Rosara during his absence. The Condi and Alberto retired early to their apartments, feeling themselves fatigued from the oppressive heat of the sun, which they had been exposed to during the whole of a long day's journey.

The Condi had not mentioned a word to Alberto respecting the purport of the letters he received at the Castello di Durazzo, which rather surprised him, as his father was accustomed to repose great confidence in him, and treated him more on the footing of a familiar friend than as his son. This circumstance gave Alberto a little uneasiness, as he dreaded lest there might be some unpleasant intelligence, which his father, out of respect to his feelings, had withheld from him. Reflection soon restored his usual serenity, and recommending himself to his Maker, he sunk quietly to rest.

Alberto the next morning arose invigorated by the refreshing sleep he had enjoyed, and dressing himself he went in quest of Rosara, that he might have an opportunity of talking over the different events which had happened during his absence, and in turn receive her confidence; but to his mortification, he found she had not yet left her chamber, and the Condi meeting him, they entered into conversation until breakfast was announced; as soon as the repast was ended, the Condi desired Alberto and Rosara to attend him in the library; having entered the room and seated themselves, he in a mild tone thus addressed them:—

"Alberto and Rosara, my children, I believe from your infancy, you have never known me sparing of my fortune, or my labors, to gratify your every wish, and form you, (as you are) brilliant ornaments to society.

"I have in every respect tried by my conduct towards you, to lessen the irreparable loss you sustained, by the early fate of your invaluable and lamented mother. I do not intend by harshness to enforce my wishes, as your happiness is my chief object; but it is my duty to point out, what is necessary and advantageous to your future prospects in life.—Thus far have your days glided on in sweet serenity and peace, and it is my fervent prayer that they may so continue to pass, until, weighed down with years, you sink into the silent tomb!—But, my children, you well know, that each one is ordained by Nature to fill some peculiar station on the great theatre of life, or else we become useless members, and a pest to society.

"To you Rosara, I now particularly address myself.—The Duca di Urbino, a nobleman of great wealth and connexions, (who has not for some time visited Venice, having chiefly resided at his Castello, therefore, probably, you have not heard his name frequently mentioned) has made the most handsome and flattering proposals to lead you to the altar."

"For Heaven's sake, my dear father!" scarcely articulated the agitated girl.

"Hold one moment, my Rosara, until you have heard me:—it is very far from my intention to compel you to this union, or bias your inclination in the choice of a husband, so long as he is suitable to your rank in society; I am also well aware of the delicacy of the subject to a young and innocent mind, but it was to be expected, that you should look forward to some future establishment; I request you will consider carefully the Duca's proposals; and on being acquainted with him, I doubt not but he will be so agreeable to you, that you will cheerfully accede to my wishes in this instance: to night the Duca will be here, for the purpose of being formally introduced to you; I have already given him every reason to suppose, that he will be well received by you, and let me not be disappointed."

"To receive him well, and to night too! indeed my father, this is a wretched hour for the unhappy Rosara; how can I refuse to do what you require of me? and yet by yielding I commit that which is repugnant to my feelings."

"Do not alarm yourself," said the Condi, "I promise you not to dispose of your hand, unless the Duca be pleasing to you—but mark me, Rosara, you must give some powerful motive for your refusal—the Duca di Urbino, is a nobleman, insinuating in his manners, and as I believe, unexceptionable in every point of view."

"Pray permit me to retire, my dear sir," said Rosara, "as my spirits are at present too much agitated to enter any further on the subject; but I will do all I can, to receive the Duca di Urbino, so as to merit your approbation."

"This indeed is being a good girl, you are ever my own Rosara," said the Condi, as he kissed her cheek, and led her to the door.

With a mind, filled with various contending emotions, Rosara sought the apartment of Signiora Luzia, and briefly related, to that worthy old lady, what had passed between herself and her father in the library.

To the different questions Rosara asked of the Signora, respecting the Duca di Urbino, she could gain no satisfactory reply, except that he was rich and powerful, but that he must have passed the zenith of his youth. The idea became still more abhorrent to her, at being united to a man, with whom there must be a great disparity of years; and it seemed almost impossible to her, that she could ever give her hand to the Duca di Urbino, even though she should forfeit the affection of her father.—Though mild and docile, Rosara possessed great firmness, when it was necessary to bring the energies of her mind into action, and though she sincerely loved her father, yet this was a point on which her own happiness entirely depended;

therefore she determined, if the Duca was not a man to whom she could give her heart, she never would her hand.

Alberto remained confounded at so unexpected a subject being entered into; but as soon as Rosara left the room, and he recovered himself a little, he addressed the Condi by asking him how long he had known the Duca di Urbino?

"I was never personally known to him," said the Condi, "until a few weeks previous to our journey to the Marchese Durazzo, and while there the Duca di Urbino did me the honor to propose this intended alliance, and conceiving it to be a matter of too much consequence to Rosara's establishment in life, I hastened my return to Venice."

"Then, sir, the letters," enquired Alberto, "that called you so suddenly back, contained these proposals?"

"Most assuredly, Alberto, they did," replied the Condi—"would it not have been highly improper to have delayed one moment in ensuring your sister's felicity?"

"Certainly, my dear sir," replied Alberto, "it is natural that her felicity should engross a large portion of your thoughts, but how can we tell that it will be ensuring her felicity to ally her to a man she does not yet know, and probably may not esteem?"

"Alberto," said the Condi, in a stern manner, "has any part of my conduct through life induced you to suspect my disposition to be tyrannical?—mean you to infer that I would force your sister, Rosara, to the arms of a man she disliked?—or do you conceive that my paternal care and fondness has been lavished on you both from childhood, that I might in your maturer years, rob you of your opening prospects, by dashing the cup of happiness from you, to make you taste more keenly the bitter one of misery?—no, Alberto, the real, and not the visionary prospects of your sister's future happiness, guide me in the choice of a husband; neither wealth, a gilded coronet, or high sounding titles, would induce me to give my approbation to any suitor, unless virtue and probity were combined."

"Forgive me," said Alberto, falling on his knee, "my dear father, I have erred, but not intentionally; far was it from my thoughts to infer that it was your wish to sacrifice my beloved sister to the Duca; no, sir, your son, could never form so degrading an opinion of you, and if my words betrayed any thing offensive, attribute them to the affection that I entertain for Rosara; the strong desire I have of seeing her happy, and the pain I felt at the violent emotions she appeared to suffer while you were mentioning the subject to her."

"I forgive you freely, my son," said the Condi, raising Alberto from his knee, "I feel convinced that you were actuated by the dictates of a generous heart, and must admire your motives; though you should be more cautious, in giving way to the impetuosity of your passions; you need not be under any apprehensions respecting Rosara, I will strictly watch the Duca di Urbino, and I will become well acquainted with his mind and character, before I yield up such a treasure to him."

"Thanks for my sister's sake, my worthy father!" exclaimed Alberto, "and let it be my care to assist in this undertaking."

The Condi and his son now separated.

Alberto, on quitting his father, mounted his horse, with the intention of trying what exercise might do in calming his spirits, which had been agitated by the morning's conversation. He reflected, as his horse moved slowly, on the necessity of gaining a more intimate knowledge of the Duca di Urbino. He had not proceeded far beyond the environs of the city, when the sound of an instrument, accompanied by a sweet and harmonious voice, attracted his attention. He immediately checked his horse, and listened with delight to the ravishing tones, drawn forth by the invisible but skilful performer.

The full enchanting notes now swelled upon the balmy breeze, then gradually sunk into a soft and mellow cadence, till rudely wafted by the envious air, they ceased to charm the enraptured listener. Who can this Siren be? thought Alberto. The villa and its situation he was perfectly unacquainted with until the present moment: he however determined to risk every thing and gain admittance; therefore alighting and perceiving a garden door ajar, he hung the bridle of his horse to a hook, entered, and ascended a flight of steps, which led to a terrace, and at the extremity saw a small summer-house, where a lovely girl sat, reclining her elbow on her harp, while with the other, she carelessly turned over the leaves of a music book, as if seeking some fresh piece to perform.

Alberto stood for a moment to contemplate her figure: the position she had unconsciously placed herself in, tended to set it off to the best advantage; she was rather above the middle size; fine long brown tresses hung down her shoulders in graceful negligence; her mouth was ornamented with teeth that might rival the most polished ivory; her soft melting blue eyes, were such as filled the soul with extacy and love; her skin surpassed the most dazzling whiteness; her neck, which the envious gauze scarce permitted to be seen, appeared more lovely than the imagination can conceive, or the powers of description convey a just idea: in short—

> Fair Flora lent her stores; the purpled hours
> Confined her tresses with a wreath of flowers.
> * * * * * * * * * * * * * * *
>
> * * * * * * * * * * * * * * *
>
> Her robe (which closely by the girdle brac'd)
> Reveal'd the beauties of a slender waist,
> Flow'd to the feet, to copy Venus's air,
> When Venus's statues have a robe to wear.

"By heavens!" ejaculated Alberto, in a transport he was no longer able to contain, "had ever mortal so fine a form! No, her angelic countenance bespeaks her to be no earthly mould."

The lovely girl started up in alarm at the sound of a strange voice so near; but Alberto advancing, most respectfully bowed, and quieted the apprehensions, in some measure, which she seemed to labour under at his unexpected appearance.

"Pardon gentle lady," said he, "pardon this abrupt intrusion; and if I have excited any uneasiness in that fair bosom, I will at the faintest bidding quit your presence."

"Truly Signior," answered Viola (for that was the lady's name) with her eyes bent towards the ground, and trembling voice, whilst her confusion added a thousand charms, "a stranger breaking in so suddenly upon my retirement, has given just grounds to cause alarm; but your appearance denotes you to be a cavalero of no mean extraction; and therefore I am willing to conclude you a man of honor: if Signior you are in want of any assistance that can be rendered you here, I will instantly summon the domestics of the villa."

"No, fair Signiora, it is not aid I seek—in riding past the villa, the soft strains drawn forth from yonder instrument, accompanied by your melodious voice, struck upon my ear, and so charmed my senses, that, maddened with delight I sought this spot, (where harmony and beauty reign) not knowing what I did; and for this my bold presumptuous conduct, I do entreat your free forgiveness."

"My forgiveness, Signior," said Viola, "you are welcome to, but let me request you to depart, as I feel the impropriety of your remaining any longer here; and should Signiora Benvoglio, who is the owner of the villa, come here during your stay, it may be the cause of drawing down her anger."

"I fly," said he, "nor for worlds would the unhappy Alberto, even for an instant, cause a pang to you lovely Signiora; my cruel fortune drives me from your sight and I must obey."

Then gracefully bowing, he left the summer-house, mounted his horse, and putting spurs to his sides, quickly reached the Palazza, to ponder on his morning's adventure, and prepare for his introduction to the Duca di Urbino, in the evening.

CHAPTER IV.

THE much dreaded evening at length arrived; and the trembling Rosara, with her amiable friend Signiora Luzia, descended to the saloon, where her father and brother already waited for her. They had not long assembled before the Duca di Urbino was announced, and formally introduced by the Condi to Rosara, Signiora Luzia, and Alberto.

"Happy am I," said the Duca, "in being acquainted with a family, in praise of whose virtues no tongue is silent:—and happier still, shall I be, beauteous Rosara, (at the same moment turning towards her, and most gallantly saluting her hand) if I can obtain a small portion of your esteem, and be permitted to bask in the sunshine of your eyes." At the conclusion of this, the Duca seated himself by the side of Rosara. "I hope Signior Condi," continued he, "that you and the Signior Cavaliero, your son, have recovered from the fatigue of your journey—some part of my domain is not very distant from the Marchese Durazzo.—Have you been long acquainted?"

"The Marchese is an old and valued friend of mine," answered the Condi, "and for whom I have the highest regard.—I had not seen him for a long period of time; and as he is infirm and never visits Venice, I could not forego his kind invitation to spend some time with him, as perhaps another opportunity might not quickly offer."

"His Castello," said Alberto, "is the seat of hospitality; and his bosom that of every manly virtue, and honorable feeling.—I know not when I felt more happy in the society of a man, so much my superior in years—and I hope, my dear father, I may be able to re-visit the Castello, when Fernando returns."

"I have heard much in his praise," answered the Duca, in a quick imperious tone, "but tell me lovely Signiora, (addressing himself to Rosara, in a softened voice) is the Marchese Durazzo also a great favorite of yours?"

At this instant the servant announced a variety of visitors, therefore the Condi and Alberto went to receive them.

"You answer not, Signiora," said the Duca, still urging a reply.

"I am not personally acquainted with him," answered Rosara, "but as the friend of my father, I must esteem him."

"I too am the friend of your father," said the Duca, "and may I hope to possess some portion of your esteem."

"Certainly," answered Rosara, "as the friend of my father."

"Oh, Rosara!" said the Duca, in an impassioned tone, "be not thus cold; cast not a gloom over my fond expectations, and hurl me from the supremacy of bliss—for bliss it is, to enjoy thy sweet smiles.—Permit me to occupy one little space within thy fair bosom, and be thy humble servitor for ever."

"I understand you not, Signior;" answered Rosara, "I am not accustomed to hear such language; therefore I request you to desist."

"You cannot be ignorant, fair Rosara," said the Duca, "that your father means to bless me, by giving me the enviable right to protect you through life—why then this distant manner to one who adores you? Whose fortune and existence are devoted to you;—and without the happiness of calling you his, the world would become void. Urbino is no common lover, though unknown to you until this evening; yet has he constantly beheld and admired the amiable

Rosara di Vincenti—I have sought an alliance with your family; and have gained the consent of the Condi—and now lovely maid, your humble slave waits but your assent to crown his proud aspiring hopes with joy unutterable."

He then ceased, and fixed his dark eyes on Rosara, as if waiting for a reply; who, ready to sink beneath the seat she occupied, at the sudden declaration of the Duca, at length replyed in faultering accents:

"It is not for me, Duca, to dispute the will of the Condi; but upon this occasion, which is so dear to my own happiness, I must consult my feelings, my judgment, and my affections; and these, I know, my father, who has been ever good and kind to me, will not force; and unless Signior," continued Rosara, who had shaken off her trepidation, and had now assumed an energy in her manners, "you can gain complete empire over these, you never can expect me to be yours—candidly, Signior, I must tell you, that as the Condi has desired me to receive your addresses, I must, but you have not any-thing more to expect."

"Not anything more to expect!" repeated the Duca, the blood receding from his cheeks, and quickly returning, whilst his frame shook with contending passions, "Not to return my love and to be treated with scorn! Did I hear aright?" Then suddenly recollecting himself, as he perceived Rosara's eyes intently bent upon him, he in a soft and gentle tone exclaimed:

> "Say that you love me not, but say not so
> In bitterness: the common executioner,
> Whose heart the accustom'd sight of death makes hard,
> Falls not the axe upon the humbled neck,
> But first begs pardon: will you sterner be
> Than he, that dies and lives by bloody drops?"

"You cannot be so cruel as to cut off all hope for ever:—but the adoring Urbino, by his conduct and assiduities, will prove he is not unworthy of the love of the daughter of the Condi di Vincenti."

Alberto, who had been engaged in conversation with some cav-alieros at the opposite end of the apartment, but was attentively observing every movement of the Duca, saw the emotion that was expressive in his countenance, and judging, that the conversation must have taken a disagreeable turn, hastened towards his sister, and arrived at the moment the Duca concluded the last words to Rosara.

The trio joined in general conversation, but it was spiritless, and frequently interrupted by long pauses; at length the Duca di Urbino, finding his stay irksome, and despairing of making any favorable impression during this interview rose to depart.

"Good night, and may the saints bless you, Signiora!" said he as he bowed to Rosara, "and may our next meeting be more propitious to the miserable Urbino!"—then turning to Alberto, he took his leave, and seeking the Condi, shortly after withdrew altogether from the party.—Alberto found his sister very much agitated, but with all the kind solicitude, that had marked his every action towards her, he seated himself by her side, and used every cheering argument to raise her drooping spirits.

"Come, come, my dear Rosara, all will yet be well, remember your brother—your friend from childhood is near you; the proud and haughty Urbino shall not make you unhappy whilst Alberto has an arm to protect you!"

Rosara, pained to the heart by the abrupt declaration, and bold manner of the Duca di Urbino, scarcely heard the soothing accents of her brother, or saw any of the objects which surrounded her; grief had within a few hours taken possession of her mind, and chased away her usual happy spirits; but yet her native energies were unsubdued, and she forgot not that the proud blood of Vincenti flowed within her veins; pressing Alberto's hand affectionately, she rose, and bidding him farewell for the evening, glided out of the salle*, and repaired to her apartment, leaving Signiora Luzia to arrange every necessary requisite for the remaining few of the party.

"Alas! poor Rosara," exclaimed Alberto, as she quitted him, "I fear the Condi has planted a thorn within thy tender bosom, that nothing but the downfall of the Duca's hopes can ever eradicate."

Alberto, though compelled through politeness to mix in the society, assembled at the Palazza, yet felt as much at a distance from the

---

* Drawing room. [Tuckett's note.]

scene of gaiety, as if he had been in a desert; so completely were his ideas absorbed with the affairs of his family, and the fascinating image of the fair incognita. It was not until an hour after midnight, that all the guests took their departure from the Palazza, when Alberto willingly retired to his apartment.

The Duca di Urbino, was a nobleman of great family and wealth:—in his younger days he had been well known in all the fashionable circles, and had been esteemed one of the most accomplished cavalieros of his day; for the Duca had now considerably passed his fiftieth year; but even at this advanced age, the Duca possessed a fine manly figure, tall, well-made and robust, he might have challenged half the youths in Venice for strength and comeliness;—he possessed dark piercing eyes; black hair, and an animated countenance, unless when any thing disturbed him, then would his eyes flash fire, and a dark scowl overspread his brow, indicative of all the base passions that struggled within his vicious mind.

Possessing a thorough knowledge of mankind, and having had a general intercourse with the world, few were more subtle, and few knew better how to use the soft blandishments of language, or were more insinuating [in] their address when necessary; but when opposed, rage, passion, all claimed supremacy over his degenerated soul, and totally excluded every dormant virtue, which might have remained within his breast; then would he plan schemes, dark and wily to overthrow the object of his hate, and set all danger, justice, and right at defiance to accomplish his diabolical purposes.

Such was the man, the Condi di Vincenti had accepted to become a member of his family;—such was the man, whose love, the gentle, amiable Rosara di Vincenti despised! and to whom she had the hardihood to express her thoughts ingenuously.

After his departure from the Palazza, and having gained his own private apartments, within his magnificent habitation, he burst into a paroxism of passion:—"What!" cried he, vehemently, and striking his clenched hand against his forehead, while his countenance expressed the dæmoniac malice of his heart, "shall a girl, whom I have honored with my addresses, dare refuse my proffered love?—No, Rosara, in spite of fate, thou shalt be mine!—Urbino has declared it, and who shall cross his will?—One short week I grant thee, and if then thou refusest my suit, tremble at the vengeance of the insulted Urbino!" Then throwing himself on his couch he sunk into an unrefreshing sleep.

Alberto, as usual rose with the dawning of day, and mounted his horse, in hopes he should be able to gain some intelligence of the fair unknown; he soon reached the well-remembered spot, and after various enquiries, was at length informed, that the villa belonged to a Signiora Benvoglio, and that she and her daughter Viola had resided there some time; this was all he could learn, but he determined to make more minute enquiries at some future period; then turning his horse towards the road, which again led to the Palazza, tolerably well satisfied with his morning's ride, he reached it, as Signiora Luzia, Rosara, and the Condi were taking their seats at the breakfast table.

As soon as Alberto had paid the usual morning salutations, the Condi enquired if he had rode far.

"No, Signior," said Alberto, "I have not, but the weather being so extremely inviting, I could not resist the temptation of taking a little exercise, *pour passer le tems,* before you had assembled, well knowing I should not keep you waiting."

When the repast was concluded, after some desultory chat, Alberto proceeded to the places of public resort, where the fashionable and gay daily thronged, with the full expectation of gaining some knowledge of the character of the Duca di Urbino, among his acquaintances; however all proved fruitless; he was well known by name, but had been so long from Venice, that nothing else of him was remembered.—Weeks passed on, and Alberto had not gained any intelligence of the Duca, though he had been particularly active in making very minute enquiries—he had frequently passed by the Villa of Signiora Benvoglio, and had often the inexpressible pleasure of conversing with Signiora Viola from the window of the little summer-house, which looked to the road: if Alberto had been struck at first sight with her accomplishments; how much more was he enchanted with the beauties of her mind!

The Duca di Urbino redoubled every effort to gain the affections of Rosara; and was not sparing of every attention he was master of, to insinuate himself in her good opinion: but Rosara, incapable of concealing her disgust, treated him with cold civility. Far from being repulsed by this line of conduct, the Duca determined to pursue the disdaining object of his wishes—tired with the etiquette of a formal courtship—and never doubting that even though Rosara might not have seen him with a favorable eye, yet she never could reject his alliance from motives of family interest—he decided on requesting an interview with her, that his hopes might be either realised or crushed.

After having once formed a resolution, the Duca was prompt in putting it into effect; therefore he repaired to the Palazza the next day, and intimated to the Condi his wish to see Rosara, on the subject nearest his heart. Elated at the prospect of his daughter's speedy establishment, the Condi left the Duca, that he might himself request her attendance, and at the same time to mention the purpose of the Duca's visit.

Rosara was thunderstruck at the order of her father, and the sudden resolution of the Duca; but collecting her spirits, she with some degree of composure, descended to the Duca, who was pacing up and down the apartment, in evident agitation. As soon as he perceived the entrance of Rosara, he approached her with all the insinuating softness he could throw into his address, and of which he was a perfect master—then taking her reluctant hand, in the mildest accents, thus spoke:—

"Thanks to you lovely Rosara, for thus kindly granting me this interview, which far exceeds my most sanguine expectations. Your sweet compliance augurs well in the miserable Urbino's cause—yes, Rosara, miserable must he ever be, if banished from your presence: see then the humble Urbino (falling on his knee) sues for the fair hand of the loveliest female in all Venice; and lays his fortune, titles, all, at her disposal—deign to accept his proffered alliance, and bestow upon your devoted slave, happiness unequalled. Let not a cloud overspread thy brow, but bend a kind consenting look on him who adores you!—Speak, oh speak! and let him hear the joyous or the awful sentence; for on thy rosy lips hangs the doom of the Duca di Urbino."

"Rise, Signior, rise," said Rosara, "that kneeling posture ill becomes you—and sorry am I, that the daughter of the Condi di Vincenti should have witnessed it."

"Those words, Rosara," said the Duca, rising, (and quickly catching at her concluding words) "bring hope again to my distracted mind; which like a balm, have healed the wound inflicted by your averted looks—oh! do but speak, my loved Rosara, the kind consenting word, and let Urbino proclaim aloud to all the world, the transport that awaits him—say on sweet maid, and bless his delighted senses!"

"Duca," said Rosara, with a firm and dignified tone, "had you waited a few moments, you might perhaps have spared yourself a great portion of pain, if your love towards me be really so great, as your high-flown expressions would lead me to believe. Your attentions to me have been marked, since your introduction to the Palazza; I have been obliged to receive them in obedience to my father's will; but my conduct can never have evinced anything more than common-place politeness: and recollect this Duca, that Rosara di Vincenti, never will give her hand where she cannot give her heart—force may compel her to yield the one, but still she will be always mistress of the other.—Know then, Duca di Urbino, the latter you never can possess—Rosara di Vincenti will always act candidly: therefore however flattered she may feel herself, at the high opinion you entertain of her, she hopes you will receive this as her final decision."

Here Rosara rose for the purpose of quitting the apartment, when the Duca springing from his seat—fire flashing from his eyes, and his whole frame agitated with rage; forcibly seized her arm, and passionately exclaimed:

"Stay Signiora, stay! Is it thus you treat Urbino's love?—Has he condescended to kneel to Rosara di Vincenti, and be thus requited? —Had you received his love, no earthly happiness that could have been procured, but Urbino would have lavished on you:—but," here he grasped the arm of Rosara with so much violence, that she exclaimed in a loud and haughty tone, her proud blood mantling in her cheeks, at the indignity offered:

"Unhand me, Signior! or I will summon the domestics:" then cooly and sarcastically adding: "this force but ill accords with *the manners of the mild, the gentle Duca di Urbino,*" then with some expression of anger, at not being released from the strong hold of the Duca, she repeated: "why do you not unhand me Signior?"

"No, Signoria, no—before Urbino quits you, you must hear him: once you led him in the silken chains of love; but now the bonds are broke:—you might have been the bride of Urbino, and the most envied dame in Venice—but you have rejected him. Fool that he was to whine and play the love-sick swain, to win you to his bed, and share his honors and his vast domains; but, haughty fair, you have to dread the utmost vengeance of his slighted love—you shall be his in spight of fate—even though all the legions of dark Tartarus, should form a solid phalanx round you, yet Urbino, the despised, rejected Urbino, would snatch you to his arms—beware and dread him!"

At the same moment he dashed the trembling Rosara from him, who tottering fell upon the floor. Alberto entered at the conclusion of the Duca's words, but sufficiently in time to hear them, and to witness his brutal action towards his sister.

"Turn villian, turn!" cried the noble-minded, the spirited Alberto, drawing his sword, "nor think the brother of Rosara di Vincenti will brook this outrage."

Quickly flew the sword of the enraged Duca from the scabbard.

"Take thy punishment, rash boy," cried he, making a furious pass at Alberto, determining to satiate his vengeance at a blow; but he was not aware of the courage and dexterity of the antagonist he had to cope with, who parrying it, evaded the fatal thrust. The combatants equally skilled, fought with various advantage. The clashing of the swords brought the domestics to the salle but not before the Duca had been wounded through the fleshy part of the sword arm.

Rosara, during the whole of the conflict, lay in a supine state, where the Duca had cast her; but the kind attention of the affectionate Signiora Luzia, soon restored her to a state of sensibility, and she was conducted by her attendants from a scene highly grating to her feelings. Within her apartment, and on the bosom of Signiora Luzia, Rosara relieved her almost bursting heart, in a flood of tears, which in a great measure calmed her spirits.

But how did the high spirit of Alberto feel the indignity offered to his beloved sister? He had in the recent rencontre wounded the Duca, but was that sufficient to wipe off the insult offered the house of Vincenti? No, it was not sufficient; and as soon as the Duca was capable of meeting him, to give him honorable satisfaction, he should then resent it to his utmost; for Alberto was too noble

—too proud of his long line of ancestry—and too tenacious of his honour, to take advantage, or to taunt a fallen foe; therefore he decided on waiting the perfect recovery of the Duca.

Not such were the feelings of Urbino, who had been conveyed to his Palazza: every dark and malignant passion taking possession of his breast, he vowed to be revenged on the house of Vincenti.

"What," cried he, "to be rejected by a girl,—and foiled by a boy! —shall the haughty spirit of Urbino bear it?—One whose will has ever been a law. Oh! here I swear never to cease my endeavours to effect the downfall of Vincenti and his heirs—*they shall fall!*" exclaimed he, with redoubled rage, "Urbino swears it, and who shall dispute his word? By to-morrow's sun, far from the splendid gaities of Venice shall I be—my firm resolve is fixed; nor heaven, or earth, shall shake it!"

Then summoning his domestics, he ordered his travelling equipage to be prepared within the hour.

The wound of the Duca was merely trivial; he felt no inconvenience from it, but that which he experienced from the loss of blood; therefore capable, after a few hours rest, of travelling.

Punctually to the time the Duca, with a few attendants left his Palazza, and set out on his journey.

The Condi di Vincenti was absent during the period the above transaction had taken place; judge then his astonishment at having a detailed account from Alberto of the events—instead of meeting his daughter as the kind consenting destined bride of the Duca, he found her spurned from him and treated with indignity: at the relation his whole frame shook with indignation—"To me," cried he, in a voice full of passion, "you shall answer for this Urbino!— these muscles are not yet so stiffened, nor the blood, which flows within these veins, so chilled with age but that I can defend my yet unsullied honor, and untarnished fame!—Poor Rosara, how can I atone to thee, my child, for presenting such a man as thy affianced husband?—No! from this moment the Duca is a stranger to these doors, and my Rosara's will shall ever be her own!"

Saying this, he left the room to visit her in her apartment, whither she had been led, and had now recovered from the terror she had experienced from Urbino's conduct.

The words that Alberto had overheard the Duca utter, sunk deep

in his mind; he now clearly saw that the whole of his specious conduct, had been but to win the lovely person of his sister—that the
Duca felt no real affection for Rosara, Alberto was well convinced,
and he rejoiced that he had so opportunely arrived, to witness his
throwing off the mask. The Duca di Urbino was powerful, and
Alberto well knew he would still use every means to possess his
sister; his late rage was but the immediate result of the supposed
indignity offered to his pride and titles, by Rosara's rejecting him.
The Condi had declared he would never force her inclinations, and
from the recent occurrences there was a stronger reason to persist
in this resolution: Alberto was glad that things had taken such a
turn, as it was the means of freeing his sister from a disagreeable
lover, and banishing a man, with whom he always felt disgusted,
from the Palazza.

CHAPTER V.

WE have now presented to the reader, the circumstances which
had occurred, and the state in which the family of Vincenti was,
previous to the period Fernando left the Castello of Durazzo, with
the intention of paying his promised visit, to his friend Alberto, at
Venice; and whom we have conducted as far as Ravenna, for that
purpose.

As soon as the sun had streaked the eastern sky, Fernando sprung
from his bed, refreshed by the tranquil sleep he had enjoyed; and
calling to Gaspardo, who was in the adjoining apartment, directed
every thing to be immediately put on board the vessel they were
to embark in; as it was his intention to lose no time in reaching
Venice. Gaspardo obeyed with alacrity the orders of his master, and
returned in a few minutes, to say every thing was ready; as every
necessary arrangement had been made with the boatmen the night
before; therefore they had only to send the light baggage off in the
morning.

With a light heart, Fernando stepped on board the vessel that was
to convey him to his friend Alberto; and leaning against the side,
watched the men while busily employed in heaving the anchor,
and unfurling the sails—they were quickly filled with a prosperous

breeze, which impetuously urged the vessel through the bosom of the briny deep.

The sailors alternately sang, and trimmed the sails—all seemed happy and contented; and as the evening came on, the prospect of their labors being soon at an end, added to their hilarity. The sun was setting fast, and in half an hour Fernando expected to be landed in Venice.

The water was covered with a great number of pleasure boats, barges, and gondolas; all of which were sailing and rowing in divers directions, as the sportive fancy of the parties led them. One above them all, moved with the greatest rapidity and majesty—dashing the white foam about her bows, as if disdaining the element on which she rode: but just as she passed under the stern of the vessel in which Fernando was, a gondola that had not been perceived, in consequence of the interesting vessel, ran with violence against her, and by the concussion, a lady, who had risen from her seat at the approaching danger, was precipitated into the sea—Fernando saw the accident, and instantly leaped in after her;—

> "He trod the water,
> Whose enmity he flung aside, and breasted
> The surge most swoln that met him; his bold head
> 'Bove the contentious waves he kept, and oar'd
> Himself with his good arms, in lusty stroke,"

and bore the sinking female, in safety to the barge. With very little difficulty they were assisted in, and Fernando seeing his fair burden in security; (ever active in succouring his fellow creatures when in danger;) flew to assist in disengaging the two boats, no exertion having been yet made by either party. The mariners on both sides, had remained mute and inactive spectators of the young lady's providential rescue from the waves; but now the wordy war had commenced between them, and threats and imprecations dreadful, followed the awful silence that had prevailed—no sooner had Fernando reached the prow of the barge, than this fierce contention ceased. His manly appearance, his skilful directions in clearing the boats, and his recent heroic conduct, inspired them with respect—amity prevailed, and the two crews vied with each other, who should be the most conspicuous in their exertions. They strove not long in vain, for again the barge and gondola were freed from their dangerous predicament.

Fernando now thought it necessary to return to the party he had merely had a glance of, and make some enquiries respecting the lady's health; but before he could reach the stern of the barge, he found his hand grasped, and at the same moment he recognised his friend.—Fernando!—Alberto!—was mutually pronounced in the same breath; and these two young cavalieros, greeted each other with all the genuine warmth of friendship and esteem; such as minds honorable and untainted with vice possess.

The Condi received Fernando with every mark of gratitude and friendship.—Alberto introduced his friend to Rosara, who had sustained no injury, (for it was her Fernando had rescued) but that of a wetting; who thanked him for the timely aid he had afforded her, with all the bewitching sweetness so natural to her, and passed high encomiums on his courage and address, such as the great service he had rendered her merited. Fernando gracefully bowed as she ceased to speak. He now proposed returning to his own vessel, from whence a small boat had been sent to convey him back; but neither the Condi nor Alberto would hear of this: therefore directions were given to the men where to land, and every thing left to the charge of Gaspardo.

The barge rowed rapidly to the landing place, at the Condi's Palazza, where they disembarked.—Fernando was, now the Condi had leisure, overwhelmed with kind enquiries, respecting the Marchese Durazzo.

"He was well, Signior," answered Fernando, "when I quitted the Castello, and I was in hopes I should have found a packet, from the Marchese, by the time I arrived."

"I am glad indeed," said the Condi, "to hear my old and valued friend still retains his health."

Gaspardo here made his appearance, and informed Fernando every thing was placed in his apartment; requesting to know if he did not wish to change his dress.—Until Gaspardo reminded him of the necessity of changing his wet garments, the state he was in was totally unheeded by him or his friend—so great was the pleasure they felt at this unexpected meeting.

"Bless me," cried the Condi, "how indiscreet have I been, to detain Signior Fernando—why Alberto did you not think of this?"

He no longer delayed, but took his friend by the arm, and led him to the suite of rooms allotted for him.

"I need not remark to you, Fernando," said Alberto, "that while you remain under this roof, I expect you will consider every thing at your disposal—such is the wish of the Condi; and by doing so, you will make Alberto feel a greater degree of satisfaction."

Gaspardo had already placed dry clothes for his master, and while assisting him in dressing, the two friends chatted on common occurrences. The light breast-plate Fernando had worn, Alberto sportively took up; when examining it, he perceived it hacked through in several places.

"Why what have we here?" said he with astonishment, "how comes your breast-plate cut through? I hope no accident has be-fallen you on the road."

Fernando then related to him what had passed on his journey from the Castello di Durazzo.

"I do not know, Signior," said Gaspardo, as his master concluded, "who the warrior can be, that we saw at the old ruined Castello where we slept, and who sided with us when we were attacked; but I should like to find out, for he seems to follow us very close.—When I was bringing up the baggage, he was standing near the steps of the Palazza; but as soon as he found he was observed by me, he glided off in an instant. He cannot mean us any ill will, or he would not have helped us out of the two scrapes we got into; and it looks very much as if he followed on purpose to watch us; but I hope yet to be even with him, for I shall look pretty sharp after him."

"It certainly cannot be the effect of chance:" said Fernando, "I have not been more than an hour in Venice, and this same unknown is at my heels."

"The circumstance is rather extraordinary," said Alberto, "but let his motive be what it will, it does not appear that it is inimical to you; he might have conceived he knew your person, and wishes to ascertain the fact, without your knowledge."

"That," replied Fernando, "does not appear to be the case, for when I turned to thank him after the rencountre, that I mentioned, he rode off, as if purposely to avoid me:—but conjecture is useless, and we must leave it to time to elucidate his real intentions."

"He is a gallant fellow," said Gaspardo, "and rendered us very essential service, when we needed it; and for that reason alone, I should not like to quarrel with him; but if I meet him prowling about, and he does not give a good account of himself, we must tilt a little."

"I have little doubt Gaspardo," said Alberto, "that you will not hear anything more of this troublesome personage.—Come Fernando, since you are equipped, we had better descend."

The two Cavalieros found the Condi, Signiora Luzia, and Rosara, already in the salle. The Condi rose to meet Fernando at his entrance, when taking him by the hand, while the warm tear trickled down his cheek, pressed it, and in a low tone said:

"Excuse my not expressing my sincere thanks before this to you more fully, my young friend, for snatching my loved child from a watery grave; had it not been for you, she would now have been numbered with the dead, and I a miserable old man:—but you are welcome to my Palazza—and doubly welcome; as well on account of your own intrinsic merit, as for the friendship I bear the Marchese."

Fernando found a renewal of the circumstances, which had recently occurred very unpleasing, he hoped they were forgotten; they had been so by him; but who was there that had once seen Rosara di Vincenti, that could erase her image from his memory? The noble youth approached the blooming maid, and placed himself in the vacant seat next to her:—he viewed her lovely countenance with rapture:—in her sweet looks, and lovely figure, were blended all the attractive graces, which captivate the heart and melt the soul to soft seductive love.

"You must be greatly fatigued, Signior Fernando," said she, "after your journey."

"Not so, Signiora," replied Fernando, "the pleasure of again seeing my friends, and finding myself among those whom I esteem, has dispelled every thought of weariness; and who could feel such in the society of Signiora Rosara?"

The color for a moment suffused her cheek, at the compliment paid her. "But the frame," said she, "Signior, after having undergone great exertion must naturally require repose, and I am afraid you are neglecting your health, merely through etiquette."

"Were I to quit," replied Fernando, "this happy circle, even in the retirement of my chamber my thoughts would be with them, and sleep be a stranger to my eyes."

The servant announced the collation ready, the party therefore adjourned to the eating room, and soon after retired for the night.

Alberto accompanied Fernando; and Gaspardo being dismissed, he related the events that had taken place at the Palazza, since the Condi and himself had returned from the Castello di Durazzo; he dwelt with energy on the offered, and rejected alliance of the Duca di Urbino, his brutal conduct to Rosara, and his threats.—He then spoke of his love for the fair Viola; and opened without reserve every secret avenue of his heart. Thou hast confided, Alberto, thy inmost thoughts to a soul congenial!—At a late hour he left his friend.

Sleep fled from the tired Fernando; the image of Rosara di Vincenti was perpetually before him; at one moment he saw the haughty Urbino kneeling at her feet, then in his phrenzied rage, dashing her from him, and the prostrate girl bleeding from her fall. —Here his feelings became too great, and involuntarily the words villain! coward! escaped his lips; Fernando, forgot Urbino was not present; but the man, who could use the charming lovely Rosara with harshness must be worse than either—"look but in her lovely countenance," exclaimed he, "and every rebellious passion must subside—even the frigid anchoret's hard and flinty heart would soften into adoration—Oh! happy, happy man, that calls thee his, Rosara; and may thy beauty and thy virtues, lovely maid, be rewarded in thy choice!"

Rosara could not banish from her mind the occurrences of the evening—she tried to compose herself, but became more restless in the attempt—the figure of Fernando haunted her imagination; sometimes she beheld him buffeting the waves with lusty sinews, and snatching her from impending fate; sometimes she compared his mild engaging manners with those of the fierce Urbino.

Would Fernando have spurned me from him?—no! his generous and noble mind would never harbor a thought injurious to the sex,

whom by nature, and the laws of honor he is bound to protect.—
Would the Duca di Urbino have plunged into the foaming billows,
and rescued me from the horrors of a watery grave? no! he who
could insult an unoffending female, would never risk his life in her
defence!—his dastard soul would never dare the brave the worthy
deed!—How different was the contrast in their address:—on the
one hand, Urbino, proud, overbearing, impatient of contradic-
tion, dictational in his opinions, and cruel in his disposition!—on
the other hand—Fernando, gentle, generous, and brave, was a far
superior being!

"Oh! my father," exclaimed she, "Rosara might have acceeded to
thy wishes, had he been thy . . . ."

Stay, stay, fair maid! not even the softest zephyr could catch thy
concluding word; but yet the modest blush that mantles in thy
cheek, too truly betrays the feelings of thy heart! Hide not thy face
—it is not the blush of shame—even virtue might share with pride
thy inmost thoughts!—Calm thy perturbed spirits, lovely maid, and
rest in peace, whilst innocence guards thy serene slumbers.

From his infancy, Fernando had been trained to manly sports,
and hardy exercise: Nature, prodigal of her gifts, had lavished them
abundantly on him.—When clad in his armour, with his helmet on,
his air appeared majestic—his strength immense; and his intrepid-
ity was such, no danger could appal. But when uncased, his noble
aspect, his looks penetrating, but mild, in which were mingled dignity with benificence; attracted universal admiration;—the most
envious, unable to injure him, became his friend.

No wonder then the young and amiable Rosara di Vincenti
looked on our hero, at the first interview, with a favorable eye—she
had heard her brother speak with fervency of the noble sentiments
of his mind, and goodness of heart—the latter she had experienced;
and doubted not his possessing every other virtue, which Alberto,
in the enthusiastic moments of friendship, had attributed to him.

At rather a late hour the party assembled round the social breakfast table.

"I am afraid," said the Condi, "by your looks, you have not rested
well, Signior Fernando, your apartment probably, is not to your
liking?"

"It is perfectly so," replied Fernando, "but I am generally accustomed to rise by break of day, and very likely my sleeping too long might have made me heavy."

He felt glad to offer anything by way of excuse, lest by prolonging the conversation, his emotion might be discovered.

"Rosara," cried Alberto, sportively, after fixing a stedfast look at her for an instant, "where have all *your* roses fled?"

Poor Rosara, at this remark, blushed the deepest crimson hue, as the recollection of the cause flashed across her mind.

"They fled I see," continued Alberto, "merely to bring auxiliaries."

Rosara bent her eyes on the ground to recover herself, but in raising them, she met those of Fernando; and as she essayed to speak, her confusion became more apparent. Alberto finding her distressed at what he had said, immediately changed the subject. The party soon separated; and Rosara, whose whole thoughts were engrossed with the idea that Fernando suffered in his health, scarcely reached her apartment, ere she sank upon a chair, quite overcome.

"How wretched shall I be," said she, in an agonised voice, "if any ill betide the brave, the generous youth—it were better far, if my days had been cut short, than I should witness such an hour."

Here she was relieved by a torrent of tears, and her spirits became more composed.

CHAPTER VI.

Time fled on rapid wings.—Fernando had been some time an inmate of the Palazza, and it appeared but as a day; each one had tended to augment the firm link of friendship that existed between the two cavalieros, and every hour Rosara and Fernando found something to admire in each other: their truant eyes had often spoke love's softest language; their every action shewed their hearts in unison; but yet their tongues had never dared reveal their mutual passion.

Fernando never felt so delighted, as when wandering through the grounds with Rosara, or seated in the alcove near the sea, reading to her, or listening to her melodious voice. Rosara never more happy, than when in the society of Fernando—all was vacancy in his absence, a melancholy preyed upon her mind, and the lagging hours seemed as if determined that the period should never arrive, that was again to bring him to her presence.

"My friend," said Alberto, while they were one evening together, "I cannot but perceive that you love Rosara—nay start not, Fernando, for there is no man breathing, in whose keeping I would prefer placing so valuable a treasure; for no one, that I am aware of, is so well formed to guard it:—tell me my friend, are my conjectures just? if so, my sincerest wishes are gratified."

"Too truly indeed, your sister Rosara possesses my affections, and unless I can obtain her hand, I shall be miserable."

"Doubt not your own worth," replied Alberto, "Rosara loves you, I am sure; this never would have passed my lips, but for the high opinion and esteem I have for you—the most unskilled in the art of love, could easily discover your secret."

"I love Rosara dearer than my life's blood!" passionately exclaimed Fernando, "but yet, Alberto, I know not, if I presumptuously threw myself at her feet, and avowed my passion, that it would be well received—besides the Condi—"

"Do not make yourself uneasy, Fernando, on that head," said Alberto, "if you gain Rosara's approbation, be not fearful of my father's; and I am well convinced my friend has made a strong impression on my sister's heart. This makes you dull, come let us strole, and try what effect air and amusement will do, in shaking off those woeful looks."

"I will be with you in an instant," said Fernando, quitting him for the purpose of procuring his cloak, which he usually threw over his shoulders in the evening. Gaspardo was busily employed in his apartment when he entered. "Give me my cloak," said Fernando, "it is cool, and I may want it before I return."

"Had you not, Signior, better put on your helmet and breast-plate? it is late, and there is no knowing what may happen."

"No," said Fernando, "the cloak will be sufficient."

"Indeed, Signior," said Gaspardo, (at the same moment presenting Fernando with his helmet, and holding up the breast-plate, to assist in accoutering him) "you will find it much better, there can be no harm in being prepared."

Fernando passively complied with the request of Gaspardo; he knew that his servant's intentions were wholly influenced by a strong desire to serve him; therefore opposed not his arming him. It was invariably the custom of Fernando, when at the Castello di Durazzo, always to wear a light plate, being more commodious than that which was generally used, when either practising military exercise, or marching against an enemy.

Alberto and Fernando amused themselves by walking in the public places, where the gay and fashionable resort. Two persons, closely enveloped in their cloaks, drew the attention of the friends, whom they observed to pass frequently by them, and examine them with a scrutinizing eye. It was quite dark, and the cavalieros wearied with their promenade, were just on the point of quitting the garden, when a well-known voice attracted the attention of Fernando.

"Good heavens!" said he, turning towards the place from whence the sound had issued, "it is the voice of the ruffian Sanguinario!"

But no human form was visible; the figures were no where to be seen.

"Are you certain you know the person who spoke?" enquired Alberto.

"Too well indeed," replied Fernando, "it is that Sanguinario, who I before mentioned to you, as inhabiting the cottage where I rested, after passing the night in the Castello di Lepanto; his voice betrayed him, and the words he uttered were too nearly connected with what had passed, to allow of doubt."

"Let us return to the Palazza," said Alberto, "every one has long since retired."

They had not proceeded far, before the figures again crossed them, as if watching their steps.

"There they are again!" exclaimed Fernando, "be upon your guard Alberto, for there is not anything which that villain is not capable of, and I am much deceived if it be not him."

"I am prepared," said Alberto, "we seek not them, nor will we avoid them. If plunder be their aim, from me they only will obtain a well tempered sword; and even that they shall purchase dearly."

They had nearly reached the Palazza, when a ruffian springing from his hiding place, struck a poignard at the bosom of Fernando;

(thy caution, Gaspardo, saved thy valued master's life) but the breast-plate which he wore, and which his cloak concealed, turned the dire blow.

Rapid as the eagle's flight he drew his sword, and with mighty strokes assailed his foe; the villain soon had paid the forfeit of his life, but drawing from his breast a whistle, collected by its shrill sound his band—fortunately for thee, thou wretch, they readily obeyed thy call, or else the warm blood that flowed around thy polluted heart, would have in purple currents trickled from thy breast, and thy wicked soul have fled through the gaping wound inflicted, to wander on the Stygian shore—but ere Fernando's raised sword could give the fatal blow, four deadly weapons were in an instant leveled against the cavalieros—urged by impetuous ire, Fernando pressed the assassins on all sides, his intrepid soul disdained the wretches, against whom he contended; his care was to avert each impending blow from his friend Alberto, who nobly fighting had received several wounds, not being armed, as were the assassins, —tottering, he fell from the loss of blood into the friendly arms of Fernando; though encumbered with Alberto, yet the gallant youth firmly stood, like the raging lion, when pierced by the hunter's spear, threatening death and destruction to all that dared approach him; not even the certainty of death would make him turn his back upon an enemy—but at this critical juncture, his friendly genius again interposed—*the unknown was at his side!*—his vigorous and sturdy blows, tempered with coolness and address, quickly routed the villains.

As soon as Fernando found they had fled, his whole attention was taken up with the bleeding Alberto, he raised him in his arms, for sense had left him, and bore him towards the Palazza, but he had not proceeded far, when lights approached him, and he joyfully recognised the Condi's domestics with torches.

Gaspardo, who was amongst the foremost, cast an anxious look at his master, and perceiving Alberto in his arms, relieved him of his burden; silently, but with an uneasy mind, Fernando followed his friend, whose life he hoped he had preserved, and whose existence he found dear to him; he deeply bewailed the misfortune that had occurred, and would with pleasure have sacrificed himself to have ensured Alberto's safety.

By the time they reached the Palazza, the wounded and insensible Alberto, had, from the motion he had received in being carried, recovered animation, and with the assistance of Paulo and Gaspardo, was enabled to walk to his apartment—with as little bustle as possible, the domestics retired, and the family surgeon sent for, to examine his wounds; but this was not so quietly effected, but the Condi and Rosara heard the noise, and enquiring the reason, were too quickly informed of the sad disaster; happily the surgeon found the wounds slight, but the loss of blood had been great, and pronounced, that with quiet, his patient would very soon be restored to health. Fernando remained with Alberto after he had been dressed by the surgeon, for the purpose of keeping every thing still, as had been recommended.

Alberto, languid with the exertion he had undergone, sunk into a profound sleep, and Fernando stole from his side, for a moment, for the purpose of seeking some one of the family:—no one save Rosara was in the salle—her eyes were wet with tears, and melancholy pervaded the whole of her beautiful countenance—her head reclined upon her hand, and deeply absorbed in thought she heeded not the entrance of Fernando, till roused by the sound of his footsteps—never did she appear so interesting in his eyes—never did he look so amiable in hers.

"I come, Signiora, to say that your domestic surgeon has announced Alberto to be free from danger, and declares his recovery will be speedy.—Oh! Rosara, how truly do I deplore the sad circumstances that have involved my friend—if by laying down my life I could allay one atom of your grief willingly would I do so! —had Fernando suffered instead of Alberto, he then would have been happy!—but the cruel fates are adverse to him, and he must submit!"

"Say not so, Fernando," replied Rosara, "you must be happy!— The debt of gratitude the house of Vincenti owes you is great, and would that I could contribute in the slightest degree to repay it!— You have rescued my brother and myself from death, and what can be more gratifying to a noble soul like yours?—your fate Fernando is most enviable."

"Though sorry for the cause, yet that I could serve Alberto, I am proud; it testifies the real friendship I profess—but still a thorn rankles in my breast, that robs me of my peace, and until it is plucked from thence I must be miserable!"

"Oh! that Rosara," replied she, "could but extract it, her utmost care would be to heal the wound."

"It would cost thee more," said Fernando, "than thou art aware of, sweet gentle maid to—"

The Condi here entered, and prevented the concluding part of the sentence, he had been to visit Alberto, who still remained in the profound sleep in which Fernando had left him.

The youth dared not raise his eyes towards Rosara; she blushing, feared to encounter those of him, who had become more dear to her than all the world contained.

"Have you any cause, Signior," said the Condi, "to suspect the persons who attacked you?"

"I cannot," said Fernando, wishing to evade the question, "recall to my memory any one, who could bear me an enmity in Venice; it certainly appeared my life was the principle object."

The Condi remained musing. Fernando trembled at the idea of having said too much to Rosara; had not the Condi interrupted the conversation, it is more than probable, that an avowal of his love would have taken place.

"Could you not discover the features of the assassin," enquired Rosara, "who wounded my brother?"

"No, Signiora," replied Fernando, "every thing was enclouded with darkness, and it was with difficulty we could observe from whence we were attacked, and to this I attribute the unfortunate wounds of your brother."

"Alas! indeed," said Rosara, "it has proved unfortunate."—

Paulo, here came to say, that Alberto had awoke, and wished to see Fernando; our hero, bowing was about to leave the room, when Rosara requested she might be admitted to her brother, as soon as he could receive her.

Alberto was much refreshed from the few hours tranquil sleep he had enjoyed, and was so far recovered as to be enabled to sit up in his bed; it was with difficulty Fernando could prevent him from rising and joining them in the salle, but this he so strenuously opposed, that Alberto reluctantly yielded.

"Those villains who attacked us," said Fernando, "cannot have escaped without being hurt, for I found the blade of my sword stained with blood; I certainly should have secured the one who first struck at me, had not the remainder of his gang come so opportunely to his rescue."

"You may think what you please, my friend," said Alberto, "but they were no common assassins, I feel confident;—plunder did not seem to be their aim, or else when they found we resisted with so much determination, they would in all probability have desisted: —I strongly suspect the two figures we saw in the gardens were among them, they certainly bore a strong resemblance."

"Sanguinario is concerned in this affair," said Fernando, "I think beyond a doubt,—it was he who spoke in the gardens, and you say the figures that attacked us bore a strong resemblance to those which passed us in the walk."

"How happened it," said Alberto, "that you had a breast-plate on?"

"Gaspardo," answered Fernando, laughing, "insisted upon it, therefore I complied."

"Something or other crossed my mind," said Gaspardo, "that all would not go well, for I saw our old acquaintance again, near the steps of the Palazza."

"Who was it came up to your assistance?" enquired Alberto, "if I could find him, I would return him my sincere thanks for his handsome conduct.—Did you not enquire his name, Fernando?"

"That would have been useless," replied Fernando, "for it was the unknown, who Gaspardo dignifies with the epithet of, our old acquaintance:—as usual, as soon as the ruffians fled, he made off, and left me to assist you home how I could.—What brought you out Gaspardo, with the torches?"

"I never thought of telling you before, Signior," said Gaspardo, "We were all making merry below, and Paulo there, was just saying what a handsome couple the Signiora and you would make.—"

"Never mind all this," said Fernando, "we want to know how you came acquainted with our situation."

"That" replied Gaspardo, "was what I was just going to tell you, Signior: Paulo was saying what a handsome couple you would make—when a rap came at the door—I ran directly to it, and a man, wrapped up close, whose face I could not even discover, immediately said—get lights, and at the next turning you will find Signior

Fernando and Alberto; the latter is wounded, and requires assistance—delay not one moment; and away he darted, before I could say a word; I did as he directed me, and we were happy enough to find you."

"Step, Gaspardo, to Signiora Rosara, and say that Signior Alberto can now see her."

The willing domestic retired to execute his master's orders, and attended the Signiora to the door of her brother's apartment.

"How fares my brother," said Rosara, kindly taking his offered hand, and affectionately saluting him, "after his repose?"

"I am quite well," said Alberto, "and wanted to join you below, but my doctor there, Fernando, will not hear of it."

"Indeed Alberto," said his sister, "it would have been the height of imprudence in you, to have attempted such a mad scheme; however, I hope by to-morrow you will be sufficiently recovered, to leave your room without danger, in spite of this misfortune."

"I consider myself rather fortunate," said Alberto, "in not having been worse off—thanks to Fernando."

"We owe him indeed," replied Rosara, "a multitude of thanks; it seems as if heaven had kindly sent Signior Fernando, to be the guardian of our house."

"Chance has thrown it in my way to assist Alberto," said Fernando, "and I am glad my efforts proved so successful. To merit Signiora Rosara's good opinion, is my utmost wish; and if I obtain that, it more than recompenses me, for any slight service I might have rendered the house of Vincenti."

Rosara wished her brother a good night, and Fernando attended her to the supper room, where the Condi and Signiora Luzia were waiting.

After a sleepless and restless night, Fernando rose by break of day, to refresh himself, by sauntering in the garden and enjoying the sea breeze. Rosara occupied his whole thoughts. He had wandered about for some time when he heard a gentle tread close to him—it was the lovely object that perpetually haunted his imagination—it was the charming Rosara.

He saluted her with his usual politeness.—They moved on close to each other, but not a word escaped.—They both felt the awkwardness of their situation, and neither had the resolution to enter into conversation. They instinctively bent their steps towards the alcove, situated close to the sea: the beauty of the situation; the calmness of the air; the perfume of flowers, which formed in festoons, hung over their heads; the gentle murmur of the water, which flowed at their feet, added to the soft langour which pervaded them. Their conversation frequently commenced, and a sudden silence as frequently ensued.—Often their eyes bent upon the ground, met in raising them, and were as speedily averted.—A tear—a sigh would escape from Rosara, as she hazarded to ask a question of Fernando, which remained unanswered, but by a responsive sigh.

A lute lay upon the table; Fernando ventured to request Rosara to play: she took the offered instrument, and touching the strings with exquisite execution, joined her melodious voice to the sweet sounds she produced. The air was a favorite one of Fernando's—it was plaintive in the extreme—Rosara did justice to it. While singing, Fernando contemplated with rapture her lovely countenance; not a sound escaped her lips, but his moist eye, and empassioned looks, spoke the tender feelings of his heart. Rosara ceased to sing, but still our hero listened to the dying strain. Embarrassed at the emotion she had evidently excited in Fernando, she covered with one hand the blushes which suffused her face; while the other wandering over the strings of the lute, drew forth wild and irregular notes.—These plaintive sounds encreased that tender melancholy, which had seized on their senses. Nothing could equal the charms, the rapture of that silent sympathy of soul, which the calm they enjoyed produced.

The name of Rosara, at length escaped from the lips of Fernando —a pause ensued.—

"Pity me, Rosara, have pity on the wretched Fernando."

Rosara attempted to speak—her voice faultered, her tongue refused to do its office; and she answered with a deep drawn sigh.

"If Rosara," said Fernando, "whose soul is the seat of every virtue, will not bestow one pitying word on me, I must be wretched indeed—farewell to happiness."

"Oh Fernando!" said Rosara, "there is not ought I could refuse thee—what can I do to serve you? Pity you indeed I do, and would feel it the proudest moment of my life, to bring back to you, that happiness you complain of having lost!"

"You know not what you say, Rosara," replied Fernando, taking her willing hand, "it is only you that can recall my peace; you have made me presumptious, fair maid; but let me rather keep my woes safely locked within my bosom, than incur the displeasure of the lovely Rosara."

"My displeasure, Fernando, you never can incur," said Rosara, with her head half averted, and in a voice so tremulous, that her words were scarcely distinct, but to the ears of a lover, "and if you deem me worthy to be intrusted with the secret of your woes, I may perhaps ameliorate the bitter pangs you seem to feel."

"Then hear me patiently, Rosara,—here on my bended knee I pray you look with mercy on one, who has dared to lift his aspiring thoughts to Rosara di Vincenti!—See at your feet, lovely Rosara, one who adores you!—and on the tablet of whose mind, thy virtues and thy image are so deeply engraven, that nothing can ever efface them!—Say, dear maid, at least you do not hate me!—my doom is irrevocable, I see it in your looks!—Even though, Rosara, you disdain my love—my life—nay, every moment of my existence shall be devoted to thy will!"—

"Rise from that posture, dear Fernando," said Rosara, in an intreating and affectionate tone, her violent agitation prevented her from saying more.

"That word," cried the enraptured youth, "dispels my fears!—say dearest Rosara," rising and encircling her waist with his arm, "say that you love, and ease my bleeding heart!"

"If," said the blushing maid, "the full possession of my heart can make Fernando happy, it is already his!—despise me not!—nothing but the anguish of mind I saw you suffer, should have ever torn the secret from my breast!"

"Despise you!—Fernando despise the beautiful Rosara!" cried he, while with an extacy of joy, he clasped her to his breast, and impressed a warm and fervent kiss upon her lips.

Rosara, overcome with the scene she had gone through, supinely rested her head upon the shoulder of her dear Fernando in a delirium of joy, he used every endearment that could tend to raise her spirits—a pleasing sensation thrilled through her veins, and her languid limbs refused to do their office.

Their hearts were too full to converse; Fernando drawing her arm through his assisted her to return to the Palazza, as the hour of breakfast was fast approaching, and he felt the necessity of Rosara's gaining her composure, before the family assembled; he led her to the door of her apartment, and then took his leave.

Fernando paced up and down his apartment, musing on his good fortune, in having obtained a return of his love from Rosara, and forming pleasing ideas of future bliss; when his attention was attracted by a letter, which lay upon his table, and had before been unobserved by him; he took it up, and finding it addressed to himself, he broke the seal, and read the following lines:

"Beware, Fernando, a secret enemy watches thy footstep; she is wily, and seeks thy life—thy friend Alberto too, is destined to be a victim—twice have I succoured thee in the hour of danger—beware!   R."

The note had merely the letter R, by way of signature; but Fernando was aware it came from the friendly unknown—he immediately summoned Gaspardo.

"How came this paper here?" said Fernando.

"I know not, Signior," said Gaspardo, "I placed it not there, nor has any been delivered to me, save what I have always presented to you."

"Is Signior Alberto stirring?" enquired Fernando.

"Yes, Signior," replied Gaspardo, "it is some time since he rang for Paulo, who is still with him."

Fernando hastened to Alberto, with the unfolded paper in his hand.—He had risen from his bed, and was nearly dressed, when Fernando entered.

"Why what has caused that dismal face of yours?" enquired Alberto, "I hope no more evils have befallen you."

"Before I answer you, my friend," said Fernando, "let me know how you feel yourself."

"Quite well," replied Alberto, "with the exception of a little stiffness—have you got a love-letter there?"

"Read it," said Fernando, as he held out the open paper to him, "and satisfy yourself."

Alberto perused it with astonishment.

"Thy life sought, and I a destined victim too!" at length he exclaimed, "surely Urbino never could be so base; he threatened Rosara, when he parted from her; but it is so long ago, his resentment must have subsided."

"It is wonderful, how well this unknown is acquainted with every occurrence that takes place about me;" said Fernando, "but I will not neglect his advice; I will act cautiously.—But now Alberto, prepare yourself to hear of things yet more extraordinary."

"I am prepared," said he, "for nothing now can astonish me."

"You know, my friend," continued Fernando, "I dared to love Rosara; I have this morning dared to throw myself at her feet and avow it.—The kind maid, with modest look, and crimsoned cheek, confessed that I possessed her heart, and promised to become my bride."

"I have watched your growing love," said Alberto, "and I deem myself fortunate, that I shall add the endearing name of brother, to the sacred one of friend.—You merit well Rosara's hand; your noble mind will justly appreciate her virtues; and days of joy open to your view—let me congratulate you then, in having succeeded in your wishes; my friend's felicity glads my heart, and renovates my languid frame.—It must be my care to pave the way, previous to your asking the Condi's consent; but Rosara's choice will be his."

Nothing could exceed the harmony that existed in the Palazza.—From the frequent opportunities Fernando had of seeing his loved Rosara, he daily told his tale of love; how happy was he, when passing the fleeting hours with her in the favorite alcove, where first he avowed his passion; or else

> "Amid the cooling fragrance of the morn,
> How sweet with her, through lonely fields to stray;
>
> *   *   *   *   *   *   *   *   *   *   *   *
>
> With her the shades of night their horror lose;
>   Its deepest silence charms if she be by;
> Her voice the music of the dawn renews,
>   Its lambent radiance sparkles in her eye."

CHAPTER VII.

Weeks had now elapsed, and each revolving day added fresh enjoyment to the amiable pair. Alberto had recovered his health completely, and was again enabled to move out; he invented every stratagem in his power to discover if Urbino had any thing to do in the late affair; to every enquiry at his Palazza, the porter answered, that he had not yet returned to Venice; he was therefore with reluctance obliged to give up all enquiries, and contented himself by keeping on his guard as much as possible.

The Condi proposed in the evening to amuse themselves by going on the water; it was the first time since the accident happened, that any of the family ever mentioned the subject. However the evening was beautifully serene, and the numerous assemblage of boats, of various descriptions, and the brilliant scene they afforded, gave ample satisfaction to the party. Fernando lost no opportunity of paying every attention that could gratify his Rosara, and she with pleasure beaming in her lovely countenance, timidly received them.

Sometimes their light barge, impelled by the strong oarsman's bending stroke, skimmed swiftly over the glassy surface of the deep, outstripping all that dared contend her speed. Sometimes, resting on their oars, they in pleasing converse with some well-known friend, beguiled the time; or else with mute attention, listened to the soft tones of melody floating on the breeze. In every passing countenance, mirth had assumed her empire; sorrow was chased from every brow, and gladdening sounds reverberated on the ear.

The party finding the evening closing in fast, and the air becoming chilly, desired the boatmen to return to the shore, they soon landed, well-pleased with their aquatic excursion.

Fernando, on retiring to his apartment, found a billet on his table, it was from the unknown—it ran thus:—

"I am about to leave Venice,—the exact time is uncertain—another opportunity may not occur, so convenient as the present, to tell you to be cautious; therefore I have thought proper to

embrace the present one.—Danger is near!—be not rash—you may
with confidence rely on me.   R."

This billet was signed as the former one, simply with an R.

"I will," cried Fernando, "place implicit faith in thee—thou hast
never yet deceived me, and if thou knowest how grateful my heart
is to thee, thou wouldst not doubt me."

It was too late Fernando thought to disturb Alberto, he therefore
conceived it best to wait until the morning, to make known the contents of this latter paper.

The sun had some time risen before Fernando woke, and he was
fearful he had kept the lovely Rosara waiting for him, as it was usual
for them to meet before that hour in the alcove, he therefore gave
the note to Gaspardo, desiring him to deliver it to Alberto. He hurried along, framing an excuse for his want of punctuality.

He approached the alcove gently, and called softly through the
trellis work—"Chide me not, Rosara, my thoughts were with thee
in my dreams;"—he heard no sounds from within; he entered—no
Rosara was there:—the lute, which had so frequently captivated
his senses, lay broken on the floor—the table was thrown down—a
scarf torn to atoms, hung over the arm of the chair, where it had
apparently caught—it was Rosara's scarf!—Quick as when the vivid
lightenings shoot across the sky, he sped towards the Palazza; he
met Alberto on the steps, who was just going to seek him, respecting the letter from the unknown.—"Where," cried he, grasping his
arm, and looking wildly at him, "where is my Rosara?—where is my
Rosara fled?"—then quitting him, he rushed towards her apartment.

Alberto followed and gently detaining him, enquired with strong
emotion, at hearing his sister's name so vehemently called upon
by Fernando—"What is it that has so agitated you Fernando—for
heaven's sake speak—"

"Look on this scarf," said Fernando wildly, "it once belonged to
the fairest maid in Venice!—dost thou not know it Alberto?—it was
Rosara's!—"

"Do compose yourself," said Alberto, "and speak more rationally."

"Even now I picked this up in the alcove, that borders on the sea, in
this tattered state, it too truly bespeaks some ill that has befallen her."

"I will knock at her door," said Alberto, assuming a composure foreign to his heart, "she may not have yet left her room;"—he struck loudly, no answer was returned;—"perhaps she sleeps,"—he tried the lock which readily yielded to his touch—the bed was vacant, and every thing in the apartment bore the marks of her having recently left it.

The whole Palazza, the grounds, and every part belonging to it, was minutely searched by the friends, but no Rosara was to be found; no appearance of footsteps were to be seen; and the only clue they could obtain, which authorised them to hazard a conjecture that she had been forcibly seized, was the disordered state of the alcove. Despair was depicted in the fine expressive face of Fernando—rage and impetuous passion became predominant in the breast of Alberto.

"Urbino! the villain Urbino has done this!" exclaimed he, "no corner of the earth shall hide from my resentment, this lurking spoiler of our peace!"

The sudden loss of all Fernando held most dear, was too severe a blow to his acute feelings; it had for the moment bereft him of his faculties; and while each was giving his opinion, and projects were forming, as to the best mode of recovering the lost Rosara, he stood as if his every nerve was paralysed; but at the name of Urbino, his terrible eye flashed fire, his brow assumed a severe and haughty aspect, and his majestic figure appeared more than human.

"Prepare my courser, and my armour, Gaspardo!" cried he, in a firm and elevated voice, while his looks declared the determined purpose of his soul.

The surrounding domestics, who had been accustomed to see Fernando gentle and affable, shrunk back with dismay, at his fierce mien; even his friend Alberto, could scarcely believe this was the same Fernando he had seen only a few minutes before.

"I will accompany you," said Alberto, "let your intentions be what they may; nothing shall ever separate me on this trying occasion from my friend and brother."

"From this moment," exclaimed Fernando, "I devote myself entirely to my beloved Rosara!—Not one instant will I rest until I find her, and rescue her from her ravishers, or perish in the attempt. Oh man! how couldst thou tear so lovely a flower from the bosom of her family, to plunge her into an abyss of grief? Could not her tears, her piercing shrieks, open a passage to thy heart? Urbino, thou hast for a moment triumphed, but here on my knees I swear, even on this same spot, where first I offered up my plighted faith, and sealed my love, to immolate thee to my just revenge.—No time is to be lost, let us equip ourselves." The youths retired.

The Condi had been informed of the misfortune which had befallen him—he cursed the hour he had known di Urbino—reproved himself for not being more thoroughly acquainted with him, before he received him into his family, on such an intimate footing.—He raved, he swore to revenge himself, and plant a dagger in Urbino's heart; but at length worn out and exhausted by repeated paroxisms of despair and passion, his domestics were obliged to conduct him, half frantic, to his apartments.

The two friends were not long in making their arrangements; they first went to take leave of the Condi, who had now become more composed.

"My brave Alberto," said he, "now the only support of thy wretched father's declining years, be careful of thyself; and may your efforts in search of my beloved Rosara, (at the repitition of her name, the emotion of the Condi became so violent, that nothing but his sobbing could be distinguished, for a considerable space of time) be crowned with success; for never again will these eyes behold her—she is gone, alas! for ever. Heavens protect you both!" taking a hand of each, "again I see, Fernando, you are ready to serve me, thou art indeed a noble youth! Let it be my care, instantly to give orders that my followers may be ready to aid you, whenever it is necessary, should your exertions prove successful."

The two youths pressed his hand with fervency, and after receiving his blessing, bade him adieu, and left him to mount their coursers.

The armour of Fernando was of polished steel, impenetrable and flexible, which defended the whole of his person; the casque, shaded with white plumes, covered his head; the buckler, round and light, armed with a sharp point, bore on it, as his device, two doves, with this motto—"*Innocence and Virtue.*" His keen edged sword depended from his shoulder; his poignard placed within the girdle that encircled his loins; the scarf he found in the alcove, belonging to Rosara, he attached to his armour, opposite his heart.

His neighing courser, whose floating mane descended to his knees, seemed with fiery eyes to view his master, and with pampered pride he champed the foaming bit. Fernando lightly vaulted on him, and was scarcely able to restrain his impetuous ardour.

Alberto was also encased in polished armour; and over whose casque waved a beautiful black plume; his shield, which was richly studded, bore as his device a phœnix, with these words as his motto *"He has no equal."* Gaspardo and Paulo, both armed at all points, attended the two youths.

Full of ardor, and burning with the desire of shortly avenging themselves, the two cavalieros moved off from the Palazza. Fernando had not imparted the line of conduct he intended to pursue as yet to Alberto; nor did Alberto think of questioning his friend with respect to it; the hurry of preparation driving every thing but Rosara from his memory; every minute of delay appeared to him an age, until he was actually in search of his dear sister; where to seek her he thought not of; where to gain any clue as to the place whither she had been forced, he knew not; but these were circumstances that had never recurred to his ardent mind, he trusted to Fernando entirely: he had intimated his intention of seeking Rosara—that was sufficient for him to join his friend in the arduous undertaking. Fernando rode musingly by the side of Alberto—he spoke not, but all the horrors of Rosara's situation perpetually harrassed his afflicted mind: if he had boldly declared to the Condi that he loved, and was beloved by Rosara, all this might not have happened. Oh, Love! what dost thou not make thy votaries feel? How many crosses do they not experience? But yet how sweet whenever the passion meets a kind return.

> "Ah, me! for aught that I could ever read;
> Could ever hear, by tale or history;
> The course of true-love never did run smooth:
> But either it was different in blood;
> Or else misgraffed in respect to years;
> Or else it stood upon the choice of friends;
> Or, if there were a sympathy of choice,
> War, death, or sickness did lay seige to it."

END OF THE FIRST VOLUME.

THE

VAULTS OF LEPANTO.

A Romance.

IN THREE VOLUMES.

BY

T. R. TUCKETT, Esq.

Murder most foul, as in the best it is;
But this most foul, strange, and unnatural.
My hour is almost come,
When I to sulph'rous and tormenting flames
Must render up myself.   SHAKESPEARE.

Oh! then at last relent; is there no place
Left for repentance, none for pardon left?
MILTON.

VOL. II.

LONDON:

PRINTED AT THE
Minerva-Press,
FOR A. K. NEWMAN AND CO.
LEADENHALL-STREET.
1814.

URBINO;

OR,

The Vaults of Lepanto.

CHAPTER VIII.

IT will now be necessary to revert to the Villa, where Signiora Benvoglio resided. From the first interview Alberto had with the fascinating Viola, he became deeply enamoured of her; his visits had been frequent at the summer-house, but he had never been able to gain an invitation to the Villa, nor had he ever yet beheld the Signiora Benvoglio, to whom it belonged: the fair Viola often urged to Alberto the impropriety of his breaking in upon her sacred retreat, and often declared her firm resolve of never again entering it unless he desisted; he as often pledged himself not to return; but, alas! impelled by those irresistible inclinations, which a lovely female inspires, he repeatedly transgressed. Viola conscious of his indiscretion, would chide him; but when Alberto gently pleaded his suit, acknowledged his error, and prayed forgiveness; then would the amiable Viola, already plunged in a delirium of delight and love, tenderly stretch forth her hand in token of reconciliation, which the enraptured Alberto would receive, as a gracious permission to err again.

It was during one of these sweet and stolen interviews, that the Signiora Benvoglio had strayed towards the summer-house; hearing the voice of a man, in converse with Viola, she burst like a torrent upon them; her face inflated with passion, and her voice choaked with rage, which for a considerable space of time, rendered her incapable of uttering a word; this however, fortunately, gave Alberto time to recover from his astonishment.

"Who are you, Signior?" at length roared she, addressing herself to Alberto, "how dare you intrude within the walls of my Villa? And you, Signiora, (turning to Viola) is it proper for you to be in this lonely situation with a cavaliero? I guessed the cause of your great regard for this place; but by to-morrow's dawn it shall be leveled with the ground!"

"For heaven's sake, Signiora," said Viola, ready to sink with fright and vexation, "do not judge harshly of me—I met this Signior cavaliero merely by accident."

"*Accident indeed!*" retorted the Signiora Benvoglio, "a pretty *accident*, truly, when a young Signior and Signiora are found conversing familiarly in a solitary place; but you shall repent this dearly; and you, Signior, I request you would never again set your foot within the precincts of my Villa."

The furious Signiora Benvoglio was about to retire, when Alberto approaching her, rather in a sarcastic tone said: "do not deprive me of the pleasure of paying my respects to the accomplished Signiora Benvoglio, for to her only can I suppose I am addressing myself."

"Yes, Signior, my name is Benvoglio, but how you became acquainted with it, I am much surprised!" said she, in rather a softened tone.

"Certainly, Signiora, I was totally unacquainted with your person," replied Alberto, "but the surrounding neighbourhood are ever dwelling on the virtues of the amiable Signiora, who resides in this Villa, (here casting a look at Viola) and to them I have long been no stranger; to this you must attribute the intrusion you have so justly censured."

"Signior," said the Signiora Benvoglio, with a voice, comparatively speaking, rendered a little milder, by the flattery Alberto had so timely made use of, "how can I with propriety admit a cavaliero to the Villa, unless I know his name and family—to you I am an entire stranger, therefore cannot receive your visits."

"I hope, Signiora, that my name and family will never exclude me from your doors; the noble race of Vincenti is, no doubt, well known to you—from them I spring: the noble Condi, who now bears the honors of that illustrious line, is the father of Alberto di Vincenti, who now addresses you."

"Had you, Signior Alberto, but declared your name," said the

Signiora Benvoglio, "I should with pleasure have received your intended visit; and I hope you will excuse the warmth with which I expressed myself." Her manner now became quite gentle, and she attempted to smile, but nothing could chase the marks of her latent fury from her bloated countenance. "Will not the Signior Alberto," asked she, "walk in, and take some refreshment?"

With the appearance of satisfaction, Alberto accepted her invitation, the better to let her remain in the erroneous opinion, that his visit was solely intended for her; though he could have dispensed with her civilities, as he clearly saw that he should not have any opportunity of renewing his delightful conversation with Viola, in the presence of the Signiora.

The length of time having elapsed, which was usual for a morning's call:—Alberto rose to take his departure; receiving many polite invitations from the Signiora Benvoglio, and many tender glances from Viola.

"How came you acquainted with the Signior cavaliero?" said the Signiora Benvoglio, as soon as Alberto was out of sight.

"He came in through the little garden gate," replied Viola, "and seeing me in the summer-house, saluted me—I was on the point of conducting him hither, when you entered." During this explanation, the face of poor Viola was of the deepest scarlet dye; she was ashamed of uttering a falsehood, but Alberto had declared his purpose was to see the Signiora Benvoglio, therefore she had no resource left her.

Whether the Signiora Benvoglio was satisfied with this answer, she did not declare, but remained thoughtful the whole of the day.

Viola was not aware, until Alberto's rencounter with the Signiora, that he was the son of the Condi di Vincenti; her heart alternately fluttered with hope and fear—could Alberto di Vincenti really love her? His conduct, his attentions, his language, his every look bespoke it; and her poor heart too truly told her, that she felt a deep interest in whatever concerned him.—Alberto had never avowed his love; but could he be acting a dishonorable part? No, it was impossible!—Nothing on earth could make her think unworthily of him. How unfortunate was it, that the Signiora should have broken in so suddenly on them; perhaps it would prevent her ever seeing him again; and even if that were not the case, it would be only in the presence of Signiora Benvoglio, who was too fond of flattery, to let the least opportunity escape of extorting a compliment; and of conversation, not to engross the whole of it. Viola became perplexed; she knew not what to think; and her mind was a prey to the greatest anxiety and inquietude.

Signiora Benvoglio, immediately after Alberto had introduced himself, and mentioned his name, thought it necessary to behave herself with the most marked respect, and to offer every inducement to the young cavaliero, by her courtesy, to repeat his visit to the Villa. The Signiora, who had been an adept in the art of love, clearly perceived by Alberto's countenance, and expressive looks, that he saw Viola in a favorable point of view. She was an orphan, entrusted to her care; therefore a speedy establishment was what she earnestly looked forward to; however the idea of forming an illustrious connexion, had never entered her thoughts; nay, it was next to an impossibility, from the secluded manner in which she lived; but now a brighter prospect presented itself to the penetrating eye of the Signiora; and Alberto di Vincenti, was marked out by her as the destined husband of Viola.

Day after day, Alberto visited at the Villa, and was always received with the greatest complacency by the Signiora Benvoglio, and with kindness by Viola. The Signiora rarely ever left her alone with Alberto, so that these interviews were perfectly monotonous; and the only gratification Alberto felt, was in seeing, and being for a time near the lovely—the blooming Viola. Vexed at the constant disappointment he met with, at not being able to converse freely with her he adored, he almost determined formally to declare to the Signiora, his intentions towards Viola. But upon reflection, he conceived this measure would be unwise: he was not certain that the lovely girl esteemed him; and he wished to know her sentiments, before he disclosed the affair to the Signiora.

He was perpetually on the watch—he almost haunted the vicinity of the Villa, to gain an opportunity of meeting the object that had become so dear to him; but his endeavours proved fruitless. The Signiora had forbidden Viola ever again to go to the summerhouse, unless attended by her; and this the Signiora was determined should be strictly adhered to, as she more closely observed the conduct of Viola than ever.

Could a youth of Alberto's impetuous disposition brook the delay, the officious vigilance of the Signiora caused? No!—the more obstacles that appeared to be thrown between his love and him, gave but an additional spur to his ardent mind, to overcome them. He therefore formed the resolution of writing a billet, as being the only mode that seemed to promise success, and of giving it to Viola, the first time the Signiora Benvoglio should for an instant leave the room: luckily for the impatient youth, an opportunity soon offered; he presented the billet to Viola, during a momentary absence of the Signiora, who trembling hardly dared to reject or accept it. During this painful indecision of Viola, the returning steps of the Signiora were heard—it now became imperiously necessary to act decidedly; he therefore dropped it in the lap of Viola, and immediately resumed his seat. Compelled in a manner to accept the folded paper, she hastily placed it in her bosom, lest the Signiora should discover it.

Alberto soon took his leave, and Viola retired, cautiously locking her door, and looking round fearfully, lest any prying eye should have invaded the privacy of her apartment; she carefully drew the paper from its concealment, and threw it on her dressing table. What, thought she am I about to do?—clandestinely to receive the letters of a young and accomplished cavaliero; it is, I am sensible incorrect, and he will, I fear, in the sequel, despise me for it.—No, Alberto! I cannot read it!—I will to-morrow return it thee. She took it up and examined it with attention. "If I give this back to him unopened, his disappointment will be great.—I do not wish to inflict pain, dearest Alberto!" exclaimed she, "but still, every rule of propriety forbids me from entering into a correspondence of this nature;—but yet it surely cannot contain anything, but what might be perused by all the world—Alberto is too noble-minded to act in any way derogatory to the strict principles of honor."

Her hand was upon the seal, while she was considering what line of conduct to pursue—she knew not what to resolve. Inclination, the secret whisperings of her heart, decided at length in favor of Alberto—the seal was broken, and the letter hastily read—it contained only these few words:

"Pardon, dearest Viola, the temerity of Alberto di Vincenti; he would not thus have dared to intrude himself upon you, but that he despairs of ever again enjoying that sweet uninterrupted converse, which had so frequently beguiled the heavy hours: he therefore prays you, as you value his life, and his happiness, to grant him a few minutes audience in the summer-house: with fear and anxiety he waits your answer—destroy not the hopes, dearest Viola, of your

"ALBERTO."

"How couldst thou make so cruel a request, Alberto?—why did I open this fatal billet?—better far that I had been ignorant I was dear to him, than have known his wishes:—this has placed me in a most distressing dilemma—thoughtless Alberto! to ask that which you must be aware is wrong for me to grant, and which, alas! my heart is too willing to allow—but by to-morrow I must determine what course to follow.—If I am dear to thee, Alberto," ejaculated she, "heaven can testify how beloved thou art by Viola!—But my future prospects are dark and cloudy—my origin is envelloped in obscurity—Alberto is yet unacquainted with my little story."

Viola, oppressed with care, remained spiritless and cheerless the whole of the day; and the Signiora was a female little adapted to chase away the gloomy ideas that tormented her.

The plan the Signiora Benvoglio intended to follow with respect to Alberto, was never to allow him an interview with Viola, but in her presence; she conceived that by adopting this mode, it would compel the cavaliero, to ask her approbation, previous to his declaring himself to Viola, for there could not be a doubt as to his love for her. The Signiora had never dropped the most distant hint, that Viola was not her niece, and she was fearful if Alberto discovered her real situation, that he would discontinue his attentions; she also knew that the integrity of mind Viola possessed, would lead her to disclose every thing to him, in the event of his having an opportunity of making known his sentiments to her; but if she could once, by raising the passions of the youth, by the repeated disappointments he met with, in not being able to tell his love, induce him first to open his heart to her; she thought it easy to bend the pliant mind of Viola to her will, and keep the secret till it was no longer a matter of consequence.

At the usual hour Alberto called at the Villa; the Signiora sat with him a long time, previous to the entrance of Viola, hoping that she might gain some clue as to his intentions; but she was entirely foiled in her views. The Signiora, much to his satisfaction, was called out, when taking advantage of it, he immediately asked Viola if she would grant his request. The roses and the lillies alternately drove each other from her lovely cheeks. "For heaven's sake," said Alberto, "do not distress yourself so, dearest Viola!—But no time is to be lost —say you will meet me this night at twelve, in the summer-house." The trembling and terrified girl could make no answer, she was ready to fall from her chair. "Say that you will;" urged the impetuous Alberto, "my life, my happiness depends upon it! (the hand of the Signiora was on the door) Say you will!" cried Alberto, with vehemence.

Falteringly, and scarcely audibly, Viola uttered,—"Yes, I will."

But the acute ears of the Signiora heard the words as she entered. "What will you, Viola?" enquired she glancing a sharp and suspicious look at her.

Alberto, fearful lest Viola should, by her agitation, betray herself, immediately replied, "I have been requesting a landscape, which I have so frequently admired, from Signiora Viola, and at last I have obtained a reluctant promise of it."

"Why" said the Signiora, "do you not give the landscape to Signior Alberto? do pray get it from the porte-feuille."

Viola rose, obedient to the desire of the Signiora, whose will was tantamount to a law; and taking the landscape from the porte-feuille, presented it to Alberto; he received it with every mark of respect, though he could scarcely contain the joy he felt, at having so completely deceived the Signiora.

Alberto with his extorted gift, soon left the Villa; but not before he had an opportunity of reminding Viola of the hour of midnight. The cavaliero considered it perfectly easy to reach the summer-house, by climbing the wall; Paulo could accompany him with a rope ladder, and by these means all difficulty would be done away with. On arriving at the Palazza, Alberto instructed Paulo in what it was necessary to obtain for the operations of the evening.

"I do not like wall mounting," said Paulo in a low grumbling tone, "we stand chances enough every day of our lives, and of breaking our necks, without seeking walls at night, to climb to shew our dexterity."

"What are you talking to yourself about?" said Alberto, "if you do not wish to accompany me, you are at liberty to remain at home, and I will procure some one else."

"No, Signior," answered Paulo, "wherever you go, I will follow: there is no danger you can expose yourself to, that I will not share it with you; ever since I was a child, I have been devoted to you, and it is not now that I will desert my master, when he has occasion for my services. If I was induced, Signior, to speak, it was because I was anxious lest an accident might happen to you."

"Very well, Paulo," said Alberto, "I know your intentions were good, or I would not have entrusted you, but no more of this for the present; be careful you execute my directions strictly."

"You may depend upon it, Signior," said Paulo, "every thing shall be ready at the hour."

CHAPTER IX.

The Signiora Benvoglio, now thought she had brought matters nearly to a conclusion, and was determined, if the cavaliero did not shortly come to some explanation, that she would forbid the frequency of his visits, or plainly ask him the cause of their constancy, just as circumstances required. She felt secure in her mind, that he had not made known his passion to Viola formally, as she had given them no opportunity of being alone, but for a very short space of time. Though she thought the cavaliero rather tardy in making his avowal; the flames of love she fancied burnt not so quick around his heart, as she could have wished. Her patience became almost exhausted, and she doubted whether his calls were only meant to pass his idle hours pleasantly, and had nothing serious in them, This was a terrible idea to the Signiora: if she had been deceived in this, she never would trust again to appearances.

The hours during the remainder of the day, seemed to move unusually slow to Viola, who feared, yet anxiously wished for the conclusion of the interview. She conceived it would be the means of destroying her peace of mind for ever; yet it was a dreadful trial she found necessary to go through. The clock at length struck the midnight hour, and Viola with an assumed composure, descended to meet Alberto. The whole family had retired for some time, and every thing was quiet within the Villa.

The cavaliero had been some time in the summer-house, waiting the arrival of the loved object; at last he heard her light tread on the terrace, and in an instant found himself by her side.—Their embarrassment was great, and the place brought back to their memories the scene that had passed the last time they met there. Alberto recovering a little, took the hand of Viola, and leading her to a chair, seated himself by her.

"You are kind in having thus granted to your Alberto his request—"

"Pray Signior," said Viola, interrupting him, "inform me of the cause of your expressing a wish to see me here?"

"Could not," said Alberto, "your heart tell you, that I loved you! —Thou art, Viola, the only woman, that has ever made an impression on me!—I love you to distraction!—but who would not, that was acquainted with thy beauties and thy virtues?—I have read in thy eyes, beaming with love and mildness, that Alberto was not indifferent to you—your faltering accents have betrayed the interest you felt in my fate—I could no longer delay opening that heart to you, where you reign sole mistress—Alberto loves you, Viola! and sues you to accept his vows."

"I cannot deny, Signior," answered Viola, with fortitude, "that you have possession of my heart—you are indeed very dear to me, but Signior I beg your attention for a few moments. It would ill become me," continued Viola, "after a noble cavaliero has confessed an honorable attachment to me, to treat him with deceit —no; let groveling minds stoop to meanness; and though my happiness is wrecked, my probity shall be untarnished.—You, Signior, conceive me to be the niece of Signiora Benvoglio—I am not!—I expected this surprise, Signior, it was but natural.—No, Alberto, no fostering mother's care did Viola ever experience—my days, even from my birth have been marked with sorrow; I am an orphan, thrown upon the protection of the Signiora Benvoglio, from my tenderest years, she has had the sole direction of me; every master that was necessary to form my education has been allowed me—

but still to all my enquiries I can learn no more—now Alberto you see there is an insurmountable barrier."

"What," said Alberto, "can my Viola, think that any change of circumstances can shake my love?—you now have a greater claim to my affection—if you were dear to me as the relative of the Signiora, you are much more so as the orphan Viola—you must be admired by all, dearest girl; nothing can equal the disinterested acknowledgment of your birth, and aught not Alberto to feel himself happy in possessing the esteem of an amiable and lovely girl, who is capable of such honorable sentiments?—yes, Viola—you are, you shall be mine!"

"Let not passion hurry you too far Alberto, my heart bleeds to see you thus; but it would not be consistent with my duty to encourage your love.—Heaven knows my joyous hours were few, but now alas! they are fled for ever!"

"Say not so, dearest Viola!" said Alberto, with emotion, "my arms are ready to receive you—say that you will become the bride of Alberto di Vincenti—he will soothe thy tortured mind, and with his kind attention, restore your wanted serenity."

"Hear me, Alberto," replied Viola, "never perhaps did woman love a youth with more fervency than I do Alberto di Vincenti!— You have a father, who from your infancy has treated you with every mark of paternal care; your conduct has been such, as to give him every degree of satisfaction; and each day he beholds with greater pride, that son, who is one day to enjoy the honors of his house. Think but for a moment, Alberto, what his feelings would be, when informed that you have placed your affections on an orphan—a friendless being without a name. No, Alberto!—Never will Viola enter the family of the proudest nobleman in Venice, where she is to meet with contempt; it is my love for you, dearest Alberto, that prompts me to this act; it would completely break my heart, to know that I caused the anger of your father."

"You know him not!" replied Alberto, in despair, "I will fly to him and ask his permission—he will readily grant it—he values my peace too much, to refuse a request in which my happiness is so nearly connected: you have indeed given a death blow to all my hopes."

"Do not, by the love you profess for me, acquaint your father that you have placed your affections on me. There was a time when I looked forward to brighter prospects; when my youthful fancy led me to exult in the idea of possessing Alberto's heart, I became intoxicated with the deep draughts of love I daily drank; but now returning reason has resumed her empire, and Viola has escaped from plunging into an abyss, that would have made her tenfold more miserable! She would have sacrificed her integrity—she would have destroyed a virtuous, an amiable cavaliero, by drawing down the vengeance of his family on him.—Farewell, Alberto!—think of me often—you never shall be absent from my thoughts. I go to pine in secret: even when the cold hand of death is on me, still the image of Alberto will be present, and his dear name be sighed out with my departing spirit."

Her tears choked her further utterance—her feelings were wound to the highest pitch of sensibility. Alberto could not speak —he gently drew her to his bosom, and imprinted a kiss upon her lips: she rejected not his freedom—she regarded Alberto as superior to the rest of the world. She had the firmest, the strongest reliance on his honor: but as if a sudden thought had struck her, she sprang from him, and without saying a syllable, ran as fast as she could down the terrace, and entered the Villa. Alberto stood transfixed— her action had been so quick, that he had been incapable of making any effort to detain her.

"Cruel, cruel Viola!" exclaimed the empassioned youth, "thus to leave me a prey to every horror that can assail the mind—my fate is peculiarly hard." Here his feelings became too powerful for him to combat; he knew not how to leave the spot, now rendered doubly dear to him.

Paulo, who remained in the road, beneath the garden wall, from the long stay of his master, began to fear that his predictions had been verified; he therefore fastened the horses, and ascended by the ladder to the terrace. Alberto was sitting on a chair, the image of woe: it required every exertion of his faithful domestic, to rouse him from the stupor into which he had fallen; and with difficulty he succeeded in the attempt. With considerable trouble, Paulo got his master over the wall, and assisted him on his horse; they moved off at a gentle pace towards Venice, while involuntary sighs burst from his distracted bosom.

Viola was thoroughly aware of the danger of her situation with Alberto, and her duty had dictated to her the propriety of refusing his hand, but her heart could not conceal its secret; she therefore as readily acknowledged the deep impression he had made upon her, as she was determined to adhere, in her line of conduct respecting him; but when she found herself yeilding to the delightful sensations that ran through her veins, and suffering the endearing, though chaste caresses of the youth she loved; the solitary situation she was in; and the lateness of the hour, flashed upon her mind, and she left Alberto in the hurried manner described; fearful of trusting herself even to say adieu once more. Gaining her apartment, she threw herself upon her bed, almost ready to faint with the load of grief that weighed upon her mind.

"He is gone—for ever gone!" exclaimed she, "Alberto, who I loved so truly, I have for ever banished from my sight. Oh, Viola! what hast thou done?—Thou hast ruined thy peace for ever, and the world is but as a blank before thee." Tired and overcome by the contending passions that warred within her breast, she became restless beyond endurance, until sleep in pity to her sufferings, waved his leaden wand over her eyelids, and by his influence, she soon sunk into a sweet forgetfulness of her woes. Alas! sweet girl, this was but a short respite to thy grief.

When Alberto arose, after a short and restless sleep, he found that the words of his adored Viola, were still fresh in his memory; and on reflection he conceived that it was impossible, but that the Signiora Benvoglio, knew her name and from whence she sprung; it was not a probable circumstance that she should have brought up Viola in so superior a manner, had she not been fully acquainted with the history of her parentage, and someway interested in her prospects in life, when every action evinced the most decided dislike to her.

"I will call," said Alberto, "tell her I love Viola, and try to fathom the depth of the mystery, which enclouds her birth."—Though depressed, and little fit for such an undertaking, Alberto hastened towards the Villa, for the purpose of putting his resolution in force; but judge of his surprise, when on knocking at the hall door, the porter refused him admittance, and delivered to him the following note:

"Signiora Benvoglio requests Signior Alberto di Vincenti would discontinue his visits, as it is at present impossible for her to receive them; it would be unnecessary for the Signiora to enter at greater length into the cause of her thus for a time desiring that the Signior would not repeat them."

"I am not awake, certainly," said the astonished Alberto; "pray," enquired he of the porter, "did the Signiora desire you to deliver this to me?"

"Yes, Signior," replied the porter.

Alberto walked out of the hall, and the doors shut him out from her, he prised more than his existence; he knew no means of getting into the Villa, nor did he know any of the servants within, whom he could entrust with a letter to Viola.

The sun had for some hours penetrated the casement of Viola, ere she arose, and finding it late, she hastily attired herself and descended to the breakfast room, where the Signiora was already waiting for her.

"You have slept longer than usual this morning," said she to Viola, as soon as she entered the apartment, "and it will be highly necessary for us to exert ourselves for the reception of an illustrious visitor, who intends honoring me, by spending some time at the Villa; and I request you will treat the Duca di Urbino with every degree of respect.—He wishes to be as private as possible, I have therefore given orders, that the Signior Alberto should not be admitted, I have also written a note to him, which merely requests him to decline his visits for the present."

"At what hour, Signiora," enquired Viola, timidly, "do you expect the Duca?"

"Not before night fall," answered the Signiora, "he will have to travel some distance, as his letter assures me: there will be two cavalieros with him; and though the Duca does not wish us to see company, yet we shall not be in total solitude."

Viola never saw the Signiora look so sprightly, she seemed as if she had made up her mind to captivate the Duca and all his party; good humour shone in her countenance, as far as she was capable of shewing good humour, for her face bore every appearance of moroseness, and Viola wondered how she could even manage to throw the small portion of vivacity she displayed

into her composition; but her illustrious visitor no doubt was the
cause.

CHAPTER X.

At the period the Signiora expected her visitors, they arrived; and
the Duca di Urbino introduced the two cavalieros, with him, as
Signior Sanguinario, and Signior Bernardo. They were then in
rotation presented to Viola; but as her eyes met those of Urbino,
his frame shook, the colour fled from his cheeks, and his half open
lips, and straining eye, shewed the inward agitation he suffered.

"Do not," said Sanguinario, in a harsh voice, "unman yourself
thus." At the same time taking the Duca by the shoulder, and shaking him violently, to bring him to his recollection.

"Thank you, Sanguinario," said the Duca, "for recalling my scattered senses; but the likeness this fair Signiora bears to one I shall
ever remember with regret, excited the degree of emotion you just
witnessed."

"Come, Duca, cease these unpleasant reflections," said Sanguinario, darting a fierce look at him.

The Signiora, who had prepared an excellent repast, invited them
to partake of it, which they with pleasure acceded to. The introduction, thought Viola, is not very flattering, but however, when they
are refreshed, I shall be better able to judge.

The Duca paid great attention to Viola, and Sanguinario eyed
him with a ferocity, that frequently caused him for a time to sink
into a sullen silence. The other cavaliero, Signior Bernardo, enjoyed
all the good things that were going forward; he never opened his
lips, but to ask for wine, which he took in copious quantities.

Happy to be freed from such society, Viola hastened as soon as
she could to her own apartment. The fineness of the night, and it
being still early, induced her to open her window, to enjoy the cool-
ing breeze; besides the summer-house was in view, and it brought
back sadly pleasing scenes to her mind. She contemplated with a
melancholy air, the little building in which she had passed many
hours of joy; and where she had also spent the bitterest of her life.
She gradually sunk into a reverie, and had remained so for some

time; when she heard the sound of voices beneath her window. A little grove of trees partly excluded the persons from her view.

"I never saw," said one of them, who she recognised by his voice, to be the Duca, "so striking a likeness to her mother—it went to my very soul; and had it not been for the shake you gave me, I must have fallen."

"It was a sudden qualm I suppose, that came over you;" said the other figure, which she now perceived to be that of Sanguinario, "they are not very common with you, Duca. Viola is certainly a lovely creature—you knew her mother, when as young as her?"

"I did," answered the Duca, "she was even fairer than this lovely rose-bud; but come, we will no longer dwell on scenes that cannot be recalled."

"More qualms;" said the savage Sanguinario, with a sneer, "but when shall we proceed to business?"

"To-morrow," said the Duca, "we must find out by what means we can most easily gain admittance into the Palazza; if that can once be accomplished, I do not doubt the issue. My person is well known there, therefore we must employ some of the party."

"That," rejoined Sanguinario, "would be imprudent, as we must not let them further into our scheme, than what is necessary."

"You are right," said the Duca, "Know you if Bernardo has collected in Venice a sufficient number of the band?"

"Never fear him at mischief," said Sanguinario, "he is never backward when that is in the way; but he is so fond of his bottle, that unless sent upon some desperate business, he never thinks of anything else."

"I intended proposing him to gain intelligence from the Palazza," said the Duca.

"No that will not do;" answered Sanguinario, "he would first get drunk with the domestics, and then cut their throats: let that be my care—we must go cautiously to work;—but remember, this service done, I instantly expect my reward."

"It shall be granted," replied Urbino. "Let Bernardo know we meet here nightly after supper."

"I will," replied Sanguinario.

They both wished each other a good night, and separated.

The conversation was too interesting to Viola, for her to lose

one word. It was obvious both the Duca and Sanguinario were acquainted with her origin; they even spoke of her mother.—Perhaps
she was the offspring of guilt!—the thought made her miserable.
Should she confess to the Duca, she had overheard his conversation, and entreat him to inform her what he was acquainted with,
relative to her birth? That her mother was no more, appeared by
the Duca's answer. She determined, as the most preferable plan, to
be at the window each night, as perhaps she might hear something
more, that would give her a clue to discover the secret of her origin.
She despised the idea of becoming a listener; but the urgency of
her situation, required her to use no delicacy in this instance. Sanguinario appeared to her to be a villain.—Bernardo was not more
prepossessing in his aspect: long, lank black hair hung over his high
forehead; his large eyeballs rolled perpetually around, as if in quest
of something; his figure was nearly as tall as that of Sanguinario,
but much more athletic; no act seemed desperate enough for him
to undertake; he hardly ever spoke at table, but when questioned
by the Duca: he looked an ungracious wretch, fit for the mountains
and the barbarous caves, where manners ne'er were preached.

My time, thought Viola, will not pass very gaily, in the society
of these accomplished cavalieros. The Signiora did not seem quite
so well pleased with her guests, as Viola expected she would have
been, from their morning's conference.

"Alberto! dearest Alberto!" ejaculated Viola, "If I should ever
prove worthy of being received into your family, then perhaps,
peace may again return to my bosom. Thou knowest not how dear
thou art to me, Alberto!"

Poor hapless maid, thy destiny is indeed severe; but yet a day may
come, when thy transcendant virtues will be rewarded with all thy
heart can wish.

The whole party did not assemble the next day at breakfast; both
Sanguinario and Bernardo were absent. To the enquiries of the
Signiora, whether the cavalieros would not attend that meal, the
Duca apologised for their abscence, saying they had gone out early
on business of importance.

"I hope," said the Signiora, "we shall have the pleasure of seeing
them at dinner."

"They seemed to express some doubt," said the Duca, "whether they would be able to accomplish the matters, respecting which they are gone, before night; but I think we may rely on their being present at that time."

The heart of Viola sunk within her, at the mention of their absenting themselves on *urgent* affairs: she well recollected the last night's conversation; and she feared, from the opinion she had formed of the two Signiors, that something not well calculated to see the light of day, was going forward. Their nightly meetings appeared mysterious.

The Duca paid Viola every polite civility in his power, but he had a boldness in his manner, that was not consonant to her feelings; wherever she moved, he followed as her shadow, and only in the retirement of her room, could she find quiet from his disgusting conversation.

Several days elapsed, and nothing extraordinary had taken place at the Villa. The Duca and the two cavalieros met nightly under the window of Viola, and she constantly took her post. Sanguinario returned home one evening just as they were sitting down to supper, pleasure seemed to sparkle in his eyes, and his gloomy countenance was expressive of secret satisfaction. He became gay, and even talkative during the repast, frequently pledging the Duca in bumpers.

The Duca was the first to withdraw, and Viola well knowing they would be punctual at their customary place of rendezvous, hastily took her lamp, and retired. She had not long placed herself at her window, before she observed Sanguinario and Bernardo coming down the avenue; the Duca was already waiting for them.

"Well," said the Duca, as soon as they joined him, "I hope you have at last some good intelligence?"

"All," answered Sanguinario, "that could be wished for—I have made myself acquainted with all the avenues of the Palazza, and every part of the grounds."

"Ten thousand thanks, dearest Sanguinario! I never shall be sufficiently able to repay thee."

"You know my reward Duca—I ask no more—but you have a rival, Signior, who is beloved—I heard the love-sick fool offering up his adorations to his divinity, and could I have reached him in time, my dagger should have drank his life's blood, and sent his canting soul to whine in hell!"

"Perdition catch the reptile," said Urbino, in violent rage—"who is he that dares my vengeance?—knowest thou Sanguinario?"

"His name," answered Sanguinario, "I could not learn; but I saw sufficient of his person, to recognise in him the cavaliero, who that old babling fool Theresa admitted to the cottage, the morning after we met at the Castello di Lepanto."

"Is it certainly him?" enquired the hitherto silent Bernardo, "for if so by mine honor, Signior Cavalero I owe you something in turn for the wound you gave me in the forest, and by way of thanking you I swear to let a little of your blood."

"That was bravely spoken, Bernardo," said Sanguinario; "it is unworthy of a man to accept such services without making a return."

"We shall find more difficulty," said the Duca, "in effecting our purpose, than I had conceived.—This cavaliero, you told me was bold, and to my cost, I know her brother is—I fear we shall be foiled."

"How comes this?" answered Sanguinario, with a sneer, "I thought the Duca di Urbino was always foremost in the hour of danger, but he seems appalled at the idea of encountering two spirited cavalieros; but remember," added he fiercely, "I will accomplish the scheme that brought me hither, and expect my reward—it is for that I serve you Duca."

The proud spirit of Urbino seemed to yield to the overbearing language of the murderous Sanguinario.

"What mode do you now propose?" enquired the Duca.

"There is but one," answered Sanguinario, "that men bent on an honorable revenge would pursue.—This cavaliero, this redoubted knight, at whose mention the Duca di Urbino turns pale, must fall! How could Sanguinario live beneath the same atmosphere in which this damned hated object breathes?—And has he not besides this, solemnly sworn to plunge his sword a thousand times within his breast? which he would have succeeded in, had not a meddling fool most timely come to his assistance;—and can I let this glorious opportunity escape? Duca, did Sanguinario ever break his word to thee?—No, never!—Then will not Sanguinario depart from his oath! Lend me for a moment, your undisturbed attention.—It is the custom of your innamorata, to meet this youth every morning in the summer-house, at the end of the grounds; there is no mode of approaching it but by water; we must prepare a gondola, from whence it will be easy to step on shore and seize the lady; as for her kneeling swain, should he live, I will poignard him; but revenge is sweet, and it must be more speedy. Nightly will we walk until we meet this dreaded cavaliero, when warily following, we will suddenly and unexpectedly make an attack, whilst Bernardo and part of his band shall intercept him, and by this means hemming him between the parties, sacrifice the victim at a blow; this branch lopped off, the Duca di Urbino will have less to fear.—How like you this?"

"Very well," said Bernardo, "only it will be better I should stab him to the heart; but should I miss my aim, with my whistle I can give notice, and then I think between us all, we can easily dispatch him, and give him to the fishes for a feast."

"Well be it so," said Sanguinario, "with you, Bernardo, I never cavil in a point of honor; but we must procure a gondola by to-morrow forenoon, and in the evening hunt down our prey."

"Thou art a trusty friend indeed," said the Duca. "Every thing now is finally settled, and all we wait for, is the golden opportunity. —Could I but once have thee in my possession, lovely maid, not all the powers combined should wrest thee from my arms!"

" 'Tis time we should retire," said Sanguinario, "it may excite suspicion."

This trio separated, after having formed their villainous schemes. Viola could scarcely support her tottering frame to her bed; overcome with every mental calamity, she was almost driven to a state of phrensy. She had hitherto supported herself with the idea of collecting some information from their nightly conversation, which might lead to a discovery respecting her name and origin; but the party seemed entirely bent on murder, and the commission of every wicked deed. Viola was in hopes something might occur to counteract the projects of the Duca and his associates; it was not in her power to avert their designs. Completely confined within the walls of the Villa, she had no means of warning the persons who were endangered; besides she did not hear a name mentioned, which totally extinguished every hope she had nourished of preventing the successful issue of Urbino's savage purpose.

The morning had already dawned, before Viola had composed herself to sleep, and then her imagination perpetually figured to her some horrid scene of bloodshed. Feverish and languid, the distressed girl arose from her thorny couch, and much to her satisfaction, found the Signiora alone. The cavalieros had all gone out but were expected back soon. Viola entreated the Signiora to permit her to absent herself from the party, as she felt extremely indisposed; with difficulty this favor was granted, and she rejoiced at the prospect of being freed for a short time, from the unpleasant society formed within the Villa.

The day passed swiftly and tranquilly with Viola, she could indulge without interruption, in reflecting on the virtues, and noble soul of Alberto di Vincenti; on his disinterested love, which even her forlorn state could not shake; in meditating upon the different conversations that passed under her window; and at the extraordinary appearance and conduct of Sanguinario and Bernardo, who had been introduced as cavalieros, but the truth of which she now suspected, struck her as being little calculated to maintain the characters of such.

The night had worn away apace, and she thought of descending for the purpose of procuring a lamp, when she heard a bustle in the hall; she anxiously listened—all was again silent—no sound was to be heard. Some fresh misfortune has happened, thought she, but assuming a degree of courage, foreign to her heart, Viola moved towards the door, when a hasty step was distinguishable, approaching down the corridor, and almost instantaneously the Signiora Benvoglio burst into the apartment: in her countenance, fear was strongly depicted; the lamp which she held in her hand, displayed to the astonished Viola, several spots of blood upon her garments.

"For heaven's sake," cried the terrified Viola, "what has happened to you?—You are not injured I hope," pointing to her dress.

The Signiora cast her eyes on the spots and answered, "No, no—It is not I; but there is a terrible business below: the Duca and Signior Bernardo have brought in Signior Sanguinario wounded."

"Some accident I suppose has befallen him?" enquired Viola.

"Their story," replied the Signiora, "is a little curious. They were walking together, and presently they heard the clashing of swords;

Sanguinario you must know, is considered as bold as a lion, and he must run directly to assist in the fray, that was going forward, and before the Duca and Signior Bernardo could come up, he was wounded; but they succeeded in driving off some villains, who had attacked a young Signior. It may be so, but I do not think the cavaliero Sanguinario so likely to assist anybody in distress, though they say he is so courageous.—I do sincerely wish that the Duca had not brought these two cavalieros with him."

"The Duca di Urbino," said Viola, "is a man of family, and appears to have a great knowledge of the world; but I must confess there is not anything prepossessing in the manners or conversation of his companions."

"I shall not regret their leaving us," replied the Signiora, "and the sooner it takes place, the more pleasure I shall feel."

"How came you to be sprinkled with their blood?" enquired Viola.

"Why when I heard the bustle," answered the Signiora, "I ran into the hall to see what was the cause, when I beheld a man leading in wounded, and almost fainting; it came into my mind immediately that it was the Duca, for my fright prevented me from observing that he had hold of one arm of Sanguinario; I therefore ran up to offer my assistance in staunching the blood, when this must have dropped on my clothes?"

"Is the Signior much injured?" asked Viola.

"Oh yes, very much," answered the Signiora. "He has a large cut on the side of his face, and another between his shoulder and his breast; but what I wonder at, is how the villains could penetrate through the great heavy armor he had got on under his cloak! I must now return, for by this time the Duca will have had him put to bed and properly dressed, and he will be expecting me in the supper room—will you not descend?"

"I would rather not," said Viola, "but you will oblige me by ordering me a lamp."

The Signiora wished Viola a good night, and hastened to meet her guests, who she was fearful might have been waiting for her.

At the usual hour, Viola took her post at the window; she felt very anxious to collect some information, from this night's conversation, respecting the progress of their diabolical schemes. The fate of the cavaliero, who she was certain had been assaulted by the bloodthirsty Sanguinario, she was particularly desirous of knowing. Her thoughts were soon disturbed by the sound of the Duca's voice, who was accompanied by the odious Bernardo.

"How could you possibly have bungled so?" said the Duca, in an angry tone. "I conceived you had been more expert."

"It was not in my power to know he had a breast-plate on—you pointed out your man, and he seemed only wrapped in his cloak.—I wanted to settle him at once, because it is a rule with me to give as little pain as possible; but had I been aware he was armed, he should not have escaped me."

"Sanguinario is much hurt," said the Duca, "and this is particularly unfortunate, as it will retard the execution of our plan, in carrying off the Signiora from the Palazza."

"He will soon recover," answered Bernardo, "and no great time will be lost.—But did you ever behold a braver cavaliero, than this same one we attacked?—He fought like the very devil—we shall have tough work with him yet."

"I fear so too," replied the Duca. "Have you got every thing ready about the gondola?"

"Every thing," said Bernardo, "is in order.—Two of the band were gondolieris, but were obliged to enlist with me, having taken it into their heads to stab a couple of cavalieros, and make free with their cash; them I have placed in the gondola, they do not know anything about what our intentions are, and they are always to be found."

"Had it not been for this cursed wound of Sanguinario's," said the Duca, "every thing might have been speedily at an end, and I have been made happy."

The conference here concluded, and these two worthies separated for the night. Urbino trembled, lest the gallant cavaliero who had so bravely defended himself, and who Sanguinario had ascertained was his rival, should be a bar to the accomplishment of his designs. Twice had he beaten back, and eluded every effort that had been made to annihilate him. Ah, thought the Duca, if Sanguinario thou couldst but inveigle him into one of the vaults of Lepanto, there thou in security mightest brain him,

> "Or with a log
> Batter his skull, or paunch him with a stake,
> Or cut his weazand with thy knife:"

and satiate thy utmost thirst for vengeance; rid me of a hated rival, and a base minion, who dares to stand betwixt me and my purpose. Dispirited from the failure of their enterprise, the Duca sullenly sought repose.

The villainous Sanguinario, began slowly to recover, and in a few days was so far convalescent as to be able to quit his room, and take exercise in the large garden of the Villa. The ill-starred Viola, was now constantly liable to his intrusion; she used every means to shew the disgust with which she viewed him; but all to no purpose—it was no easy task for the virtuous lovely girl to repel the advances of the rude ruffian, who could coolly plot the murder of a fellow creature.—Each day Sanguinario became more familiar in his deportment towards Viola; he looked upon the beauteous maid with lascivious eyes—a dishonorable passion raged throughout his burning veins, which could only be quenched by possession. For hours frequently they were alone, at which periods he always gave a distant hint of the flame she had kindled in his bosom, which she invariably affected not to understand, but this was not satisfactory to Sanguinario, he therefore in the most unequivocal language addressed Viola.

"No exertion of mine," said he, "to please the Signiora Viola can avail, but I love her and will make her happy!"—here he took her hand, she drew it back as if an adder had stung her—he saw the aversion she had towards him depicted in her countenance—"you shall reign," continued he, "my fancy's queen, and have pre-eminence over all my mistresses!"—he threw his arm around her, and forcibly kissed her blushing cheek and neck.

The indignant spirit of Viola could not brook this degrading proposal or violent conduct.—"Monster," said she, "how dare you violate my ears with your unlicensed speech, and so far forget the character of a cavaliero as to insult me beneath that roof where you are so hospitably received?—But the Signiora shall be made acquainted with your unparalleled effrontry, that measures may be taken to liberate me from your base importunities.—If thou wert here, dearest Alberto, I need not want a protector!"

"Alberto!—of what family is he?" eagerly enquired Sanguinario.

"Of a noble one," answered Viola; "he springs from the house of di Vincenti!"

"Heavens!" exclaimed Sanguinario, "Alberto di Vincenti is then my rival?"

"*Your rival!*" scornfully, said Viola, "the generous, the virtuous Alberto, *the rival* of such a *wretch as thou!*—pollute not his honorable name, by coupling it with thine!"—she attempted to retire, but the ruthless Sanguinario restrained her.

"In spite of all your scorn—in spite of the virtuous Alberto di Vincenti," said he in an ironical and malicious tone, "you shall be mine!—look at this dagger," drawing one from his bosom; "even this very dagger, will I bury in his heart, and bring it to thee, reeking with his warm blood, as a surety of his fate! then will I take thee to my arms, and revel in thy beauties undisturbed—then may you call upon your dearest Alberto to witness my joys.—Aye! those very hands that will caress thee shall first have made the hated Vincenti rest in eternal sleep!—To this thy beauteous form has urged me.— Reproach not Sanguinario with the bloody deed!—thy fairness has set his soul on fire, and thou hast tempted him to this!" He still held the dagger in his hand; she was terrified lest in his rage, he should plunge it in her bosom.

Nearly frantic with apprehension, Viola, broke from his strong gripe, and fled precipitately beyond his reach. The malignant expression of Sanguinario's features, caused her spirits to sink within her, lest his threats should fall upon the head of the devoted Alberto.

Thoughtless, hapless Viola, to be thus thrown off thy guard by this treacherous villain; by thy inconsiderate rashness, thou has endangered the life and security of him, thou wouldst even suffer death to save. With a mind fraught with woe, weighed down with care, and oppressed with sorrow, the disconsolate maiden in secret brooded over her afflictions, without a friend to assist in alleviating her distress, or in whose breast she could confide the pains that corroded her heart, and sapped the foundation of her peace. Before her late conversation with Sanguinario, she was miserable, and pined with hopeless love; but now accumulated grief nearly bereaved her of her faculties, and with difficulty she was conducted to her bed. She wildly called on Alberto; accused the Signiora of forbidding him the house, and despoiling her of her happiness.

For the first time the Signiora shed tears—for the first time she felt for the piteous state of Viola, and her depraved heart accused her for the multitudinous injuries, she had heaped on one, it was her duty to foster in her bosom. The fever of Viola advanced to so great a height, that it was necessary to call in medical aid: she passed a sleepless night, incessantly calling on her Alberto, and declaring she was the innocent cause of his death; for her wandering imagination had now tortured into reality the threat of Sanguinario.

Thus passed the tedious night in the Villa. The morning brought welcome news to the Signiora; a billet was handed to her; it was from the Duca; it ran thus:—

"Circumstances have compelled me to leave Venice at a moment's notice, and the cavalieros Sanguinario and Bernardo accompany me.

"URBINO."

"This is rather sudden," said the Signiora, "but thank God, that I am rid of such uncourteous visitors." Every domestic in the Villa rejoiced at the information, that the Duca and the two Signiors were not to return, though they wondered at their abrupt departure.

CHAPTER XI.

It will now be necessary to account for the apparent flight of Rosara.—She had as usual gone to the summer-house, in the expectation of meeting her loved Fernando, and had not long seated herself, when she heard the sound of footsteps, and two men in masks almost immediately entered, and seized her rudely; she rent the air with her piercing shrieks—she struggled violently to free herself: but with united strength, the strangers raised her in their arms, and bore her to a gondola, which was in waiting only a few paces from the summer-house; they had no sooner placed her within it, than they wrapped her in a large cloak, so as to conceal the whole of her person. The men were deaf to her tears, her lamentations, and entreaties; she offered large promises of reward for her liberation, but they were not to be bribed.

The gondola, after rowing swiftly for a considerable time, made for the shore and landed them; she was then lifted into a carriage that was in readiness, the two persons stepping in after her; they were driven off furiously, as if fearful of a pursuit. They travelled during the whole of the day, and towards evening they stopped at a little cottage, some distance from the road, to obtain refreshments, as they had not tasted food during their journey. She was again handed out by the two men, who silently offered her every respect her situation required. In the little room of the cottage, an homely repast was provided, and her companions invited her to partake of it.

The one who seemed to be the superior, said, "You have some distance yet to travel, Signiora, and perhaps we may not meet with an opportunity of again procuring such accommodation, therefore you had better profit by this. In two hours we shall again be on the road, and if you feel fatigued, there is a bed within, where you may rest in security."

"Where, for heaven's sake! are you conducting me?" enquired the unfortunate Rosara.

They both shook their heads, and placed their fingers to their lips, to imply their silence on that head. All her artifices proved abortive, in trying to draw them into conversation; they were well skilled in their profession, and Rosara looked upon them in the light of bravos. As soon as the two hours had elapsed, Rosara was again compelled to resume her place in the carriage; they still moved with the same rapidity, as at their first setting off. The features of her companions were undistinguishable, as they kept their masks on, and they yet maintained a most determined silence. Naturally the thoughts of Rosara were bent on those that were most dear to her: the shock that her disappearance must give her aged father; the grief her affectionate brother would feel; and above all, the heart-rending pangs, her adored Fernando would experience. Amidst these painful reflections, she heeded not the objects around her, nor did she perceive that they had struck into a thick wood, until aroused by the carriage stopping, and the hum of voices. The person who had before addressed himself to her, now let down the window, and spoke to some of the people assembled on the outside.

"We must now alight, Signiora," said he, "and proceed on horseback, the remainder of our journey."

Rosara cast a look out of the window, and perceived the horses were ready saddled. The door of the vehicle was opened, and Rosara assisted to alight; she was then placed behind one of her conductors, who immediately galloped away with his lovely prize, followed at some little distance by two other men.

What next will become of me? thought the afflicted girl; had murder been their intent, they had passed numerous situations where the tragic deed might have been perpetrated with facility and security; and where probably no other foot but that of the assassin had ever trod. She had offered them rewards, but that had little weight with them; their suspicious natures, perhaps led them to suppose she would withhold the liberal offer she had made, when placed beyond their power. The horses were now checked by the riders, as the branches of the trees crossed the road so low, that it required the nicest care, lest they should be struck from their seats.

After travelling some time in this perilous and disagreeable manner, the road gradually began to widen, and disclosed to the view of the forlorn Rosara, the dismantled and decayed walls of an old Castello. At the near approach, a bugle was sounded by one of the horsemen who accompanied her, which was answered immediately from the old building; by this time they had passed over a broken drawbridge, into a court yard, overgrown with long weeds, and nearly filled with fragments, which had fallen from the once proud battlements. Rosara's conductor lifted her from the horse, and taking her by the arm, led her through the large portal, into a hall, when pushing a pannel aside, they began to descend; at the bottom of the stairs they entered a small chamber, from whence they proceeded down a long arched passage, and at the extremity of this, her conductor thrice struck upon the door which impeded their further progress; it was directly opened, and as it grated heavily on its hinges, the whole subterraneous vault harshly echoed its discordant sounds, and as it closed upon the harrassed and distracted maid, an icy coldness ran through her veins, who nearly fainting, was compelled to lean against the humid wall, to sustain her tottering steps. Incapable of moving, and petrified with fear at the prospect of being immured within this desolate building, deep and hollow groans burst from her full and agonised bosom. The wretch who had conducted her thus far, raised her in his arms, and quickly conveyed her to a small apartment, and gently placed her on a bed; he left her for a few moments, and returned with wine, of which he pursuaded her to drink. The lovely girl soon found the benefit of this renovating cordial; her conductor seeing her sufficiently recovered, prepared to depart.

"This, Signiora," said he, "is the room you are for the present to occupy; in that basket you will find sufficient provisions, and to-morrow you will be again supplied.—Farewell Signiora." And closing the door after him, locked it.

Rosara taking the lamp, began to examine her apartment: it was small; the furniture consisted of a bed, a chair, and table; there was neither window nor aperture to admit the light; a door which had before escaped her, now attracted her attention, it was low and appeared to be barred on the opposite side; she tried if it would yield to her force, but it resisted every effort her delicate frame could use. Tired with these futile exertions, and wearied with the fatigue she had undergone, she sparingly partook of the frugal, but wholesome food that was left her; and throwing herself upon her humble bed, gave an unrestrained license to her sorrows.

"Here," ejaculated she, "I shall find my tomb;—perhaps murdered, and denied the holy rites of burial, by the remorseless villains who dragged me hither; or else my limbs be wantonly mangled, to glut their savage ferocity; or left to linger out a miserable and loathsome existance. Perhaps compelled to undertake some menial occupation, and be obedient to the will of a band of murderous ruffians.—Oh, Fernando! had I been thy bride, or thou hadst been within my call, on that too fatal morn, the lost Rosara would not have been thus. Even as the sturdy oak protects the tender vine, and with its foliage guards it from the tempestuous wind: so wouldst thou, my loved Fernando, have stretched forth thy arms, and shielded me from these my cruel foes." Then piously offering her prayers to heaven, she sunk into a calm repose.

Rosara on the following morn, was disturbed by a loud noise at the door; she started from her bed, forgetful of the place she was in, when the turning of the heavy wards of the lock, too quickly brought back all the horrors of her situation; she had, however, sufficient resolution to request the person who was on the outside, to allow her a little time to attire herself; this was granted in a grumbling tone. As soon as Rosara had notified to the person that she was ready to receive him, he opened the ponderous door, which creaked upon its rusty hinges, as he sullenly and violently threw it back. It was not the same person who had attended her on the evening before.

"I have brought you provisions," said he; "as soon as you have concluded your meal, I will conduct you hence."

Rosara sick at heart, felt no appetite, and requested to be immediately conducted whither he pleased. He motioned to her, without speaking, to follow him, and silently led her to a large room, where several lamps were burning, and which from the cursory view he had of it, appeared to be well furnished. A cavaliero from the opposite end approached her, and her conductor withdrew. On his coming so near her, as to enable her to discern his features distinctly, she recognised the well-known ones of the haughty Duca di Urbino.

"Can the lovely Rosara forgive her devoted slave," said he, in a tender tone, "for having caused her so much uneasiness? Believe me, dearest Rosara, it was not your Urbino's intention to place you in so unpleasant an apartment; but owing to your being unable to proceed further, you were carried there to restore your fainting spirits, and where it was conceived most proper to allow you to remain the rest of the night."

"Then," said she, the blood mounting into her face, and with a scornful look, and firm determined voice, "I am *to thank* the Duca di Urbino for this restraint, and the indignities I have suffered;— what right, Signior, had you by violence to take me from my paternal roof, and lodge me in a dungeon?—was this well done?—"

"Do not upbraid me, beauteous maid," said the artful Urbino, interrupting her; "heaven forefend that I should disturb the calm of thy fair bosom.—Urbino loves you! and death, without thee, would be most welcome:—take pity on my sufferings, and let me call thee mine."

"Call me thine!" replied she, in a sarcastic tone, "sooner would the tender lambs herd with wolves, than Rosara di Vincenti, so far forget the duty she owes her birth and fame, as to unite her fate with that of the despicable di Urbino. I told thee once before, I never could be thine; but now a stronger tie forbids it: know then, that I love, and am beloved by a noble and amiable cavaliero; one as far thy superior, as the lofty poplar to the noisome weeds beneath. This tyrannical act of oppression, in detaining me against my inclination, only strengthens the mean opinion I ever entertained of the Duca di Urbino.—Return me, Signior, to my family, from whom you have surreptitiously torn me!—then perhaps some of your crimes might be cancelled, for having performed one act of justice."

"Hold thy accursed tongue!" vociferated the enraged Urbino. "Thy proud spirit shall be taught to yield; and like the pliant osier, bend it to my will. Thou art beneath the roof of Urbino—thou art within my power, as fast as bars and chains, and trusty vassals can secure thee. For this same youth, that thou dost speak so highly of, I will, ere long, make feel my direst vengeance; even within the Vaults of Lepanto, will I plunge a dagger in his heart, or feast my eyes, by seeing him linger out his days, and sighing out Rosara's name, like a love-sick fool; until exhausted nature can no longer support the accumulation of misery, and death rescues him from my rage: even then his limbs will I have scattered for the beasts of prey, and leave his bones to whiten on the burning sands."

"I do not doubt thy cruel disposition," said Rosara, "and know thou wouldst not hesitate at anything, to accomplish thy bloody purpose—thou art such a villain. The brave Fernando fears not thy empty vaunts—the terror of his eye would strike thee dead— thou wouldst not dare encounter him. It would not have accorded with the character of the Duca di Urbino, had he not threatened to satiate his vengeance like an assassin. How camest thou to possess boldness sufficient to oppose the youthful Alberto's sword? But from that there was no retreating. View now, haughty Duca, the manly conduct of that cavaliero with thine own:—quick to resent an injury offered, but having once received an honorable satisfaction, he no further persecutes his fallen enemy; but thou wouldst fly an equal contest, and have recourse to the hired bravo's steel;— thou art a coward, for thou art cruel. The glorious actions the Duca di Urbino can boast, are, that he has seized a helpless female, and vows to assassinate the man she adores.—"

"One word more," said the Duca, agitated with rage, "and with this dagger I will silence thy tongue for ever!"

"That was spoke," answered Rosara, "like the Duca di Urbino; one more murder can balance little in the scale of his iniquities."

"Hell and furies!" vociferated the enfuriated Urbino, and rushing towards Rosara with the uplifted weapon, would have struck the fatal blow, had not at that instant a warrior arrested his arm. He turned to his unwelcome intruder, foaming with rage, as if to wreak his vengeance on him; but no sooner had his eyes met those of the warrior, than the intended instrument of death dropped from his nerveless arm—with a groan he fell senseless to the ground, bathed in his blood, which ran fast from a contusion he had received.

The warrior waved his hand to Rosara, and in a solemn tone pronounced,—"Be firm; remember your plighted faith to Fernando—the virtuous need not tremble at the machinations of the wicked." And slowly going to the extremity of the apartment, disappeared in the gloom.

The trembling maid called loudly for assistance, and her late attendant, with her former conductor, both hearing her loud cries, and the noise that had preceded them, rushed into the room.—For a moment they stood agast, at seeing the Duca on the ground, weltering in his blood, and no one present but Rosara. These trusty servants raised him up, and chafing his temples, brought back his senses.

"There—there he is!" said the wretched Urbino, as soon as he opened his eyes, and bending them on vacancy, "I see him now—'tis he!"

"What phantom is it thus disturbs your brain, and robs you of your reason?" said one of the persons who had assisted in raising him.

"Oh! it is no phantom;" said Urbino, "too well I know his features;—it was a damned deed—and the shade of the murdered Rhinaldo revisits the earth to torture me with his detested sight."

"Be more composed, Duca," replied the person who had before spoken; " 'tis nothing but a heated imagination that has conjured up this silly idea."

"Even but now he stood by me and his image is too deeply engrafted on my memory, not to know him."

Rosara's late attendant reconducted her back to her place of confinement; she was happy to find the Duca di Urbino really conceived he had beheld a spectre, it might prove of the utmost importance and benefit to her. Whoever it was that had so seasonably entered the room, had indisputably saved her life. She shuddered when she reflected that she had stood on the brink of eternity. Urbino had called the supposed spectre, the murdered Rhinaldo; if he had not been the actual perpetrator of the foul deed, she doubted not but that it had been committed by some of his barbarous agents. Her courage died within her, at the dreadful recollection that she was within his power, without the least prospect of escaping, or of giving information to her father, brother, or lover, of the cruel situation in which she was placed. Immured as she was, in the Vaults of the Castello di Lepanto, Urbino could at any time accomplish undiscovered, his fell purpose—her life was not safe; and at any period, if she roused his passions, he might in his ungovernable fury, put an end to her existence.

"Never—never again!" exclaimed she, "shall I see my revered father, my Alberto, or my loved Fernando. Better would it be to suffer by the remorseless di Urbino's dagger, than bear the pangs that rage within my tortured bosom. When death shall close my eyes, then all will be at peace; yet no pitying hand will rear a sod upon my grave; but here, unheard, unheeded, fall a victim to the ferocious Urbino. Assist me, heaven, in this trying scene, and grant me patience and fortitude to bear against the insults, and indignities heaped upon me."

The Duca di Urbino was conducted to his apartment, where he was restored to his senses. The two persons who had so luckily heard Rosara's calls, were Sanguinario and one of the Duca's confidential domestics. The Duca could give no account to Sanguinario respecting his fall, or any of the circumstances that took place, all that he could remember was, that from the taunting language of Rosara, he was urged by impetuous passion to rush headlong on the innocent maid, for the purpose of sacrificing her, when he was prevented by the interposing *spirit*.

"A *spirit* indeed," retorted Sanguinario, with acrimony, "what next will the pusillanimous heart of the Duca, not distort things into; before long you will have a body guard to attend you from room to room, lest some of the airy gentlemen should fly away with you."

"As incredulous as you appear to be," replied the Duca, "had you but beheld the countenance of Rhinaldo, for it was him, your boasted courage would have vanished."

"Granted Duca," said Sanguinario, "*if I had seen* a spectre, it might have discomposed my nerves for an instant, for never having had the pleasure of being in the society of such personages, the honor might have overcome me:—but this is little to the purpose —I have now performed every part of our agreement, I have placed Rosara in your hands, and if she slips out of them it is your own fault—I come to claim my reward!"

"Why, Sanguinario," said the Duca, "thou dost not mean to persist in claiming Viola for thy mistress—think again upon the subject —dost thou suppose, she will ever submit to thy embraces?"

"*Not mean* to persist in claiming Viola as my mistress!" reiterated the astonished Sanguinario, "some phantom surely still disturbs your brain.—Thou hast promised me Viola, as a recompense for my services, and I will not yield up my right to any mortal breathing!—I shall not ask her consent, let me but have her once in my possession, and that is all I wish.—Come, Duca, write a note to the Signiora Benvoglio, to deliver up Viola to me, as I wish every thing should be done in quiet."

"Give thee a note!" replied the Duca, "how couldst thou, fool-like, dream I would ever sacrifice so much beauty to thee—I did but tempt thee with the bait, that I might more securely bind thee to my purpose."

"I long suspected you," answered Sanguinario, "to be a treacherous villain!—if thou respectest not thy honor to thy followers, to whom will it be secure?—Idiot and trembling coward as thou art, think you that your high sounding titles can protect you from my just resentment?—I am thy equal!—thou hast admitted me to thy secrets; I have witnessed all your daring acts:—the forest—the Castello di Urbino—and vaults of the Castello di Lepanto, still conceal deeds of thine, monstrous for the human ear to hear!—It is now too late, Duca, to retract;—remember, thou must keep thy inferiors at a distance, to make them respectful, but once they are entrusted with thy utmost secrets, and find themselves necessary to thee, then will they, when you dare to break your promises, throw the mask aside, and shew they hold thee in bonds of adamant.—Thou hast promised Viola to me, and possess her I will, even though hell itself should yawn the next moment to receive me!"

At the conclusion of this he rushed from the apartment, leaving the Duca appalled at his determination to possess himself of his promised reward.

The Duca knew the character of Sanguinario too well not to be uneasy at his threats, he began to fear his personal safety might be involved. It was highly necessary that he should take some prompt measure to humble the insolence of one, who was so much beneath him, and on whom he had lavished his confidence and friendship; therefore the turbulent spirit he had shewn rendered him more dangerous. The first thing that struck him was to put him aside, but that was a scheme not so easily put in execution. Sanguinario was desperate and brave; besides he was subtle and wary; he despaired of any opportunity offering, in which he could himself dispatch him; and he was so strongly leagued with the band, who inhabited the vaults of the Castello, that he doubted even if their chieftain Bernardo, could persuade any of them to undertake the business. What therefore was to be done? While Sanguinario remained in the Vaults di Lepanto, all would be well; but the moment he left them, some mischief would be going forward; he decided that the instant Sanguinario departed, he would denounce him to the inquisition. His name and rank would crush any tale that Sanguinario might relate; besides it would be impossible for him to know his accuser, as it was always the custom of that terrible tribunal, to conceal from the accused, the name of the person who had denounced them. Thus forming a plan, in which he thought he would be perfectly secure against any of the attacks of his colleague, Sanguinario; he without loss of time, began to prepare a paper, ready to transmit to the holy inquisition, as soon as circumstances should require.

As soon as Sanguinario quitted the Duca, he reflected on what course it was best to pursue; he called Bernardo, his faithful friend in iniquity, to aid him with his counsel, in this distressing dilemma. The Duca had broken his word, and had determinedly refused to give up Viola to him.

"What is to be done, Bernardo? What wouldst thou advise me?"

"Cut his throat first," said Bernardo, "for being a deceitful rascal, and we can soon bring off Signiora Viola."

"This would be a dangerous scheme; his people would be making some enquiry after him, and all would be discovered," answered Sanguinario.

"Well then," replied Bernardo, "if that will not do, take two of the band with you, and set off to night for Venice; the old Signiora will let you in, and if you cannot manage the rest, why you do not deserve to have the girl. There is plenty of room here, without the Duca knowing any thing about it; he is not acquainted with half the passages and vaults. I would go myself, with you, but it will be necessary for me to be present with the band;—there will be some rich booty in a day or two."

"I like your proposal very well," answered Sanguinario; "to night I will depart. I know the Duca's inmost secrets too well, to fear any thing from him; and when once the Signiora Viola is beyond his reach, all will again be well; but I must keep a sharp eye over him; for since this late dispute, I will not trust him."

"What does he mean to do with the Signiora he has got here?"

"I do not know," said Sanguinario. "Let the horses be ready with two of the band, by night-fall."

"They shall be punctual," said Bernardo, and these two ruffians separated: the one to prepare for his expedition, and the other to meditate on fresh crimes and enormities.

Rosara shut up in a gloomy dungeon, without a ray of light, except what she received by the faint glimmer of a solitary lamp; without a book to divert her thoughts; a prey to solitude and grief; conceived the idea of removing her bed from its present situation, and placing it in the opposite corner; it was very light, and her strength was equal to the task. She had busily employed herself in removing the clothes, and then the bed, from the miserable frame on which it lay, when she perceived beneath it, something that shone brilliantly; she pushed the frame aside, and found it to be a dagger corroded with rust; it was richly set with stones, and she fancied she could perceive the Urbino arms upon the haft. In going round to the spot for the purpose of examining if there yet remained any thing where she had picked up the dagger; one of the flag stones on which she trod, rocked under her, which composed the pavement of the room. With the dagger she attempted to raise it, and it easily gave way to her efforts. Having completely taken it from the place it covered, she found a packet of papers, neatly folded in a cambric handkerchief; it was nearly decayed from damp, and probably from the length of time it had been buried. With care she replaced the stone, and taking up the bed, returned it to its original situation. Seating herself by the lamp, she carefully untied the handkerchief (her heart beating high with expectation,) willing to preserve every part of it; on one corner she distinctly observed the letter V. It was obvious, it had been the initial of some wretched person's name, who in all probability had been confined within the vaults. She opened the package of papers, in which was a ring of apparently great value; this, thought she, I will keep for thy sake, poor devoted victim; and not knowing where to deposit it, she tried it on her finger, and it fitted with exactness. "There remain," said Rosara, "there I hope it will be in safety." The papers were nearly in a perfect state, though the handkerchief had been so much decayed. They ran as follows.—

CHAPTER XII.

"Whenever the tyrannical hand of power shall force any unfortunate into this abode of misery, (which may heaven, in its infinite mercy forbid) perchance the melancholy story of Viola Marchesa di Lepanto, may beguile their solitary hours, and assist in bringing her ravishers to condign punishment. But years, nay centuries may roll by, ere this may reach the hand of mortal; and my cruel oppressors be numbered with the dead. It has been with difficulty that I could obtain the indulgence of writing utensils from one of my guards; who with more pity in his nature, has compassioned my forlorn state, and kindly procured them for me; but with strict injunctions to conceal them, lest they should be discovered by his employer.

"By my lamp I daily add something to my narrative, and when my fingers grow weary with writing, I weep the loss of an adored husband, basely and inhumanly murdered; an infant son and daughter, snatched from me in their tenderest years; who perhaps have shared the fate of their unhappy father;—but why dwell I thus on scenes of woe.

"Born at Venice, of noble parentage, and educated by the best masters that city could afford, and under the immediate eye of my father and mother, I was generally considered to be highly accomplished, and at the early age of fifteen, was introduced to the world by my fond parents. Being an only child, the Condi di Rivarola hoped, by my forming an advantageous alliance, to perpetuate the honors of his family. The gay and fashionable were ever welcome at the Palazza, and nothing but mirth, and a continual round of amusements followed on each successive day. Ah, happy days of peace! fled, alas! for ever, from my bleeding bosom, then volatile and happy, no care ever intruded on my mind. It was not natural to suppose, that a girl of a good person, young and accomplished, and above all, the heiress of large domains, should remain long without having an extensive list of gallants in her train. Many noble cavalieros had made overtures to my father, but as it was his determination to leave me a free agent in the choice of a husband, he invariably rejected them with politeness, stating to them that it was necessary to win my affections first; but none of them had hitherto been able to make any impression on my virgin heart. Things were in this situation, when every tongue in Venice was busy in rehearsing the accomplishments of two cavalieros, who had just returned from France, where they had been sent together, to finish their studies; they were no other than the Marchese di Lepanto, and the present Duca di Urbino, whose father was then alive. These two cavalieros had not been long in Venice, before they became visitors at the Palazza. I cannot but acknowledge that I felt a secret pleasure, at having these young Signiors as my attendants at every public place I visited. The whole *beau monde* now gave me away as their fancy directed, either to the Marchese, or the young Duca. Thus assailed, it was impossible that my heart could hold out against the attacks of so much worth. The young Duca lost no opportunity of paying every attention that could win me: his address was particularly insinuating, but yet he possessed an imperious manner, which rather imposed respect, than conciliated esteem. Not so the Marchese: his figure was the most perfect symetry; his mind was stored with every virtue that could adorn a man; graceful and polished in his manner, he won the love of all; valiant to a fault, and tenacious of his honor, even the tongue of slander had not found a speck upon his fair name. To this amiable nobleman I gave my heart, in preference to his friend and relation, the young Duca di Urbino. My father was transported with joy, at my judicious choice; and my young mind teemed with delight, at having afforded such satisfaction to my beloved parent. He consented with pleasure to the proposal of the Marchese, and I was now considered by my family as his affianced bride, and all seemed happy and contented, at my having at length fixed on so noble and worthy a cavaliero. I became the envy of every unmarried female in Venice. I had for some time observed that the young Duca and the Marchese, were not so frequently together; and when the Duca heard that I was shortly to be united to his friend and relative, he expressed considerable surprise; from that day his countenance became clouded and sullen. Even in the midst of festivity, I have watched his varying features, alternately expressive of haughty pride, and gloomy reserve. I feared, lest the rivalship of these two cavalieros, should cause some alienation in their mutual esteem. I intimated as much to my beloved Marchese, but he quieted all my apprehensions in that respect, by expatiating warmly on the good and great qualities of the young Duca. Ah! little didst thou think, at that period, how great a villain had gained your confidence, and that at the very moment you were striving to do away every idea, which had been formed to his disadvantage, he was meditating your destruction. I must be less prolix in my story: the happy day arrived that irrevocably united my fate with that of the Marchese; surrounded by all my nearest relatives, and a large portion of the nobility, my father gave me to my beloved Marchese, and bestowed his fervent and sincere blessing on us. Every one noticed the absence of the young Duca from the ceremony; nor did he make his appearance, either at the hour of dinner, or join in the dance in the evening.

"After our marriage was thus happily concluded, we spent some time in receiving the visits of our numerous acquaintance, and in returning them: but it became necessary for us to leave Venice as the Marchese received letters requiring his presence at the Castello; every thing was prepared for our immediate departure. We journeyed by gentle stages to the Castello; and on our arrival, we were greeted by all the vassals, who had collected for the purpose of welcoming their young lord, and beholding his bride; with enthusiastic joy, they took the horses from the carriage, and dragged it into the court yard of the Castello; my heart unused to such adulation as was paid me on all sides by the vassalage, throbbed with tumultuous pleasure. This was the first period I had ever been separated from my loved parents; it affected my spirits considerably at first, but the kind attentions of my husband, soothed my inquietude, and my days passed on again in peace.

"We had not long remained in this undisturbed state, before the author of all my woes made his appearance at the Castello. The Duca had come post from Venice, and had a long conference with the Marchese, but took his departure after an hasty dinner, contrary to my husband's earnest request; he excused himself by alledging there was a necessity for his immediate attendance at the Castello of his father; these reasons weighed sufficiently with the Marchese, who no longer pressed him on the subject, and my heart felt as if relieved from a violent oppression, when the gates excluded him from my view.

"Shortly after the Duca had quitted the Castello, the Marchese informed me that he had left Venice in a great hurry, in consequence of an affair of honor, which occured at a gambling table, and he had come to request a loan to free him from some pressing embarrassments: though neglected for a long time by the Duca, the Marchese forgot his pointed rudeness, at never having attended at the marriage ceremony, or even paid a complimentary visit since it had taken place, and acommodated him with the required sum; his benevolent heart always felt for the misfortunes of others, and his mind was too noble to harbour the base idea of revenge.

"Not long after this, a courier arrived with the distressing intelligence, that my father was dangerously ill, and little hopes entertained of his recovery. That very day we set off for Venice, fondly expecting we should reach it in time, to receive his blessing.— Oh! vain delusive hope—my lamented father, on our arrival had breathed his last, praying for the prosperity and happiness of his child; my grief was of the most violent nature, not all the tenderest care of my husband could for several days assuage it; whole hours did I sit and weep, and spend my time in unavailing sorrow.—I was pregnant at this period with my first child; the Marchese feared the consequences of my despondence, but the ameliorating hand of time, dried my tears, and left me a prey to melancholy. The Marchese, as soon as delicacy would permit, opened his doors to receive visitors, and lost no opportunity in leading me into society, which in some measure succeeded in chasing away the gloom which I had contracted since my father's death. It was in these gay circles that the Marchese heard the real story of the Duca's conduct respecting his affair of honor: he had for some time been addicted to play very high, and had plunged into every degree of extravagance; but not contented with this, he formed a friendship with a needy adventurer, who was a constant attendant at all the public gaming tables, and whose mal-practises became so glaring, that he was shunned, even by those who were in a similar situation in life; this man did the young Duca countenance, and he began again to be received; for there are always plenty of those fawning sycophants, who will readily caress or despise a great man's favorite as he rises or falls in his estimation; but there were many virtuous young noblemen, that rather conceived the Duca degraded himself, without being able to raise his associate, they looked upon him as little better than his intimate; under these impressions, whenever the Duca played at any game of chance, some one or other in the room strictly watched him; he had lately won considerable sums, which were quickly dissipated in every species of debauchery: one evening while playing, a young cavaliero expressed his suspicions that every thing was not fair; stung with anger at this public insinuation; the Duca retorted severely; their language became high, and both inflamed with passion used the most opprobrious epithets; the consequence was, the Duca drew his sword, and before the young cavaliero could place himself in a posture of defence, his antagonist ran him through the body, and he fell, weltering in his blood; the Duca and his new acquired friend took advantage of the confusion, and made their escape from Venice. The friends of the cavaliero, wishing to hush the transaction, as it had passed in a place that could not reflect honor on him, dropped all persecution against the Duca.

"Our delay at Venice was prolonged, as the Marchese wished me to be confined at the Palazza in preference to the Castello. Every day some new circumstance confirmed the Marchese in his opinion of the unworthiness of his relation.

"The report now reached Venice that the old Duca had died suddenly; this made a wonderful alteration in the affairs of the present Duca; every one anticipated the splendor and elegance that would be displayed by the young heir; but nothing could exceed the wonder that took place, when information was received that the late Duca had been buried privately on the same day of his death, and the present one, with his constant companion had set off for France, as it was said, to divert the grief he felt at the melancholy event that had taken place. The busy tongue of calumny again spoke loudly against this young nobleman, and he did not even escape the finger of suspicion being pointed at him, as the *murderer of his father!*—Villain as he is, it is my earnest prayer, that at the awful day of retribution, he may be cleared of this foul and damning deed!—my heart sickens at the thought—I must for a moment lay down my pen."

"Good heavens!" exclaimed Rosara, "what a load of crimes must the detested Urbino have hereafter to answer for!"

She more than ever dreaded the effects of Urbino's vengeance, for now she was fully aware, from the tenor of the Marchesa's tale, that he was capable of executing his threats to their full extent. Exhausted and fatigued, she folded the manuscript, and lay down for a few hours, to taste repose. Her food was regularly brought her once a day, with a sufficiency of oil and cotton to trim her lamp. She made enquiries of her attendant, as soon as he came with her usual allowance, if the Duca had been much injured by his fall.

He answered in a surly tone, that he had not yet been able to leave his bed, from weakness; but the contusion was nothing.

Rosara felt overjoyed at the prospect of a short respite from the importunities of the Duca; she entreated the man to allow her pen, ink, and paper.

"If you have anything to communicate to the Duca di Urbino, you shall be provided," said he.

"Perhaps," said she, "you might procure me a book?"

"No," answered he, "you are not to be allowed a book."

To the Duca she had not any subject to write on, but to request her liberation, and that she had strongly urged at her late interview, without the least shadow of success.

"Have you anything to communicate to the Duca?" enquired her attendant, "speak at once, for I cannot waste my time in trifling."

"I have not," said Rosara.

He took up the empty basket that had contained the provisions of the preceding day, and departed. As soon as the door was fastened, and the dying echo of his steps could be no longer heard, she tasted her food, and taking her manuscript, now her only solace, from beneath her pillow, and trimming her lamp, seated herself by the little table, and unfolding it, again began to read the narrative of the unfortunate Marchesa di Lepanto.

Continuation of the Marchesa's History.

"I have again taken up my pen, to resume the unpleasant task of retracing events which have long passed by; but it feeds my melancholy, which has now become habitual; and even in the bitterest moments of my grief, the recollection of those times, in some measure, tends to alleviate the sorrows that gnaw the very fibres of my heart;—but, to my tale:—

"Not long after the departure of the Duca, from his Castello di Urbino, I became a mother—the infant proved to be a boy; the Marchese was overjoyed at this pledge of our mutual love. Who can describe the raptures of a mother?—A thousand times I pressed my infant babe to my bosom, and in my imagination, saw him raised to man's estate, treading in the virtuous path pointed out by his noble parent, and affording every source of comfort to our declining years; but, alas! my visionary hopes are for ever fled; yet a secret whispering tells me my beloved child still lives, and will one day avenge the murder of his father. Why longer dwell I upon this heart rending theme? As soon as I was sufficiently recovered to move, the Marchese thought the air of the country would be of service to me; we therefore went thither. Every thing looked cheerful at the Castello, and my time passed happily, in the exercise of my maternal duties. If possible, the Marchese became more attached to me than ever; he hardly ever went from the Castello, but to inspect his vast domains, which had become extremely extensive, since the death of my regretted father.

"I again became pregnant, which caused a general rejoicing of the vassalage; for so greatly was the Marchese beloved, that they omitted no opportunity of shewing every testimony of their fidelity and esteem. How could it have been otherwise?—He was more the friend than lord of his vassals.

"The Marchese had formed an intimacy with a young nobleman on his travels, whose Castello was not far distant, who frequently retired there for some months in the year, from the fashionable and gay scenes of Venice; and whenever that was the case, we constantly visited; and as he was an amiable, and a pleasant companion, became a great acquisition to our domestic party: this constant intercourse ripened into a sincere and lasting friendship. This young nobleman had been spending some time at the Castello di Lepanto, when our quiet was again molested, by the arrival of a messenger, who delivered a large packet from the Duca di Urbino: it was for the purpose of asking another loan. The Marchese, who concealed nothing from his friend, asked his opinion; and they concurred that it was necessary he should give a decided refusal to this mode of levying a contribution on his purse; for though two years had elapsed, the Duca had never shewn the least disposition to disburse the first loan.

"The Marchese wished me to go to Venice, during the period of my confinement, but I had made every arrangement for its taking place at the Castello, and the Marchese was too indulgent to oppose my wishes. At length I blessed my husband with a lovely girl; this added greatly to my happiness, as it was natural to expect that I should lose in the course of time, a great portion of the society of my son; and I promised myself a great source of amusement in superintending the education of my child.—I must conceal my papers, footsteps are fast approaching."

CHAPTER XIII.

BERNARDO, faithful to his promise, had the horses and two of the band ready to attend Sanguinario, at the appointed hour, and after wishing each other success in their respective enterprizes, Sanguinario rode off with his companions, and Bernardo retired, to give necessary directions to his band.

Impatient to be in possession of the lovely person of Viola, and fearful lest his intentions should be discovered by the Duca, and some circumstance occur to counteract them, Sanguinario urged his horse to its utmost speed, with the view of reaching Venice before his departure could be known by the Duca, and his fair prize by that time secured.

As far as it was possible for any object to make an impression on Sanguinario, Viola certainly had: this villain's unhallowed love burnt with such violence, that every impediment seemed easily to be surmounted, that could be placed in opposition to his passion; his determination was to sacrifice every thing or gain his immediate object; filled with these unprincipled ideas he continued journeying on with rapidity.

It is now necessary to return to the Villa. Viola had for some time been in a convalescent state, and had began in some measure to recover her spirits: the Signiora Benvoglio had shewn, since the cavalieros had left the Villa, more tenderness towards the amiable girl, who had been placed under her protection.

One evening, as they sat conversing as usual, they were alarmed by the loud knocking of some one at the gates. The porter hesitated for some time to admit strangers at so late an hour; but the men, who composed a part of the family establishment, being summoned to attend, the gates were opened. The hall was instantly filled with armed men, headed by two officers of the holy inquisition; at the appearance of these members of this formidable tribunal, the whole party stood dismayed, momentarily expecting that one or other of them would be seized, and borne away for some crime committed.

One of the officers, advancing, said, "you are the person, commonly known by the name of Signiora Benvoglio," at the same time pointing to her; "and you bear the name of Viola," at the same time addressing her, "and are an orphan, placed under the protection of this Signiora—let your attendants retire."

This order was immediately obeyed. The officer then spoke in a low voice to the people who had accompanied him, and they silently dispersed themselves in different parts of the Villa.

The Signiora requested the officers, who still remained standing in the hall, to walk into the inner apartment, with which they silently complied. The Signiora and Viola, both trembled with fear, a cold perspiration bedewed their foreheads, and their varying countenances betrayed the terror and mental agony, under which they laboured; they expected every minute to be informed of their having been denounced to the holy tribunal by some enemy; tortured with this anxiety and suspence, they were both nearly sinking with apprehension.

The officers maintained a most solemn silence, and only occasionally cast a glance at the two terrified females. Suddenly one of the attendants, who had accompanied the officers, entered, and waving his hand to them, they rose and retired. Scarcely had they departed, before the door was rudely thrown open, and the well-known figure of the supposed cavaliero, Sanguinario, presented itself before them. He advanced with an air of confidence towards the Signiora, and presented her with a letter; "this," said he as he offered it, "is from the Duca di Urbino, who wishes the contents to be strictly complied with."

The Signiora read aloud the billet—it ran as follows:—

"Deliver up Viola to the bearer; he has my directions where to conduct her.—Comply with this immediately on its receipt.

URBINO."

The Signiora stood pondering on this strange mandate, while the treacherous Sanguinario regarded her with a piercing look, as if to read the inmost recesses of her mind; he did not like her not readily complying with the order, and the expression of hesitation, which was strongly marked in her countenance, appeared not to auger that prompt and implicit obedience he had conceived would have been the effect of the perusal of the letter.

"Every thing is ready for the departure of the Signiora Viola," said Sanguinario, "and every moment is of consequence, therefore I request there may be no further delay."

"You do not surely intend to take her from the Villa at this hour of the night?" said the Signiora, "it would be barbarous to a degree."

"Such are my directions," said Sanguinario, "and I must obey them," at the same time advancing toward the affrighted girl.

The peculiarity of her situation inspired her with a determination, almost bordering on phrensy: on one side dreading the vengeance of the holy inquisition; and on the other threatened with being conveyed whither she knew not; she recoiled from the fiend-like Sanguinario, as dreading the envenomed touch of a serpent.

"Prepare directly," said he, in an imperious tone, "my time is precious."

"I tell thee," answered Viola, "I will not attend thy bidding.—By what right does the Duca di Urbino exercise this authority over me? I am placed under the protection of the Signiora, and only am amenable to her. Think you I will obey the usurped power of the Duca di Urbino?—Or think you I will accompany such a wretch as thou; unattended by a protector, at this awful hour of the night? You know me not Sanguinario, therefore you may return to your employer, and inform him of the failure of your mission."

"Is it your intention, Signiora Benvoglio, to deliver to me Signiora Viola?" enquired Sanguinario in an exasperated voice.

"Yield not, I entreat you," said Viola, "to the request of Signior Sanguinario—place me not in his power, for by doing which, you will entail on me everlasting misery."

"It will be proper," said the Signiora, hardly daring to resist, and yet unwilling to give up Viola, "for me to consider this order more maturely: besides I cannot conceive the actual necessity of so speedy a removal—at all events, a few hours can be of very little consequence; therefore I shall not decide until the morning."

"If you Signiora," replied Sanguinario, with a savage and menacing look, "have forgotten your duty to the Duca, I have not; and it would ill become me now, to swerve from that fidelity and friendship I have always professed: know then, it is his intention, as the forerunner to my further aggrandizement, to bestow the Signiora Viola on me, as my bride."

"Thy bride!" exclaimed the indignant girl, "never will I join my fate with his, whose hands have often been imbrued in the blood of his fellow creatures.—Oh, save me Signiora! save me from the wretchedness which awaits me!"

"I will hear no more!" said Sanguinario, clapping his hands, and taking Viola round the waist, who, with all the strength she was mistress of, attempted to release herself from his rude grasp. His signal was obeyed, and two men directly came to his assistance, and were rapidly conveying the shrieking maid through the hall, when they and their leader, Sanguinario, were seized before they were able to make the least opposition: without delay they were hurried into a carriage in waiting.

The disconsolate and fainting Viola lay upon the floor, where she had been placed, when Sanguinario and his accomplices were seized. The Signiora, petrified with terror at the violent measures Sanguinario had adopted, stood incapable of making any exertion, either in calling upon the domestics, or of urging any argument that might have been conducive in averting his prompt and decided mode of acting: she gave Viola up as entirely lost to her, for she could not collect resolution sufficient to venture into the hall, or attempt to gain the wing of the Villa the servants occupied; nor probably would she have attempted to move from the spot she was in, had not her attention been arrested by a deep groan, which she fancied proceeded from a corner of the apartment. Expecting every moment to behold some preternatural object, her straining eyeballs almost started from their sockets; her hair became stiffened; her blood, chilled round her heart, and flowed through her veins in icy streams. Another groan, deep and lengthened, animated her with a desperate courage, and snatching the lamp from the table, darted rapidly into the hall, where the first object that struck upon her view was the fallen, and almost lifeless body of Viola: this unexpected appearance, added to the fears impressed on the imagination of the Signiora, was too much for her; and with a loud and piercing scream, dropped senseless.

Let us now leave the Signiora Benvoglio and Viola, and return to the hapless Rosara, in the dreary Vaults of Lepanto: with her let us trace the enormities of Urbino, contained in the melancholy manuscript of the Marchesa.

Continuation of the Manuscript.

Rosara laid the manuscript for a moment on the table, and sat sympathyzing at the melancholy situation in which the Marchesa di Lepanto had been placed. The narrative, hitherto, had been plain and simple, though it appeared to have been written when her feelings were wound up to the highest state of despondency. So deeply interested did Rosara find herself in the fate of the unfortunate Marchesa, that she again took up the manuscript, and perused it as follows:—

"Horror, upon horror!—the Duca di Urbino has been with me—he has left me more miserable than ever. All that I have now to look for, is, either a tame submission to his base designs upon my honor, or to free myself by death. Oh, how dreadful the alternative!—To rush headlong and unprepared before my Maker, as the only means of preserving myself from the detestable embraces of the Duca. Oh, heaven! in pity to my miseries, look down upon me with a benignant eye, and inspire me with fortitude to bear against my accumulating woes!—I must hasten with my tale:—

"My little infant encreased each day in health and beauty; nothing could exceed the happiness that prevailed at the Castello. Love and friendship combined to make our days glide on in peace; but Urbino, fiend-like, sought but for an opportunity to revenge himself upon his noble kinsman. Lulled into security, by conscious integrity, the Marchese rejected every caution his friend gave him, respecting the Duca, and by this fatal error, has innocently caused the downfall of his house. How shall I now describe the horrid scenes that followed?—I must assume courage to relate them, in the hopes, that one day or other, this record of Urbino's villainy may appear in judgment against him, and bring the guilty miscreant to that punishment his crimes demand;—but I wander from my subject.—

"The nurse who attended my little girl, was frequently in the custom of walking beyond the Castello gates with her, though strictly enjoined to the contrary; but the cool shade of the forest, which ran close to the Castello, was too inviting to be resisted. Having been sent for the purpose of taking the usual airing on the terrace, with the infant, but remaining a longer time absent than I thought necessary, I desired one of my females to order her immediately to return: my messenger came back with the information that she was not there; my heart sickened, and 'sad forebodings shook' my frame. I instantly directed that enquiries should be made of the porter, if she had passed the gate?—The reply was that she had. The Marchese, who had used every endeavour to quiet my fears, now became seriously alarmed himself: the domestics, headed by him, were dispatched in every part of the forest to seek her—the wood rang with loud calls, but nothing, save the echo, was returned. Spent and wearied with their exertions, they were returning to the Castello, conceiving their further search to be futile, when they discovered the unfortunate female bound to a tree and gagged; they flew to relieve her from her distressing state: they could scarcely allow time to disengage the gag from her mouth, before my loved Marchese anxiously enquired for his child—she could return no answer; the instrument had been forced so far, as to retard the freeness of respiration, and assistance, alas! was offered when too late; she drew her last breath before they could convey her to the Castello, without being able to give the least clue, relative to the circumstance. Think what my feelings must have been, when the Marchesa, in a wild and agitated manner, rushed into my apartment, where in silent agony I waited the result of the search that was making, and throwing himself upon a seat, exclaimed,—'She is lost—she is gone—your lovely child is torn from us!'

"If, reader, thou ever knewest the pleasures of a mother, or the pangs of being separated from your child, by the indispensable decrees of Providence; or if thou hast experienced the keen sensations of parting with a valued and sincere friend, whose mind, congenial with your own, had been the repository of your woes, and whose tenderness had solaced you in your afflictions; judge of the distraction, horror, and dispair that racked my soul, at this communication—it is indiscribable: let me draw a veil over this part of my little tale; the recollection of these events is too painful to be borne. The young nobleman who I before mentioned, was on a visit at the Castello; he did every thing in his power to console us, and at length he became gratified at our returning composure: having thus sacrificed a large portion of his time to friendship, he took his leave with the must unfeigned sorrow for our recent loss. Some weeks had elapsed since the late melancholy catastrophe had taken place; when we were again broken in upon, by the Marchese receiving a letter from the Duca, saying he had just returned from France, and would be with him on the ensuing day, to pass some time. Though we could with pleasure, have dispensed with this ill-timed intrusion of the Duca's, (for such I always deemed his presence) yet I gave every necessary orders that a suite of apartments should be prepared for him; and tried to the utmost extent to hide the dislike I felt to his society; but my chief aim had always been to render my husband happy, and I conceived it would give him pleasure, at my receiving his kinsman with cheerfulness. The Marchese had been brought up from an early age with the Duca; and though he could not help seeing a great number of his faults, nay, of his vices, still he could not entirely break off from his acquaintance. Since my refusal of his hand, the reports that came to my ears of the general tenor of his conduct, were such as to raise the greatest abhorrence of him in my breast; and though I frequently attempted to expel all these disadvantageous opinions, yet they would return; and the more I laboured to see him in a favorable point of view, the more forcibly his vices appeared to me.

"Thus situated were we when the Duca, attended by a suitable retinue, arrived at the Castello at the time he stated in his letter; he took the Marchese by the hand, and pressed it apparently with the most enthusiastic friendship; my noble and unsuspicious lord, with real and unaffected warmth, welcomed him: to me he paid every attention, that shewed him the most finished gentleman; he decked his countenance in artificial sorrow, and condoled with me, in such eloquent and moving terms, that I must confess, the villain deceived me, and I thought him sincere. The hypocrite will one day be unmasked, and stand exposed in all his native deformity. In a private conversation with the Marchese, he acknowledged his past errors, and laid down plans, by which his future line of life should be guided.—All at once, the dissipated, the gay Duca di Urbino, was to give over his vicious courses, and to become again an ornament and a member of that society, in which he was highly entitled to move, from his rank and talents. I dreaded much this sudden and unexpected change; I imparted my fears to the Marchese, but he felt confident that the Duca's contrition was genuine—oh! *fatal, fatal* infatuation! Urbino lost no opportunity in displaying his acquirements—every day he gained a firmer footing in the esteem of the Marchese, and the whole catalogue of his former erroneous conduct, seemed to be expunged from the memory of his kinsman.

"The Duca had dared occasionally to hint at his former passion for me, and to give me to understand, that though he had not succeeded, still it suffered no diminution: these conversations I generally turned, or affected not to hear; but the wretch, conscious of his influence over my husband, whose better judgment he had deceived by his specious arts, boldly avowed his love, and dared to tempt the chastity of his kinsman's wife.

"Indignant at the insult offered me, and that too beneath my own roof, I spurned the wretch from me with contempt. 'The Marchese shall be informed of this,' said I, 'and then he will perhaps better know how to appreciate the valued friendship of the Duca di Urbino.'

"The fawning sycophant, seeing me about to quit him, and fearful lest I should instantly inform my husband of his insolent proposal, caught my vest, and with tears in his eyes, entreated my forgiveness. 'My presence,' said he, 'I find is unpleasant—but forgive me this fault, and by to-morrow's dawn I will retire from the Castello.'

"'Duca,' replied I, 'you must be well aware that after this presumptuous avowal, and violation of every rule of hospitality, in wishing to subvert the honor of your friend and relative, your further stay at the Castello must be unpleasant—upon the condition alone that you depart to-morrow, I will be silent on the subject to the Marchese.'

"'I will obey your distressing mandate,' said he.

"I silently waved my hand, and left him without further reply.

"When I entered the breakfast apartment in the morning, the Marchese informed me, that the Duca had left the Castello: I secretly rejoiced at this, and felt as if freed from a load of misery; I returned to my avocations again with a light heart, comparatively speaking. The Marchese appeared very frequently pensive and absent; the loss of our little girl, preyed upon his mind, and was fast undermining his health: I exerted every talent I possessed to make his time pass smoothly; I was ill calculated to succeed in this arduous task; a melancholy had long seized me, and perpetually brooding over my sorrows, had tended considerably to encrease it.

"The Duca had not long left us before we learnt, with regret, that the young nobleman, who had recently been with us, was extremely ill. The Marchese wished to fly to his friend, to soften the miseries of a sick bed, but he could not resolve on leaving me at the Castello. Several days passed, and fresh intelligence was brought, that his disease had arrived at an alarming crisis; my beloved husband could no longer resist the imperious call of friendship; and attended solely by a domestic, long attached to him, he set out on his journey: in due time I heard from him; the young nobleman was recovering; his case had been exaggerated by his attendants, fearful of losing so valuable a lord, their apprehensions for his safety had magnified the danger; my husband, however, was gratified, at having shewn every attention, when it was supposed to have been necessary. The Marchese sent couriers almost daily, informing me of the progressive amendment of his friend's health; laying strong injunctions on me to preserve mine; and making a thousand enquiries of my amiable boy. At length the Marchese wrote to say that the young nobleman's health was so far re-established, that he intended to return, mentioning a specific time, and hoped that his friend would soon follow him, as the change of air might prove salutary. It is impossible to say how much pleasure this notice of the Marchesa's speedy return gave me. I directed all the household to appear in their most splendid liveries; and the vassals to be collected to greet their lord on the happy day, I anticipated with delight, the satisfaction the Marchese would feel at this testimony of my affection. The wished-for day arrived, and the banners of the noble house of Lepanto, placed on the highest tower of the Castello, waved in the air, and proudly displayed the ancient armorial bearing of the family, with which they were richly worked. The vassals were drawn up at their respective posts; and joy brightly shone in the countenance of every individual. I now began to count the tedious moments, and wondered at the want of punctuality in my lord; the time of his arrival had, for some hours expired; every little noise I heard in the court beneath, made my full heart leap with joy. I determined to ascend one of the turrets that commanded an extensive view of the forest, that I might catch the first sight of his approach; but hardly had I proceeded half way, when the bugle at the gate loudly sounded, and I heard an unusual noise in the court; with quick steps, and palpitating heart, I retraced my way, not doubting but I should clasp the Marchese in my longing arms; but as I hurried on, I could not help observing the gloomy visages of the vassals.—Who is there that will not pity my sufferings?—On entering the hall, the first thing I saw was my bleeding husband brought in by the domestics. The effect of thunder could not have been more sudden: without the power of uttering a shriek, and incapable of moving, I fell prostrate on the marble pavement; my head struck upon the steps—the blood ran trickling from three wounds; and my inanimate body lay extended at the feet of the attendants, who were bearing their lord: some of them came to my assistance—they raised me, but nothing could recall my senses. They carried me with the Marchese, pale, bloody, disfigured, resembling my loved lord, who was no more. Our livid countenances touched each other; our blood mingling, sullied our vestments: it might be said that the same blow immolated us both. At length after many hours I opened my eyes, but it was only to shed tears: surrounded by my women, who dressed my unfortunate wounds, and coldly rejecting the proffered attentions; I answered only by signs to the expressions of tenderness, which they used to ameliorate my unhappy state. Recoiling within myself, but resigned to my fate, I requested firmly to be conducted to my husband: it was in vain that they entreated me to renounce the painful wish of adding to the cruel misfortune which I had already experienced; I mildly, but with a fixed resolution persisted—my prayers availed; and with a steady step I entered the apartment where the bleeding body of my beloved Marchese was deposited. I stopped opposite the bier on which he was placed, and for a long time bent my eye towards him with a vacant stare, without pronouncing a word, or without a sigh escaping from my bosom. The females terrified at this awful silence, and dreading lest I might rashly resolve to put a period to my existence, hastily removed a dagger that had been negligently left in the apartment: I perceived the act, and viewed them with an acrimonious smile. I approached the body of my husband, and took his hand, which I kissed, and drew from it a brilliant diamond ring, which he usually wore. I bent before him, and offered up a fervent prayer for the repose of his soul; then joining my pallid and cold lips to his, I pressed them in an agony of grief: this was too much for my feelings to sustain, and again I became bereft of my reason, and fell into the arms of my attendants. How long I remained in this state of insensibility it is almost impossible for me to say; but the first moment reason dawned on me, I found myself in this loathsome dungeon. I waited in anxious expectation of some one coming, but several hours elapsed before I heard approaching footsteps; my heart beat feebly, but quickly, with trepidation, lest my door should be passed; but heaven in its mercy heard my prayer. With pleasure I saw the massy door open, and though a grim gaunt figure entered, yet it was a fellow creature, and my heart joyed at the sight. I almost inarticulately requested something to quench my thirst, and wet my parched lips; he complied, and gave me a little wine and water—it revived me considerably. Perceiving I was about to speak, he motioned me to silence. He placed some drink within my reach, and left me to reflect on all the horrors of my situation.

"It would be tedious and uninteresting to whoever may peruse this, to give in detail the gradual state of my recovery, or the wretchedness I endured during that period; but little did I conceive that I had merely been rescued from the yawning grave for the purpose of gratifying the lustful passion of Urbino.

"No sooner had my emaciated form in some measure acquired strength, than I received a message from the fell destroyer of my peace, the detested Duca, that he wished for an interview. In some little time after this communication he came to my dungeon; and with all the warmth and ardor of a lover, pressed me to forget my sorrows, and find a solace in his arms: he urged his suit with all the art that he was master of; he used the most persuasive arguments to dazzle my reason, and gain my consent; but I too well knew the villain I had to cope with. With disdain I rejected his addresses.—I upbraided him with the murder of my husband—with the unjustness of my detention: I demanded of him my infant boy—he smiled maliciously, and looked—

> "A devil, a born devil; on whose nature
> Nurture can never stick."

"'You are completely in my power, lady,' said the wretch, 'therefore do not spur me on to vengeance by this stubborn conduct.' 'Flatter yourself not,' I replied, 'by supposing that all your threats will induce me to see you in any other view than the ravisher of my child, and the murderer of my husband!' 'Thy son,' said he, 'who would have inherited the wide domains, and proud titles of Lepanto and Rivarola, now sleeps in peace, and the disdained Urbino now is lord of all. Remember well, lady, when next we meet you are mine, or instant death awaits you!—Ponder on the alternative, and do not rashly excite my displeasure.' He then left me. What painful reflections at this moment crowded on me: my husband murdered —my children torn from me—and myself detained in a loathsome dungeon, liable to the insults of a depraved wretch, and perhaps destined to fall a victim to his resentment."

Here there appeared to have been a long interval elapsed ere the Marchesa resumed her pen, it then ran as follows.—

"Urbino has not returned; pray heaven something has occurred to soften his flinty heart, and stay him from his dreadful intentions."

The manuscript here became quite detached, it spoke only of her daily permission, attended by a guard, to take exercise, it then continued thus.—

"After an uninterrupted quiet in my confinement for the space of twenty years, during which period I have never beheld Urbino, or could in any way discover the cause of his absence, a message has just come to say he will be with me in a few hours.—My trial will be severe, but I bow to it with resignation."

Here the Manuscript concluded.

END OF THE SECOND VOLUME.

THE VAULTS OF LEPANTO.

A Romance.

IN THREE VOLUMES.

BY

T. R. TUCKETT, Esq.

Murder most foul, as in the best it is;
But this most foul, strange, and unnatural.
　　　　　My hour is almost come,
When I to sulph'rous and tormenting flames
Must render up myself.　　　SHAKESPEARE.

Oh! then at last relent; is there no place
Left for repentance, none for pardon left?
　　　　　MILTON.

VOL. III.

LONDON:
PRINTED AT THE
Minerva-Press,
FOR A. K. NEWMAN AND CO.
LEADENHALL-STREET.
1814.

URBINO;

OR,

The Vaults of Lepanto.

CHAPTER XIV.

FERNANDO and Alberto rode on for a considerable time, still maintaining the same silence; until Alberto roused his friend, by demanding what was the nature of the plan he had formed for the recovery of Rosara? At that beloved name, Fernando started as if from a trance.

"Excuse my inattention, in not before having laid open to you my designs," said Fernando; "but you, my friend, know the anxiety of my mind, and therefore can easily account for this forgetfulness. I can scarcely say that I have decided on any particular mode of conduct; but the first idea that occurred to me, was to hasten our departure from Venice—seek Urbino at his Castello—and demand Rosara of him; as my heart tells me that it is him who carried off the lovely girl. Should he not be at the Castello di Urbino, we will then proceed to the Castello where I slept, when journeying to Venice, and where I heard the extraordinary expressions, which I have already mentioned to you: by searching the vaults and every part of that dreary, but once magnificent pile, we may gain some clue to assist us in leading to an ultimate discovery. We are four in number, and should there be banditti, it is more than probable they will not be stronger than our party; but even should it prove to the contrary, in such a cause as this, every prudential idea must be laid aside, and our only thoughts bent on surmounting every obstacle that may present itself to us, and success must crown our endeavours, impelled as we are, by virtue, love, and honor."

Alberto assented to the arrangement Fernando had made. "We might," said he, "be able, by suddenly taxing the Duca with the enormity of the crime, and insult offered to an ancient and noble family, cause him to repent of his hasty act, (if it be really him) and induce him to restore Rosara to us."

"Remember," said Fernando, "this is no trifling indignity—by heaven I swear, if I can once meet this proud and haughty Duca, my sword shall seek his recreant soul, and send it to perdition! unless his more fortunate steel should pierce my breast, and rob me of all that is dear to me on earth—my life without Rosara would be of no value, for it is alone her sweet accents that can calm the raging tempest in my bosom—oh! it will burst, and with such fury on Urbino's head, or else the fell destroyer of my peace, that even the stormy winds that root up sturdy trees, dismantle towers, and set resistance at defiance, shall be but as a zephyr to my unbounded rage. Forgive me, heaven, if the impetuous feelings of my soul hurry me beyond the dictates of my reason; but spurred on as I am, by the all-powerful influence of love; anxious to rescue a lovely and unoffending maiden from the trammels of some despicable villain, and to redress her wrongs; my mind, indignant spurns at the base act, nor can I suppress those feelings, when thus goaded on to madness! But thou knowest me, Alberto—thou art well aware that mine are not the empty vaunts of a base coward heart, whose actions only lie in words—no, my firm nerves never yet shook before man; and in thy cause, my lovely Rosara, they are doubly knit."

"Indeed I know thee, Fernando," said Alberto. "I know thee to be cast in honor's mould—I know thy friendship to be stable, and thy love sincere.—Never shall Fernando stand in need of aid, while Alberto has the power to raise a weapon: but, hapless Rosara, my heart bleeds at the thought of thy cruel situation: my own, alas! is not unmixed with care; and even now the recollection of my beloved Viola, raises the tender sigh within my grief-worn breast, and impels the warm unmanly tear, to start unconscious to my eye."

"Cease, cease, Alberto," said Fernando, "we must chase sorrow from our brows: let not our finer sensations give way to those of a more imperious nature;—melancholy, my friend, and the free indulgence of those feelings, can only tend to relax the energies of our minds, and make us unfit for the enterprise we have embarked in: let us perish, rather than our noble blood and reputation should be sullied by the slightest inference, that our zeal has not been exerted to the utmost extent, to search out the concealed abode of Rosara."

"Your censure is but just," said Alberto, "and from this instant I dash the intruding tear from me; and in this swollen sigh, send forth all tender thoughts and brace my nerves for hardy deeds: thus do I banish every tender impression that has been engraven on my heart, until a more genial air shall breath upon me, and bring me happier hours. The trial, my friend, is past—all, all my softer thoughts are plucked up by the roots, and cast out from me. Now welcome strife and death, and sad turmoil.—Forgive me, God of love, if in this I aught offend.—Viola, the lovely blooming Viola still holds her empire over my heart; but anger, love, and bloodshed, cannot be inhabitants where you preside; and thus have I discarded thee, unless my breast commixed with peace, again can offer thee sovereign empire:—thou art—thou ever must be dear to Alberto di Vincenti."

The conversation becoming painful, Fernando called to Gaspardo to approach.

"How far think you," said he to him, as soon as he had come sufficiently near, "are we from the Castello di Urbino?"

"Not more than two hours fair riding from here, Signior," said Gaspardo; "full well I know the road—before long we shall see above yon forest of pine, the lofty battlements of the Castello—it is a noble edifice."

"Is it," said Fernando, "capable of holding a numerous body of men? And does the Duca keep a proportion of the vassals constantly in readiness, in case of emergency?"

"I cannot say, Signior; the Duca has not been there for some time, as I have heard; and in his absence, only the necessary guards are kept up."

"Had we but here," cried Fernando, "the vassals of Durazzo, whose dauntless souls no danger know, or peril can appal; thy turrets, proud Urbino, would totter on their fabric!"

"Yes, Signior—yes, my beloved master," said Gaspardo, with vivacity, "led by thee, the vassals of Durazzo would be invincible; they would be happy in shedding their blood at thy bidding.—The

Marchese, good and virtuous, would exult in seeing you, Signior, point out to them the road to battle: but two days journey hence, we can with ease reach the Castello di Durazzo; and then our vassals will be proud to shew their fealty; not one but will in an instant arm, to assert the right, uphold the honor, and avenge the insults offered to their lord."

"Peace," said Fernando, "I know the hardy valor of our vassals well, and their firm attachment to the noble house of Durazzo. How could I reconcile it to myself, to withdraw them from the vast and fertile domains of Durazzo, to engage in needless warfare? No!—at present it might be attended with evil; but when the moment arrives that is necessary to call forth the valorous vassals of our house, then will I summon them to rally round the standard of their lord, and gloriously shew the way to victory, or to death."

Fernando ceased:—his firm, animated look, plainly shewed the impetuous ardor of his breast; but yet his countenance, mild and serene, evinced a courage tempered with humanity. Alberto, who had drooped, through the dreadful conflicts that raged within him, now assumed his wonted fire and energy of character: his piercing eye appeared as if it would, like his well tempered weapon, penetrate the deepest recesses of the soul; or with its terror, strike his destined victim dead.

Thus proceeded they, until Gaspardo drew their attention, by pointing out the lofty towers of the Castello di Urbino. The noble and magnificent pile, burst on their view as it were almost by inchantment. On an eminence stood the Castello, overlooking the deep and gloomy forest by which it was nearly encircled: the massy battlements seemed to bid defiance to the ravages of time, and to present a secure asylum to its lord. Superbly proud, the lofty towers lost amid the clouds, frowned, indignant, on the meaner neighbouring edifices.—So as when wintry winds, with boisterous force, threaten with destruction all around; the sturdy oak, unbending, braves the raging element, and with its waving branches, seems to mock its impotent efforts; whilst the more feeble shrubs are torn up from the earth, and left to wither on the naked soil. So stood the Castello di Urbino, magnificently pre-eminent, and firm and unsubdued, against the united powers of the dark tempest's blasts, and the more subtle art of man.

The cavalieros had nearly reached the drawbridge of the Castello, which was raised; and every thing from the external appearance, indicated that it was always held in a posture of defence. Gaspardo, at the desire of Fernando, approached and loudly sounding a horn, which was suspended at the gate, was almost immediately answered from one of the turrets, by the warder of the Castello, who demanded the cause of their visit.

"The Cavalieros," said Gaspardo, "whom you perceive, wish to hold converse with the Duca di Urbino."

"The Duca di Urbino," said the warder, "inhabits not the Castello at present, and his return is uncertain.—Where are your followers?"

"These two noble cavalieros are attended but by their squires," answered Gaspardo.

"From what family do they spring?" demanded the warder.

"From the noble houses of Durazzo and Vincenti," answered Gaspardo.

The warder mused for some time, then addressing himself to Gaspardo, said, "if the cavalieros, as the day is fast closing, will accept the cheer the Castello affords, they shall be welcome for the night—bear this message to them."

Gaspardo returned to Fernando, and related the substance of the parley. Disappointment was strongly pourtrayed in his countenance, on hearing of the absence of the Duca.

"I hope, Fernando," said Alberto, "you mean not to accept this offer of being accommodated for the night. Urbino, artful himself, no doubt is served by those, equally as treacherous and base; therefore let us decline entering the Castello."

"We came," answered Fernando, "to seek the Duca di Urbino in the bosom of his vassals, and therefore if we dared to brave him when surrounded by his satellites, what more have we to dread from these, his minions? No, Alberto—some clue may still be gained, respecting the concealment of my adored Rosara. I would not put my foot beneath the roof of the hated di Urbino, did I not fondly cherish the pleasing hope that something fortunate might transpire."

"Let it be as you will," answered Alberto, "I fear some treachery lurks beneath this seeming hospitality."

"Go," said Fernando to Gaspardo, "and tell the warder we will repose within the Castello."

Gaspardo quickly obeyed Fernando's orders. Some time elapsed before the ponderous bridge was lowered—as soon as this was effected, the cavalieros rode over, and entered the spacious court, where, to their astonishment, they found a greater proportion of armed men drawn up, than they could possibly conceive was actually necessary to guard the Castello, when not at war, or to prevent the chances of a surprise; but the cavalieros springing from their horses, appeared not to notice this extraordinary circumstance. They were courteously conducted through a large range of magnificent apartments, until they reached one which was destined for their reception: it seemed to be nearly at the extremity of one angle of the building, and commanded a most extensive and romantic view. The bed rooms they were to occupy, were within one another, though it was apparent, from there being several doors, that apartments lay contiguous to them.

The cavalieros sat for some time, as if unwilling to express their sentiments, but Fernando at length broke silence, by expressing his opinion of the great strength of the Castello.

"It would," said Alberto, "require a powerful force to reduce it, if it be at all possible that such an enterprise would eventually be successful."

"I do not doubt," answered Fernando, "but that the Duca, must have some very strong inducement to keep up so large an establishment, but probably the extensive scale of the Castello requires it, for their common safety; should that be the case, Alberto, I can scarcely think that even the vast domains of Urbino could furnish men sufficient to make a great defence when engaged in war.—"

Fernando was here interrupted by the entrance of the domestics, who brought in refreshments for them. The cavalieros drew near the table, and cheerfully partook of what was set before them, and as little conversation passed, their meal was quickly ended; neither of them conceived it proper to question the domestics, who were attending, and they also thought that it might cause some suspicion. Previous to their retiring, Fernando desired that their servants should be conducted to them, which was complied with after some considerable time elapsing.

"Our horses," said Fernando to Gaspardo, as soon as he perceived that he was present, "have been well taken care of I hope?"

"Yes, Signior," answered Gaspardo, "they have been well taken care of, and, if I am not much mistaken, before morning, some of the soldiery in the Castello will shew a strong inclination to do us a greater service than we could wish for."

"How mean you, Gaspardo?" said Fernando. "Have you discovered aught that leads you to suppose that any treachery is intended?"

"Gently, Signior," answered Gaspardo, "walls have ears: I do fear that our situation is perilous, but we must put the best face upon it, since it has so happened that we have ventured within the Castello."

"But to the purpose, good Gaspardo," said Alberto, who had been hitherto silent; "all this we are already aware of—inform us what has caused this alarm, and roused the ideas you seem to entertain of some perfidious act being on foot against us, by the soldiery of the Castello?"

"Why, Signior," answered Gaspardo, "Paulo and I were refreshing ourselves, when we heard voices as if not very distant from us, rather in high words. 'I tell you, Hugo,' said one of them, 'that it is he—I recollect his person well—not a day passed, but I saw him at the Palazza.' 'Was I not at Venice,' answered the one who had been called Hugo, 'as well as thou? And think you I would not know his person?—And did not Sanguinario place me to watch daily at the Palazza?—would he were here, and then all would go well.' 'I wish with all my heart he was,' replied the one who had first spoken, 'we should then be directed to seize these cavalieros, and the Duca would reward us well.—I suppose, Hugo, you will next deny that one of them is the Signior Alberto, brother to Signiora Rosara: but if I can prevent their slipping through our hands, it shall not be my fault.—I dare say I shall find nobler souls than yours in the Castello —men who will faithfully serve their lord.' 'I have always served the Duca,' answered Hugo, 'as an honest vassal should: I have bled in his defence, and in a right and just cause, am always ready to do my duty; but I like not this butchering trade; and for the Duca's promises of reward, I know how to value them well—let the cavalieros depart in peace.' '*In peace!*' retorted the other, indignantly. 'If you, Hugo, set so little estimation on the favor of the Duca, I do not.' Their conversation then became quite indistinct. From this,

Signior, I have concluded that we are not safe in this Castello, and I am fearful that we shall be detained against our inclination."

"So great a violation of the rules of hospitality, can hardly be attempted," said Fernando.

"What would not the Duca di Urbino and his base hirelings be guilty of?" replied Alberto, interrupting him. "It is now clear that we have been inveigled, and all this seeming attention is but a cloak to some villainous designs; but in the morn, should the warder even intimate the foul desire of detaining us, that very instant will I sacrifice the hoary wretch for his perfidious conduct!"

The two cavalieros desired Gaspardo and Paulo to prepare every thing in the adjoining apartments; they then took it into serious consideration, what was best to be done. At length it was determined, that any appearance of distrust on their part, might prove detrimental to them; but at the same time, it was highly necessary to keep a strict watch. It was also agreed on, that Gaspardo and Paulo should occupy one of the rooms belonging to the suite, so as to be near them; and they would remain cased in their armor, by the fire, during the night, and at the first dawn of morning, take their departure; by this arrangement, whatever danger menaced them, they were prepared to repel it. After having thus decided, their minds became more quieted; and as the danger appeared nearer, so did their resolutions become more firm. Some of the domestics belonging to the Castello, brought in wood, and requested to know if the cavalieros wished for anything further.

"No," said Fernando, "we shall not, our own attendants will be sufficient, therefore for this night we shall not require anything more of you."

Silently bowing, they withdrew. They had not long departed, before Gaspardo came to inform the Cavalieros that one of the doors in the next apartment opened into a library, which appeared by the light of the lamp, to have been entirely neglected. This was indeed a fortunate discovery for the cavalieros, as they would be enabled to procure a book, to beguile away the hours. Fernando and Alberto, followed by their servant, immediately repaired to the library. The furniture had fallen into decay, and the volumes which once graced the shelves, were grown musty, and covered with thick dust; every thing remained in confusion. A cold dampness struck through them, and Fernando hastily taking a volume, they quitted the gloomy apartment. The night was far advanced, and Alberto proposed that a few more logs should be thrown on the fire, and to commence amusing themselves by reading. Directions were given to Gaspardo and Paulo, to be ready the instant they were called, and every thing being arranged, the cavalieros drew round the fire, when Fernando thus read.—

The Legend.

"It was at the awful hour, when ghastly goblins issue from their tombs, and unquiet spirits wander over the earth, to fright the guilty with their misdeeds; or to some chosen friend or kindred, make known the wrongs they suffered, while inhabitants of the terrestial globe, and with deep and solemn injunctions, urge them to avenge their cause, that there perturbed spirits might repose in peace; a dreadful spectre appeared to the Marchese, who had retired early to his couch—his dear and faithful friend, who he had long mourned, stood at his feet, his countenance beaming with beneficence; beneath the foldings of his winding sheet, a deep wound was seen; while the hot blood smoaked as it trickled from his breast. The spectre slowly raised his arm, and with his finger, pointed to the horrid gash, then with a hollow voice pronounced, 'I was murdered!—The tale of my supposed death is false—revenge my untimely fate—speak, I command you!'

" 'I will, my friend, if on the earth the foul murderer lives.'

" '*He lives*,' re-echoed the spectre. 'Seek Rosalba—it is he that cut my thread of life—beneath the ruins of the Abbey, still my bones lie unburried.' The spectre slowly retired, emphatically saying, '*remember!*' and vanished.

"The terror the Marchese felt at beholding the shade of his friend again visiting the earth, awoke him from the profound sleep into which he had fallen. The lights were extinguished, and every thing seemed enveloped in impenetrable darkness. He loudly called to the pages, who rested in the anti-chamber—his well-known summons was obeyed. The Marchese had a sorrowful, but determined air—he dismissed all his attendants but his faithful page, to whom he related the extraordinary visitation he had from his departed friend.

"'This very night,' said the Marchese, 'will I go to the ruined Abbey, and inter the relics of the unquiet spectre, that his restless spirit might no longer wander, disconsolate, through the midnight gloom, or break the searments of the grave.'

"As the Marchese concluded, seraphic music floated on the ambient air—the full tones swelled on the balmy breeze—then the gently-dying strains were lost, and all was hushed. The Marchese and the page stood wrapped in astonishment, till the former recovering himself exclaimed, 'Heaven applauds my pious purpose, and this instant will I go to serve thee, dearest friend.—Order my courser to be prepared, and then assist me to encase.'

"The page obeyed the Marchese. He then descended the marble stairs to his spacious halls, where many a foeman's banner hung, bravely won in honorable strife. No dastard heart possessed the Marchese—Noble and valiant as the lion, his ambitious soul aspired to deeds of glory. The stately portal opened at his approach; the neighing courser champed his bit, and with exulting pride, pawed the earth. Accompanied by his faithful page, who was provided with torches, necessary to search the dark vaults of the Abbey, they crossed the drawbridge, and took the road that led them to the ruins pointed out by the spectre. Spurring their coursers, they soon reached the destined spot. The torch being lighted, they opened a small door, and descended into the subterraneous passages. They had not proceeded far, before a deep and lengthened groan reached them:—quick as electric fire, the Marchese drew his faulchion, and rushed towards that part of the passage from whence the sound proceeded; but no entrance could be found; the walls were mildewed, and from them depended long dank weeds. Disappointed, but not appalled, the Marchese, with a dauntless air pursued his way; when a voice exclaimed, 'Oh! spare me—in pity spare me!' It was that of a female—he stood unresolved. The exclamation brought back tender thoughts to him.—The Marchese loved a beautiful and accomplished lady, who conscious of his worth, returned his passion; but a relentless father's stern decree, dashed all his prospects to the ground. The lovely maid, true to her plighted faith, resisted every effort of her cruel parent to join her to another, and pines in solitude, with vows unbroken. With briny tears the Marchese nightly wets his pillow; and vainly sighing, still preserves an inviolable attachment. While the Marchese remained in this state of perplexity, a faint glimmering light, only a few paces from him, attracted his attention: hastening to the place from whence it issued, he found a door, which led into a low vaulted chamber—a lamp hung from the roof. In the inner apartment he beheld a sight which overwhelmed him with horror:—stretched on a miserable pallet, lay the object of his adoration, while a warrior of gigantic stature, with upraised arm, grasped a dagger, in the attitude of striking the fatal blow, and his meditated victim, with her hands clasped, seemed waiting with resignation the assassin's stroke. This was no time for debate—the Marchese entered the room, and as he raised his weapon against the warrior, a piercing shriek from the female, caused him to turn, and for a moment drew his attention from his bloody purpose, but at that very instant the unerring steel of the Marchese penetrated his breast, and falling, his cumbrous weight made the hollow caverns echo. The Marchese bending a stern look on the prostrate wretch, was about to speak, when the well-known features of Rosalba met his eye.

"'Heavens, thou art just!' ejaculated the Marchese, 'for in slaying thee, I have revenged my murdered friend, and rescued thee, dear maid.—Wretch, where hast thou scattered the bones of my departed friend, the worthy—the valiant Francisco?'

"At that name, Rosalba bit his lips; his eye-balls glared; and his distorted visage shewed the agony of his mind; large drops bedewed his face.

"'Dark deeds pollute my soul—there is no hope for me!' cried Rosalba, in broken accents, while the purple current streamed from his wound. 'Within the vault, near the entrance of the passage, lies Francisco['s] bones.—My soul will shortly wing its way—assist me heaven!—I dare not call upon the name—I die!' and prone he fell at the concluding sentence—the vital spark became extinguished, and his body now lay inanimate.

"The Marchese cast a look of horror, mingled with pity, at Rosalba; then flying to his adored, raised her in his arms, and bore her from the scene of death, as soon as she had recovered.

"The Marchese with his faithful page, collected the bones of the disturbed spirit, and placing them in a case, brought for that purpose, they left the gloomy ruins and returned towards the Castello. The Marchese used soft language to sooth the agitated feelings of the object of his heart, and urged his courser to his utmost speed, that she might the sooner obtain that repose, her delicate frame required."

Here Fernando laid down the book; he had been so intent upon the tale, that he heeded not the distant thunder's roll; but now the lowering clouds discharged themselves, and the swollen torrents, dashing against the craggy rocks, sent forth a hollow murmuring noise. The forked lightening, by its glare, rendered the darkness of the atmosphere more horrible.—Peals of thunder rolled on successive peals—but one more tremendous than the rest, which seemed to shake the arched vaults of heaven to its foundation, made the cavalieros recoil.

The Castello was filled with the screams of the domestics, and the more dreadful imprecations of the soldiery—a silent solemn pause ensued, as if Nature, tired of the struggle, had sunk into eternal rest. Fernando and Alberto, who had been joined by Gaspardo and Paulo, remained mute; their breasts were filled with awe, and fervently they offered up a prayer to the Almighty.

A light now broke in feeble rays through an aperture of the door of the library; wound up to the height of expectation, they bent their straining eyes towards the spot, when the door opened, and a figure, bearing a lamp, advanced to the center of the apartment—it spoke not—firm and immoveable, it appeared to contemplate the cavalieros attentively.

Fernando, incapable of longer containing himself, accosted the figure—"if it be true, as they do say, that long departed spirits oft quit the peaceful mansion of the dead, to revisit the earth—speak if thou hast power, and inform us of the cause of thy unusual appearance!"—Fernando paused, the figure still remained in a fixed attitude.

"Speak, poor spirit," said Alberto, "and if our swords can render thee essential service, thy will shall be obeyed."

The figure turned towards the open door of the library, and beckoned to them.

"It bids us follow," said Fernando.

"Thou will not follow!" exclaimed Alberto. "This may be a fresh mode of practising some hellish act of treachery against us."

The figure looked sternly at the cavalieros, and stamped upon the floor with seeming violence; then solemnly moving on, again beckoned.

"I will follow thee," exclaimed Fernando: "thou invitest, and I will obey."

Fernando advanced, followed by Alberto.—The figure slowly moved on, until they reached the open door. The two servants remained in the same place they were in when the figure first made its appearance; they had not attempted to remove from it, not having received directions for that purpose, from the cavalieros. The figure now looked towards them, and waved its hand, as if intimating a wish that they should also follow. The cavalieros desired them to keep close, and they felt themselves more inclined to pursue the steps of the figure, from the addition of their domestics. They had not noticed whether Gaspardo and Paulo were advancing with them; and the domestics were unwilling to join in the party, unless directed by their masters—they all together passed through the library. The figure seemed to touch a spring, and a concealed door immediately opened. They proceeded to be led in this manner for a considerable space of time, until they came to a small room, in the centre of which stood a trap door, thrown back on its hinges; the figure descended, and the cavalieros, with their attendants, followed. The figure looked with a peculiar meaning at the corner of the vault in which they were: the lamp it bore, shed but a faint light, and its feeble rays were but sufficient to make the gloom appear more horrific.

"What is that I see," exclaimed Alberto, "which sparkles on the ground?"

Paulo picked it up—it was a dagger, and near it lay a paper, folded. The figure raised the lamp, as if to give them a better opportunity of viewing the apartment.—The ground was stained with blood! and the scattered relics of human bones, confirmed the cavalieros in the opinion, that some most bloody, foul, and barbarous deed had been committed. The dagger was encrusted with blood, except a small part near the haft, on which the gleam of light had struck, and had been the cause of attracting their attention; a name was engraven on it, but it would be necessary to clean the dirt with which it was covered, before it could be legible. The folded paper was a short note, which they could not decypher at that moment; but the superscription bore the name of Colloredo. There could be no doubt but that the person to whom the letter was addressed, bore a great portion in the tragic scene that had been acted. The figure turned into a narrow passage, and proceeded with great care; the cavalieros kept close up with it. They continued winding along the passage, when the figure suddenly stopped, and waved its hand; it placed the lamp within a niche, and again moved on. The cavalieros were a little surprised at this; but they were determined, as they had thus far entrusted themselves to the guidance of the figure, they would not hesitate to follow. The cold air began to blow down the passage, and a few streaks of light began to appear at its extremity. They now came to the foot of a flight of steps, at the top of which a door stood open: the figure stopped and pointed to them, to precede him. Fernando immediately led the way—the rest of the party followed. Great indeed was their surprise, when they found themselves in the forest, which ran close to the Castello, whose frowning battlements proudly towered above them; they turned to look for their conductor, but the door was shut, and with all their united efforts they could not raise it.

"This is very strange," said Fernando. "I know not whether this be kindly meant of our conductor; but we shall find it difficult to travel without our horses."

A low hollow voice answered as from beneath—"to the right, within twenty yards of this, you will find your horses, with every thing necessary; but depart quickly, for your doom is fixed, if you loiter beneath the walls of the Castello di Urbino!"

"We thank thee, generous stranger," said Alberto, "whatever may be thy condition, for having thus freed us from the toils of our enemies."

The cavalieros, with their attendants, took the road to the right, as they had been directed, and found their horses, as they had been instructed. The heavens were filled with innumerable stars; and the pale moon shone in all her brilliancy. A serene calm had now succeeded the late tempest's howl; and every thing around, bore testimony to the fury of the contending elements. Their minds became inspired with awe; and the loneliness of their situation, with the late scenes they had gone through, impressed upon their minds a sentiment of religion: they silently bent their knees before their Maker, and with the utmost purity, offered up a prayer to the Almighty.—This concluded, Alberto urged Fernando to mount, that they might immediately retire from a situation so replete with danger: this caution was attended to; and without any further conjecture on the late events, the cavalieros struck into the path before them, and put their horses into a gallop.

For several hours they journeyed without resting, until it was thought necessary to take some refreshment, and bait the horses. Some provisions had been placed on one of the animals, which were spread upon the ground, and the cavalieros heartily partook of their meal. Their conversation naturally turned upon the events of the night, and in conjectures to whom they were indebted for their liberation from the infernal deceits of Urbino's satellites.

"Where, Alberto," said Fernando, "hast thou placed the letter and dagger, which you picked up?"

"Here they are," answered Alberto, at the same moment producing them.

They both looked over the note and after some little difficulty decyphered it—the contents were as follows:—

"Be ready to meet me in the forest, near the Castello; thou knowest well the old place of rendezvous—fail not to be there, as you love me, Colloredo. First I shall try my infatuated cousin, the Marchese di Lepanto, to assist in extricating me from my difficulties: and if the Duca, my father, is not likely soon to leave me undisturbed possession of his vast domains, which my necessities require to be speedy; the dagger that I gave thee will, if well applied, save a multitude of misery and delay:—that done, dearest Colloredo, all I can command shall be for ever thine.

"Urbino."

"Thou art indeed a horrid villain!" exclaimed Fernando. "Had not mine eyes beheld the contents of this paper, I could not have believed mankind to have been so degraded; or could I have supposed a son would seek the assassination of his parent. Oh, wretched Urbino! the possession of thy wealth, thy rank, thy vast domains, must daily haunt thy accursed soul—I would not for one atom of thy guilt, be master of thy magnificent Castello, and lord of all thy vassals."

"Carefully," said Alberto, "will I put this by; and if justice can be found in Venice, I will strain my every nerve to bring to light the conduct of the Duca, as far as refers to this, and let him answer at the holy Inquisition, who this Colloredo is—whose is the dagger —and the real interpretation of this mysterious letter. But say, my friend Fernando, whither shall we now bend our way? For though I droop not in my zeal to serve my dearest sister Rosara, still we are rendering her but little service."

"This much affects me too, Alberto. I had hoped within that villain's spacious courts, to have learnt some happy tidings of my loved Rosara—hear me for a moment, my friend and brother, and once more let me point out to you the course I would pursue—'tis this:—to repair to the Castello di Lepanto, and search the vaults; if we are then unsuccessful, we will hasten to Venice—lay the letter we are in possession of before the holy Inquisition—and make the Duca answer at that terrible tribunal, for all his monstrous and accumulated villainy. Could I but have met him within the length of my sword, I should not have sought the means I now propose; but it is our duty to drag him from his lurking place."

"I do approve," said Alberto, "of your scheme; but let us know if Gaspardo is acquainted with the road, and how far distant the Castello di Lepanto is."

The faithful Gaspardo was called, and to the joy of the cavalieros, they found they were not more than a few hours journey from it. The cavalieros proceeded gently towards the dilapidated Castello di Lepanto; and when they were sufficiently near, they placed food before their horses, and fastened them to the trees.

The evening had now closed in and it was almost dark—Fernando and the party moved with the utmost caution, they passed through a small postern, and shortly gained the large hall; they could not find any passage that could conduct them to the chambers below, though they sought for one with the utmost scrutiny; while thus occupied, they heard the distant tread of footsteps, they immediately concealed themselves; a warrior, completely clad, entered the spacious hall, and looking cautiously round, seemed to be retiring, when Fernando rushed from his concealment; the undaunted veteran drew his sword to defend himself, and as the noble youth raised his weapon, the warrior exclaimed—"What is it thou Fernando! and where is thy friend Alberto?" It was the well-known voice of the *unknown*. "Where is thy friend?" again demanded he, before Fernando could recover from his surprise; at this moment Alberto, with Gaspardo and Paulo, joined Fernando.

"It is our old friend!" said Gaspardo; "what new scrape is he now going to get us out of?"

"Thou needest not to fear, my friend," said the unknown; "follow me, Signiors, I was in quest of you—I shall unfold that which is necessary for your ear." The unknown led them to an apartment; as soon as they entered, he addressed himself to Fernando. "Here, Signior, is an order from the Marchese di Durazzo, who is now at Venice, directing you would proceed to his Castello, collect his vassals, and lead them forth against the powers of Urbino:—the Signior Alberto will accompany you; and seven days hence the vassals of Vincenti will join with those of Durazzo, to hurl destruction on the villain, Urbino!"

"I forgive you," cried Gaspardo with joy, "I forgive you, my old fellow, all the uneasiness you have caused me on my master's account, since you bring the news, that my lord's intrepid vassals are to be led forth by my brave young master.—Oh! what a lucky set we are, that the ugly figure should have shown us the secret passages of the Castello di Urbino!"

"What secret passages," cried the unknown, "art thou acquainted with, appertaining to the Castello di Urbino?"

Fernando related to the unknown the circumstances that had occurred; when he had concluded, the unknown turned to him with a serious aspect.—"How couldst thou, Signior Fernando be guilty of so much rashness, as to trust thyself in the hands of thy avowed enemies?—let reason, Signior, bear greater sway in the direction of your actions—of what avail is all your courage, virtue and probity? —will this save you from the villain's grasp?—no, Signor, all these shining qualifications, unaided by reason, can be of little service.— Remember, Signior, you are now entrusted with a noble enterprise

—no less than the humiliating the proud, the haughty and despotic Duca di Urbino.—Let reason and valor keep an equal balance in thy breast; your counsels then will possess firmness, and your hot intemperate courage be curbed by reflection—your arms will be doubtless prosperous—your vassals will cheerfully spill their blood in your cause, as they will be convinced that not one drop will be wantonly shed:—bear this in your mind, Signior, and excuse an old man's warmth in thus having freely spoke, but when you know me better, you will be better able to judge the reason from whence my anxiety flows.—The letter I have given you, will inform you how to proceed.—The vassals of Vincenti are already in arms, but until those of the Marchese are also collected, it would be imprudent to move them forward. Expect to meet me on the seventh day from this.—The Marchese and the Condi are both well, they are in Venice —and for Rosara, her recovery depends upon your exertion."

"Upon my exertion!" exclaimed Fernando, "tell me how to save her and I will sacrifice my existence for her—oh! tell me where Rosara lies concealed?"

"Moderate your transports," said the unknown; "though thou art brave, still thy single arm, cannot cast down walls, and pierce through embattled ranks of warriors—even yesterday the crafty Urbino conveyed the lovely girl, from the vaults of this Castello, where he had kept her close confined since she was so basely taken from the Palazza, to his Castello, and there as I do know, he has assembled a large portion of his vassals, and in addition has hired the hoard of banditti, who infested this forest, to join him till the threatened storm shall have blown over; but there shall be such a tempest raised, that not all the wily arts of Urbino, or the savage fierceness of his troops shall appease—no, Urbino, thy crimes have at length become too glaring, and sleeping justice is aroused at thy innumerable acts of murder, fraud and rapine.—It is Signior, for the purpose of liberating the young and beautiful Rosara, that you are to lead the vassals of Durazzo forth; our plans must necessarily undergo some alteration, since you are acquainted with the passages of the Castello di Urbino; but we must be cautious in making use of this advantage.—You must both," turning to Gaspardo and Paulo, "now shew the fidelity you have always professed to the generous cavalieros you have served.—The Signiora Viola,

Signior Alberto," addressing himself to him, "is well, and I hope, before long she will prove her birth and origin to be equal to that of the heir of the house of Vincenti."

"What dost thou say?" exclaimed Alberto, "let me again hear thee; my ears unused to happy sounds can scarcely credit what they hear; I thank thee stranger for this news—perhaps Alberto might be happy—but does Viola still remember me—has she not forgot Alberto di Vincenti?—no, no, her heart is too faithful, and too noble; it was ungenerous in me to harbour such suspicions."

Alberto walked backwards and forwards in violent agitation, during which time the dagger and folded paper inadvertently fell from his belt, beneath which he had placed them; the unknown, who was nearest, stooped and picked them up, but on seeing the superscription of the letter, suddenly started back—"how procured you this?" exclaimed he with energy, "it is Urbino's hand, and addressed to that villain Colloredo!"

"I found it," replied Alberto, "in one of the vaults belonging to the Castello di Urbino, on the night we were escaping from thence —read it, the contents will still more astonish you."

The unknown perused it—"this is indeed," said he, "a fortunate document—now Urbino thy long suspected guilt is clear—will you, Signior permit me to take this with me to Venice? I will deliver it into the hands of the Condi, who well knows how to make a proper use of it."

"You may make what use of it you think proper," said Alberto.

The unknown bowed, and placed the paper and dagger in his vest.

The cavalieros were perfectly satisfied that the unknown was a person on whose probity they could depend. The letter he had delivered to Fernando, spoke of him in the highest terms, and directed him to pay attention to whatever he might suggest, and to lose no time in following the orders he would communicate. Fernando already lay under a load of obligation to him, but this was not a moment to play the courtier, and speak his thanks in soft set phrases—no, the star of his adoration claimed his thoughts—and he meditated schemes deep and noble, to rescue his loved Rosara from the abominable Urbino.

The unknown reminded the cavalieros that no time was to be

lost; he intended immediately to proceed to Venice, where matters of the greatest import called him—"I shall inform the Marchese and the Condi, how and where I parted from you, it cannot fail to give them pleasure; but I must yet do more for you: necessity will compel you to pass through a part of the Duca's vast domains, and probably, he might have sent some of his vassals in pursuit of you; I shall therefore add four of the troop I have with me, to your number, but let discretion guide you, entrust them not with where you are journeying; they must be kept profoundly ignorant, and you will find them ready to obey you."—The unknown drew a small bugle from his breast, and thrice sounded it—thrice a responsive blast, sent back the sound; steps were almost instantly heard in the corridor, and twelve men, completely armed, entered the apartment.—The unknown selected four of them, and desired them to attend the cavalieros and obey their orders implicitly; they bowed in token of compliance. Every thing being thus arranged, they all descended to the court-yard; and Gaspardo and Paulo, who had been dispatched to bring their horses, now arrived, and the gallant party mounted.

"Success attend our enterprise!" said the unknown, "and may the beautiful Rosara di Vincenti be soon freed from her hateful captivity!" He spurred his horse and took the road to Venice with his followers; the cavalieros turned into a road in the contrary direction, and were soon lost in the gloom of the forest.

CHAPTER XV.

It will now be necessary to return to Rosara, and di Urbino.

As soon as the Duca was informed that Sanguinario had quitted the Vaults di Lepanto, his rage knew no bounds. He paced the room with furious mien, and execrated the hour that first leagued him with the perfidious Sanguinario. He thought this the best opportunity of compassing his downfall, and freeing himself from any further connection with this man of blood. The Duca summoned his faithful servant, and dispatched him with the packet he had prepared, containing charges against Sanguinario. The intelligence was so circumstantial, that he conceived it would be impossible that his victim could escape from the wary agents of the holy Inquisition. It was no matter to the Duca, if his colleague suffered death immediately, or languished under the more protracted mode of punishing —by the rack. Within the tomb of Sanguinario, his secrets would be entombed; and with his death, his fears of being betrayed would expire. No eye had ever witnessed his criminal conduct but Sanguinario's; and when that Sanguinario slept in peace, he vainly thought his agonised bosom would regain its wonted calmness and repose. But thou art yet to learn, that a conscience stained with guilt, and still continuing in the wild career of injustice, can feel but little consolation, even though lulled into self security, by the removal of an object that was feared; or at the prospect of being released from the tormenting idea, of escaping for ever from the hands of justice; still a secret monitor will always goad it with the horrid recollection of the past. The Duca clearly saw that the secret Vaults di Lepanto, would not be capable of longer affording him a secure asylum. He was now completely in the hands of the horde of banditti; and though the Castello was his own, by the death of the late Marchese, still the ruffians that inhabited it, claimed a right to occupy it, and to expel any one who had the temerity to enter it.

The Duca thought it would answer his purpose exceeding well, if he could gain Bernardo and his troop over to his interest, so as to accompany him to the Castello di Urbino. It was composed of daring fellows, and would be a valuable acquisition to him, in case of any rupture. He dreaded in secret, lest the Condi should arm his vassals, and make head against him: to obviate any ill consequences, resulting from such measures, he had sent private instructions to the warder of the Castello, to collect a large proportion of the vassals, and to be cautious who he admitted, and none in numbers, as he was suspicious of some of the neighbouring lords. If Sanguinario should be induced to confess anything respecting him, he doubted not but he would be able to crush it; and if the circumstances bore a more serious aspect than he conceived would be probable, the Castello di Urbino afforded him sufficient security against the whole state; and in the event of that failing, he would fly with Rosara to some distant country, with the money and jewels he could collect, and live in retirement, unknowing, and unknown. This plan seemed to promise the Duca every thing he could wish; for, ultimately, Rosara would be his, and in that all his thoughts centered. All that now remained was but to gain Bernardo over, and instantly, with Rosara, to leave the Vaults di Lepanto, for the more safe Castello di Urbino. For this purpose he summoned Bernardo: as soon as this chieftain entered, the Duca, in a familiar tone accosted him.

"How now, Bernardo," said he, "how fares the gallant troop?—Have you of late been successful?"

"The lads," answered Bernardo, "are well, and ripe for anything; but business has lately been very scarce; we have not cut a throat these two days past."

"I think," said the Duca, "I could put thee in a way of spending your time in pleasant quarters, free of expense; and it may so happen, that before long, there might be some cutting of throats —thou rememberest well the cavalieros at Venice?"

"The devil take them!" answered Bernardo. "I never was so served before; but if I could again have an opportunity of meeting this Signior Cavaliero, one or the other of us, would certainly go to the other world."

"But, good Bernardo," said the Duca, "you do not answer the first part of my question."

"True," replied Bernardo. "About *free quarters.*—I have no objection Signior; but I could never agree to lead a *life of idleness.*"

"Thou shall not, honest Bernardo," said the Duca. "I deem it to be impossible, that a man, used to active life like you, could ever rest contented in an inert state: but my friend Bernardo, I have to propose to you the removal of the troop to the Castello di Urbino; there you will, unquestionably be safe; there you will be provided with every thing you can wish; and at parting, a handsome reward shall be presented to you. The lady Rosara I mean to convey thither; and as I will never yield her up, but with my life, the Condi, her father, might be fool enough to try the force of arms; Should that take place, Bernardo, a glorious field will open to us, to avenge ourselves. One of those same cavalieros is the brother; the other, the avowed lover of Rosara.—What sayest thou to this, Bernardo?"

"Why Duca," answered Bernardo, "thou hast not performed thy promise with respect to the reward, in bringing away the Signiora Rosara."

"That," said the Duca, "shall be paid thee, the moment we arrive at the Castello—I pledge myself to the performance of this, by all the faith of man!"

"Well, well, Duca," replied Bernardo, "that settled you are to recollect that here I am, chief of as brave a set of fellows, as ever drew swords—cut a throat—or took a purse; and if we join your vassals at the Castello di Urbino, I shall then be compelled to do as you direct. But now every man is under my controul: I order as I please; and death is the immediate punishment of disobedience."

"You are not just, Bernardo," said the Duca. "I could not treat my friend so unworthily. It is my intention that thou shouldst still retain the command of thy troop, without any interference on my part—be admitted to our private councils—and share the splendors of the Castello."

"But, Duca," said Bernardo, "what is to be Sanguinario's post?"

"Him—the villain!" exclaimed the Duca. "He is not worthy to be trusted with a post of honor.—Has he not clandestinely stolen from hence—basely deserted me? And perhaps by this, his coward soul, affrighted at our daring deeds, sinks within him, and to secure himself, betrayed us!"

"No, Duca," replied Bernardo, "Sanguinario, is an honorable man; he never will impeach his associates, even on the rack, or tortured by the engines of the hellish inquisition, would he ever unclose his lips, to give utterance to so vile a sentiment—no, Duca, with him all is safe—Sanguinario's absence is to be accounted for in a far different way—you promised, Duca, to yield the Signiora Viola to him as a recompense for his vast services—he performed his part of the agreement to the full extent; but when he demanded the price of his toil, you mocked him—refused him—and drove him insultingly from you.—He then proceeded as an honorable man should—he took horse for Venice, to seize the Signiora Viola; in that he does no wrong, for she is his by right, as much so as the giving one thing for another can make it; he bartered his repose and bodily fatigue for a woman—before this I hope he is master of her person.—Had Sanguinario, Duca, been a coward, he never would have served you with half the zeal that he has done.—Hadst thou served me, as thou hast done Sanguinario, I would have plunged this dagger at the moment in thy heart—a man's feelings, Duca, are not to be trifled with—Sanguinario will yet return."

"Be it as thou sayest, Bernardo," said the Duca with a sneer, "Sanguinario shall be *welcome at his return!*—I must and do acknowledge his vast services, and shall be proud to do aught that in me lays as some atonement for my harshness; I wish him happy hours with the Signiora Viola—he should have excused my pettish answers, when he urged the yielding of the lovely girl to him; thou recollectest, Bernardo, I was not then completely recovered from the agitation I experienced on the evening before; it was an improper moment to torment me with his claim, it galled me, that he should have so little respect for my sufferings, as to move his suit when I lay oppressed with woe; but what I just now said, was the warmth of speech, and I meant not to cast any reflection on the valiant Sanguinario."

"I am glad, Duca," said Bernardo, "to find that you bear no enmity to Sanguinario; I confess it was not proper as you say, to trouble you while you were in that horrible fright, and he ought to have taken your words as those of a man who had lost his senses, for certainly the Signior ghost scared them away, but that is of no consequence, the business is now done; Sanguinario has by this time got his mistress, and no thanks to you Duca. There is one thing, Duca, I would advise thee to: whenever thou hast necessity to converse with Sanguinario on a subject, on which there might be some difference, put your dagger on the table."

"Why, Bernardo," said the Duca, "should I do that?"

"Because," answered Bernardo, "you first shew him you are not to be trifled with; and secondly, if he offends, you may instantly stab him to the heart. It is a custom I always have, of placing my weapon before me, when I think I have to do business with a troublesome fellow. Though Sanguinario is an honest, hearty, honorable fellow, he is sometimes a little lofty; but with me all runs smooth, and we are excellent friends."

"Thy plan, my friend, is a good one, and henceforward I will practice it. But say, Bernardo, wilt thou and thy troop accompany me?— Thou shalt have for them and thyself whatever may be demanded; in case fierce war should spread itself over my peaceful domains."

"I can with safety say, that the brave lads will follow me wherever I go; and if thou wilt pledge thyself, that the promised reward shall be paid on entering the Castello di Urbino, I will be thine, and we will all remove there: but mark me Duca, before I go one inch further, let me tell you, that if you fail to perform the contract, myself, and brave followers will destroy every vassal serving in the Castello. —Do not think that numbers will intimidate us; the lazy hinds, decked out in arms, could never, though thrice as many, contend with the hardy veterans I lead; whose bed is often the bare earth; and pillow, the hard flinty rock. There is not a man among us who cannot show some honorable testimony of his valor; therefore, Duca, do not look for security in your numbers; for once offend Bernardo, and he will knock the stones of your Castello about your ears."

"I do, Bernardo," said the Duca, "pledge myself to the performance of every thing I have promised.—Prepare the troop, and at night-fall we will all retire to the Castillo di Urbino; and by tomorrow's dawn, we shall be beyond the reach of all our enemies."

"I hope we may, Duca," replied Bernardo. "I will now get my brave fellows to equip—that will not take long, for they are ever on the alert. I feel a little sorrow at leaving my old place of abode; it is now fifteen years since I first entered this place; but, adieu, Duca— at night fall we shall meet again."

"Adieu," said the Duca. "I shall be ready."

Bernardo, with his troop, were assembled at the appointed time; and placing Rosara on one of the horses, caparisoned for her, they all set forth. They travelled all night, and the "sun had just began to peer above the eastern hills," when they passed the stately portal of the Castello di Urbino. The fatigued and miserable Rosara was conducted into an apartment, richly furnished: her lowly garments but ill accorded with the splendor of every thing that surrounded her. Within the dreary vaults of the Castello di Lepanto, where she was denied even the common comforts that were necessary, she felt resigned to her fate; but the magnificent appearance of the Castello di Urbino, too strongly reminded her of the elegant Palazza at Venice, where she first drew her breath, and had passed so many happy hours. Exhausted with the journey she had taken, she threw herself on the bed and sunk to sleep.

The Duca, accompanied by Bernardo, and the warder of the Castello, viewed the ramparts, and found them in perfect repair.— The sullen eyes of Bernardo sparkled as he passed along the ramparts, at the happy idea, that before long, the plain beneath would be covered with hostile troops. The Duca arranged all the different guards, and saw the sentries placed at their posts; this done, he made enquiries of the warder respecting the internal regulations of the Castello. A large quantity of provisions had been laid in, sufficient to last a seige of great length; therefore no apprehensions could be entertained on that head; and since Bernardo's troop had joined the Duca, their force would be enough to contend with any foe that might approach the walls. The warder, after some prefatory conversation, informed the Duca that two noble youths, one of the house of Durazzo, the other of Vincenti, had sought him at the Castello; and that he had permitted them to repose in the Castello, with the firm intention of refusing them permission to depart, until his arrival; but that during the tempestuous night they had lately experienced, even in the midst of the storm, they must have escaped, for they had not since been seen; and though the most diligent search had been made, yet not the smallest clue had been gained, how they could have departed: their horses too were taken from the stalls, and contiguous to them, lay some of the most faithful of the vassals. "Suspicion has, however, pointed at Hugo; I have therefore ordered him to be confined in one of the dungeons. —Not all the threats that I could use, could make him aught confess —he is a gallant fellow, and has often served you well."

"Oh!" cried the Duca, "what a noble prize has slipped between our fingers! Had we but held Alberto, and this same puling lover of Rosara's, we had not anything to fear; I then should have made my own terms; and in spite of every thing Rosara would be mine —would be mine?—She shall be mine!—I have her fast; and if the devil comes for her, he shall have me too. But where is Hugo?— Bring him hither: I must try to fathom if there be treachery among my vassals—I must be wary. What thinkest thou Bernardo?"

"Pluck the execrable villain's heart out by the roots, and throw it for yon vultures to feed on.—A fellow who basely betrays his lord, or brothers in arms, deserves no pity; and I could with pleasure steep my dagger in his blood!"

"If there be the least appearance of Hugo," said the Duca, "being guilty of aiding these cavalieros in their escape, the most inventive tortures shall be practised on his menial body, to tear the secret from him!"

"If he has offended," said Bernardo, "and in the way you do suspect, hang him on one of the loftiest towers, as an example. He must be wretched enough in his own conscience, at having betrayed you, without inflicting further punishment than death.—I should do that in mercy to him, to free him from the damning thoughts of being a *treacherous villain.*"

Every word the blunt Bernardo spoke, was a dagger to the heart of Urbino. Aware of his own base conduct, towards his quondam friend, and abettor in vice, he shrunk, lest the banditti chieftain should discover him to be the person who had exhibited charges against Sanguinario. The Duca, whilst holding the last conversation with Bernardo, in the Vaults di Lepanto, did but temporize with him, and by his crafty conduct, gained him to his purpose; but he clearly saw that Bernardo was faithful in whatever he undertook, and Sanguinario had so completely wound himself round the ruffian's heart, that he sickened when the thought intruded itself, that it might yet transpire, that he was the betrayer of Sanguinario. If so, he had the utmost vengeance of a most hardened and ferocious chieftain of banditti to dread; even that of one he had made his equal, and introduced into his Castello: this train of unpleasant reflection was broken off, by the warder appearing with Hugo.

"What hast thou to say for thyself, base wretch?" exclaimed the Duca. "Confess the full extent of thy guilt:—how, when, and by whom the cavalieros were assisted to leave the Castello."

"I have been mute," said Hugo, "to every question that has been asked me; but at the desire of my lord, I hold it my duty to answer.—The cavalieros, aided by me, and at the awful hour of night, sought their safety in flight."

"But how passed they the walls, without being noticed?" enquired the Duca.

"Frighted from their posts like timid deer," answered Hugo, "the soldiery fled, at the last tremendous peal of thunder, that seemed to rock the Castello to its foundation; on that memorable night, when the tempest raged with such unbounded fury, they seized the favorable advantage, and the cavalieros passed free and unmolested; and had a host of feeble women chosen to have possessed themselves of the Castello, they would have met with no opposition from your chicken-hearted vassals."

"Thou art bold of speech," said the Duca; "but I will bend this proud spirit of thine; for I will keep thee fast confined within the dreary dungeons of the Castello, until thy withered skin shall shrink upon thy bones, and thou hast but the form of man; then will I have thee brought forth, and on yon lofty tower's summit hung to scare away the birds, that seek their prey within the precincts of the Castello.—Bear him away, and let the coarsest food be allotted him."

"He deserves to die immediately!" said Bernardo. "Had one of my troop served me such a scurvy trick, I should have sent his treacherous soul to the other world, long ere this—but, Duca, it is your own affair."

Hugo was conducted by the guards to his place of confinement. He was a favorite among his fellow soldiers; and every one commiserated his unhappy doom. The Duca and Bernardo left the works of the Castello, and retired to one of the apartments, to partake of refreshment.

The Duca began to reflect that the part he was performing would eventually bring down the resentment of the Condi di Vincenti. He had never been able to learn the name of the cavaliero, who Sanguinario had seen in the act of paying his addresses to Rosara, but he could no longer doubt that it was the same cavaliero, who accompanied Alberto to his Castello, and who the warder informed him was of the illustrious house of Durazzo; yet he could not well reconcile that, as the present Marchese was never known to have been married, and with him the title became extinct. It might be some youth of his adoption; this again was another blow to all his schemes, for should the Marchese approve the object, this youth had chosen, he would join with the Condi in the recovery of Rosara. His mind became considerably disturbed, at his having acted so hastily with respect to Sanguinario; at this moment he wanted his counsel more than in any exigency of his life; he lamented the headstrong passion that had blindly urged him to so ungenerous and treacherous an action. It was that proud overbearing spirit that could never brook an equal, that had been the bane of his life. In the present dilemma the Duca hardly knew what to do; Bernardo was a person who was ill qualified to assist in beguiling the heavy hours—as the chieftain of banditti, no man knew his duty better—or was there a more valiant man, but the woods and rocks had been his place of residence, and lurking assassins had been his companions—he had no other tutor, save Nature—fidelity to the horde that he commanded, and strictly adhering to any promise given, comprised the whole code of honorable and just sentiments, in his opinion—such was the force of constant practice and example.

The gloomy aspect of the Duca's affairs, daily soured his temper, and added considerably to the ferocity of his disposition; and his now constant companion Bernardo, tended if anything to encrease it. The Duca had not as yet heard of the arrest of Sanguinario, though he felt convinced it had taken place. The servant he had sent with the packet, containing the charges, had immediately on its delivery returned according to his instructions; he used this precaution lest his absence from the secret Vaults di Lepanto, should have aroused suspicion, but shut up as they now were, there was little probability of any intelligence reaching them. This at all events was one source of comfort, that if the detention of Sanguinario by the inquisition was likely to remain unknown at the Castello, it freed him from all fears as to the vengeance he might have brought down upon himself.

Their repast being concluded, all the vassals that were in arms were paraded for the inspection of the Duca; every thing appeared to be as he could wish; and assuming a smiling courteous look, praised the obedience of his vassals; he made them take an oath of allegiance. This and a variety of other circumstances occupied him the remainder of the day. He determined to have a final interview with Rosara, and if she still resisted his offers, he would lead her to the altar, and there compel the chaplain of the Castello to join their hands, and take possession of her person by force; no other alternative could be resorted to; as it would inevitably heal the breach between the two houses. To carry this into effect, he sent a messenger to Rosara, to say that he would visit her, in her apartment shortly. The messenger entered her room, and found her overwhelmed with sorrow; the big tears chasing each other down her lovely face, and ever and anon, a deep drawn sigh burst from her swollen bosom; in mild and pitying words the ruthless ruffian, made known his lord's desire; Rosara, in silence received the unwelcome tidings of the Duca's intention to visit her, and at the conclusion of the message, waved her hand for the person who had brought it, to retire. After having tasted of an unrefreshing sleep, Rosara had risen from her superb couch, and seated herself at the window, which commanded a most beautiful and extensive prospect; not far off was seen the foaming waters of a cataract, whose loud fall resembled the distant thunder's roll; while contemplating this magnificent scene, Rosara, almost unconsciously sunk into deep meditation.—Her happiness had been but as a fleeting hour, when balanced with the misery she had undergone, deprived of the society of him she loved beyond every thing on earth, and locked within a loathsome prison until she should consent to the more loathsome embraces of the Duca di Urbino.—That never should be the case while reason held her empire over her mind. The day of retribution yet would come, and this proud Urbino would shrink within himself, and hide his dastard head.

"Could ever woman," exclaimed she, "love more truly than I do? Had ever woman a more worthy object to adore? My Fernando— my loved and betrothed lord!—Heaven can only witness the purity and strength of my affections! If I am to die, it shall be calling on thy name: I will call on it, until I make Urbino mad; and in my expiring moments, Fernando still shall hover on my lips! Had I, Fernando, but been thine, perhaps this cruel, cruel separation never had taken place. But heaven's will be done!—No vow of mine has yet been broken; and no force shall ever compel my tongue to utter what my heart disclaims. But I must collect my scattered thoughts, to meet this hateful Duca di Urbino, with the firmness that becomes the daughter of the Condi di Vincenti."

The disconsolate and unhappy Rosara tried to arrange her scattered thoughts; but the long confinement she had suffered had enfeebled the energies of her mind, and weakened her frame. The roses which once shone conspicuously in her lovely face, now fled affrighted at disease, and left the drooping lilly triumphant. Rosara was but the former shadow of herself; her long confinement had made a considerable alteration in her person; for the wholesome air from heaven (until her arrival at the Castello di Urbino) had not blown on her; her only solace had been the manuscript, that contained the little narrative of the Marchesa di Lepanto—she always carried it about her, with the dagger she had found. The steps of the Duca were now heard coming down the corridor; Rosara hastily recommended herself to her Maker, piously relying on him for aid, in the moment of extremity. The footsteps were now close, and she heard the Duca giving directions to his domestics, who had lighted him, to be in waiting, ready to attend him at a minute's notice; and immediately after he entered the room. He started back at seeing the change in Rosara, and for once the consciousness of the unjust treatment he had used towards her, made him feel a pang, that had a long time been a stranger to his bosom. Soon recovering from his surprise, the Duca advanced with his usual courteous manner, when he had an object to carry.

"The lovely Rosara, I fear, has suffered considerable fatigue from her late journey," said he; "but I hope the pleasant accommodation the Castello di Urbino will afford, will soon restore the roses to her cheek.—Speak but thy wishes, lovely Rosara, and they shall be obeyed."

"Why dost thou jeer me so, Duca?" said Rosara. "Thou art the cause of this grief-worn countenance, and should I tell thee my only wish, it would be denied."

"Say, lovely Rosara," replied the Duca, "what it is thou wilt, and if it be in the power of your devoted Urbino, he will readily grant it."

"Then set me free," said Rosara. "Thou hast long enough held me in thy captive chains.—I think it is time thou shouldst be satisfied with this, my degradation."

"Rosara—dearest maid!" said the Duca, in a mild and gentle voice, "thou hast asked the only thing I cannot grant thee.—It is not just to rob me of my existence; for in thy smiles only can I live. It is cruel in thee, Rosara, first to pierce my heart with those bright eyes, and then deny me the only happiness I have of being near thee. Do not think, Rosara, that I meant to degrade thy sweet person.—No, your late room but ill accorded with the magnificence you had been accustomed to; but none other could be prepared for your reception—in it you were secure: in every thing Urbino has been sedulous to protect the bewitching Rosara from intrusion.—Here, in this splendid Castello, Rosara shall be queen of all, where naught shall enter but mirth and pleasure."

"Did I not tell thee, Duca," said Rosara, "thou didst but jeer me? —What couldst thou think was more dear to me than liberty? Thou dost not surely conceive that I will ever accept thee, and thy boasted magnificence? Do not deceive yourself—it can never be! Too well I know you have been careful of me; and too well I know for what cause that care was exercised: it was not out of respect to me, as thou wouldst have me think, but to conceal me from the prying eye of my friends and relatives; and to hide thy dastard head from the impending vengeance of my brother Alberto, and the noble Fernando.—Did they but know that I was here, these massy walls would not protect thee and thy hirelings!"

"Be pacified, sweet maid," said the Duca. "Reflect again—though thou hast not favored Urbino's love, yet is he one of the most sincere of thy suitors.—Forget the past, and Urbino's utmost care shall be to make thee happy. The chaplain of the Castello shall indissolubly join our hands, and with speed we will hasten to Venice, where joy will await you, in being restored to your friends.—Does my Rosara consent to this?"

"Have I not told thee, Duca di Urbino," replied Rosara, "that thou never shalt be the husband of Rosara di Vincenti?—Again I solemnly declare, let the consequence be what it will, that I will never join my fate with thine!—Thou hast not gone the way to win my love:—confine me in a noisome dungeon, and tell me it is through thy great love.—No, thou artful fiend! thou canst not deceive me now.—I know thee to be a villain—to be a murderer! Thinkest thou I would repose upon the bosom of a murderer?"

"What dost thou mean, rash girl?—Urbino a murderer!" said the Duca, while his countenance underwent a variety of changes. "What could conjure up so wild a phantasy in thy brain?"

"It is no chimera," answered Rosara. "I have proof; and one day yet, thou will expiate thy offences on a scaffold!—Begone, and do thy worst, as long as thou dost not offend mine ear!"

"By heavens! thy scornful looks become thee," said the Duca. "Thy threats I do despise; nor will Urbino longer waste his time in idle converse; but take thee to his longing arms, and make thee his for ever!" At the conclusion of this, he attempted to seize the lovely girl; but the dread she felt, lest the Duca should accomplish his diabolical purpose, gave her courage, and stepping back, she drew the dagger from her bosom. "Oh, gracious heavens!" exclaimed Urbino. "What is that I see?—The ring!—The dagger! Oh, Rosara! thou art revenged, indeed!—Take it—oh, take it from my sight! It harrows up my soul!—Look, there it stands, pointing to its bleeding wounds!" The Duca kept his eyes fixed, as if fearful to withdraw them from some object they were bent on. Rosara became almost as much terrified at the appearance of the Duca, as at the threatening tone he had a moment before assumed; but calling all her courage to her aid, she tauntingly said to the Duca—"Where is now the intrepid spirit of Urbino?—How despicable art thou, to be thus frighted by a woman! But let me tell thee this—while I have power, thou shall never triumph over me!—Me thinks thy villainous blood would grace this dagger's point, which thou hast already steeped in human gore.—Try to appease the manes of the Marchesa di Lepanto by freeing me from this hateful bondage."

"What ho!—attendants, there!" cried the Duca, in a half stifled voice. "This, Rosara, is too much.—Thou hast probed the very bottom of my heart—thou shall repent of this!—In three days hence, I will lead thee to the altar, and then shalt thou become the bride of Urbino!"

"Look but for a moment longer at this dagger," said Rosara, holding it up. "This shall again sooner be bathed in innocent blood, than thou shall have thy wishes gratified! It can do its office well; and why should Rosara, to preserve her honor, fear the fatal dagger's point, more than the Marchesa di Lepanto?"

"Whip me ye devils!" said the Duca; "but cross not my sight with these horrid phantoms.—What ho!—attendants—why come ye not at my call?" The attendants all came hastening to the room, at the loud call of their lord. "What you," continued he, darting a fierce look, "have leagued against me too, base caitiffs!—Why did you not more readily obey my summons?" then addressing himself to Rosara, "three days hence, Signiora, we meet again!" and turning to the domestics, he bid them lead on, and took his departure.

Rosara had, in grasping the dagger for her own defence, exposed the well-known ring she wore on her finger to the Duca; his tenacious memory quickly recognised it, and his guilty conscience smote him. Rosara thought it a good opportunity to impress upon his mind the atrocity of his conduct, as she found the sight of the dagger and ring appeared to affect him; but his hardened nature returned, and she despaired of ever impressing him with a due sense of the heinous offences he had committed.

"He is indeed lost," said Rosara, as he quitted the room. "I do not think it is in the power of mortal to change his vicious course; for though the sight of this weapon, and this ring, raised a storm within his breast, and his haggard countenance betrayed the inward terror of his soul, yet at the appearance of his satellites, he assumed all his former insolence." Rosara, fatigued with the exertion she had undergone, threw herself on her couch, as the evening was far advanced, and sought to bury in sleep, the recollection of her sufferings.

CHAPTER XVI.

As soon as Sanguinario was seated in the carriage that waited, it drove furiously off, and as the distance was but short, they soon arrived at the doors of the holy Inquisition; one of the officers, who rode on the outside of the carriage, knocked, and as soon as the heavy gates were thrown open, the carriage drove into a large court, and there the party discended. Sanguinario was entirely separated from his accomplices; his guards rudely seized him, and led him through the dark passages of this gloomy pile, which were only lighted, so as to render darkness visible; they conducted him to a miserable cell, without any other comfort but a little straw, and took their departure. Sullenly Sanguinario threw himself on the ground, and revolved in his mind, the cause of his being thus suddenly apprehended; he could not fathom how it could have been possible, for him to have been traced to the Villa of the Signiora Benvoglio, as he had not even entered Venice, but struck into the bye and unfrequented roads that led round the city; but these reflections were of no avail, they could not free him from his unpleasant predicament. "Urbino," cried he at length, "if thou through vengeance, hast betrayed me, thou art indeed a detestable villain, and deservest well for thy enormities, to die by the hands of the executioner—if I can discover that thou hadst ought to do in this base treacherous act, I will unfold the multitude of crimes thou hast committed—but let me acquire that fortitude, which is so necessary to bear me through in the hour of trial.—Oh, God of mercy!—ah! how dare I lift my voice to my offended Maker?

—how can I appeal to him for succour in my distress?—Away with this unmanly conduct—Sanguinario ever was and ever will be firm in the hour of danger!—come, let them rack my body, break my bones, and tear my starting eye-balls from their sockets, still will Sanguinario rise superior to it all!—Do thy utmost, I defy thee all!"

Many hours elapsed and Sanguinario was left a prey to his unpleasant thoughts; till at length he was roused by the unbarring of the door of his cell, and the entrance of two of the officers of the holy Inquisition, attended by guards; in silence they stripped the wretched and fallen Sanguinario, and placed a garment over him, entirely closed up, except two small holes for him to see through, and his waist was bound round with a cord; on his feet they fastened a pair of sandals, and then led him forth; for a considerable time they continued walking, until they came to a door, on which one of the guards struck, and it was immediately opened; they passed beneath the doorway, and Sanguinario found himself in a small room; here they tied a bandage round his eyes, and he was again led onward.—"Be careful," said one of the guards, "for you are going to descend." At the bottom of the flight of steps they entered another room, where the bandage was removed; they had not waited many minutes, before a figure, clad entirely in a black garment, made a signal, and Sanguinario was conducted into the tribunal hall. Seated on an elevated place, at the extremity of a table, were two of the judges of this terrible court, and beneath them sat a secretary, and on each side were several of the inferior officers. The whole hall was hung with black, as were also the habits of those who composed the court; an iron tripod hung from the roof, which gave but a feeble light. The hardy soul of Sanguinario still remained unappalled at this scene of terror.

"Stand forth Sanguinario," called out the secretary—Sanguinario advanced to the foot of the table.

"You will answer truly to the questions that shall be put to you," said the secretary.—Sanguinario bowed as a token of obedience.

"Thy name is Sanguinario?" said the secretary—"answer this."

"It is," answered Sanguinario.

"Is it thy real or assumed one?" enquired the secretary.

"It is my real one," said Sanguinario.

"Write that answer down," said one of the judges—"you are to remember," said he to Sanguinario, "that this court have full documents of thy guilt, therefore a denial of facts will but encrease your punishment."

"Were you not employed," said the secretary, "by the Duca di Urbino, to carry off the Signiora Viola, residing at the Villa of the Signiora Benvoglio?"

"No," replied Sanguinario, "I was not."

"For what purpose did you intend to carry off the Signiora Viola?"

To this Sanguinario refused to answer.

The judge advised him to make a free confession, but it was of no avail. The torturer was desired to do his duty; the guards seized him, and placing him on the rack, they bound him down with strong cords; the torturer took a pair of red hot pincers, from a furnace, and only waited for the signal to be given ere he began to do his duty; at the sight of this tremendous instrument, Sanguinario felt his courage sink within him, but yet he was determined to bear his fate with fortitude.

"Before I repeat my former question," said the secretary, "as the humane judges of this holy tribunal always wish to act with mercy towards the guilty, who are brought before them, they permit you to reflect before they proceed to extremities.—First of all, dost thou know thy accusers?"

"No," replied Sanguinario, "nor the charges exhibited against me."

"Dost thou know this hand writing?" said the secretary, handing the paper to him.

"Does this bear the charges?" enquired Sanguinario.

"It does," replied the secretary.

"I know it well—it is the villain Urbino's hand!"

"Mean you the Duca di Urbino?"

"I do," replied Sanguinario.

This was a great object to be gained by his wily judges. The paper was in fact the hand writing of the Duca, but not the one that contained the charges.

The holy Inquisition had long marked the detestable courses of the Duca di Urbino, and therefore now they thought it a favourable opportunity to entangle him in their toils. It was necessary to work upon the fears of Sanguinario, that they might gain from his confession, some cause to summon the Duca to appear before them; but the undaunted manner of Sanguinario, induced them to pursue a different mode; they therefore presented the letter to Sanguinario, that had been found by Alberto in the vaults of the Castello di Urbino, and he not doubting but it contained the charges, asked the question: the secretary aware that if Sanguinario was roused to a spirit of revenge, by supposing the Duca had exhibited charges against him, his confession would be free, and that he would answer fully to implicate him, therefore he replied in the affirmative; besides, it was a matter of importance that the hand writing should be recognised, and particularly of that letter.

The secretary, after a short pause, enquired if he was now willing to answer to the questions asked him?

Burning with revenge, to have been thus treacherously caught, Sanguinario cared not what he said to criminate the Duca—"I will," he replied.

One of the judges desired him to be released from the rack on which he lay stretched.

The secretary again enquired—"for what purpose did you intend to carry off the Signiora Viola?"

"She was granted to me," replied Sanguinario, "by the Duca, as a reward for service done him—and I should have been united to her in the holy bands of wedlock."

"What was the service done," enquired the secretary, "for which thou wast to receive so great a reward?"

"The Duca di Urbino," answered Sanguinario, "long loved the daughter of the Condi di Vincenti, who rejected his offers with disdain; but he determined to possess her; and on my securing her, I was to receive the Signiora Viola—I performed my promise."

"You then," said the secretary, "seized the Signiora Rosara di Vincenti?"

"I did," replied Sanguinario.

"And where did you convey her?" asked the secretary.

"To the secret Vaults of the Castello di Lepanto," answered Sanguinario.

"Is not the Duca leagued with a horde of banditti, who infest the forest of Lepanto, and who usually shelter themselves in the Vaults of the Castello?"

To this Sanguinario would return no answer.

"Speak," said one of the judges, "or the rack instantly awaits you."

"Let all your tortures," said Sanguinario, "be exercised on my body yet I will never reply to that, which is not consonant to justice! —'Tis but to revenge myself on the false perjured Urbino, that I have thus submissively answered."

"Put him to the question," angrily called out one of the judges, "we have too long trifled with him—if mild and gentle measures, cannot influence him to reveal the guilt of his accomplices, the torture shall."

The torturers seized him, and again stretched him on the rack.

"Do your office," said the judge who had before spoken.

Instantly the cords which were fastened to his legs and arms, were drawn with violence; his joints were almost dragged from their sockets—his eyes swelled, ready to start from his head—his tongue hung from his mouth—yet no groan, no sigh escaped the wretched, the deserted Sanguinario, who lay extended a victim to justice, without a single cheering thought to bear him through in this awful hour of distress. He was again asked if he would confess; but with disdain he refused. A heavy stone was lowered from the roof upon his chest, so as almost to rob him of respiration; when this had remained a sufficient portion of time, and Nature became nearly exhausted, it was then drawn up; again he was desired to confess; but no, his stubborn heart would not yet yield—the heated pincers were then directed to be applied, instantly the ready executioner lacerated his body with this torturing instrument—Sanguinario writhed with anguish; the flesh quivered as each wound was inflicted—it was more than human fortitude could bear.—

"Oh! give me," said he, at length in a languid voice, "one little drop of water, to quench the burning flame which consumes my very vitals!"

These were the first words he had spoken since he had been placed upon the rack.

The judge ordered the executioner to stay his hand—"if thou wishest," said he, "to merit the lenity of the court, thou must make a full confession of all thou knowest, on these conditions, thou shalt be released from the further infliction of punishment, and relief instantly afforded thee."

Sanguinario, raised his heavy eye towards the terrible instrument of torture, and feebly assented to the proposal offered. Immediately he was released from his tormenting situation; cordials were administered to him, and he was conveyed to a cell, and laid upon a miserable pallet; thither the secretary followed to take the confession of Sanguinario; every attention had been paid him, that could be suggested to renovate his languid frame, and their exertions had been crowned with success.

The secretary then addressed Sanguinario—"it is necessary that you should divulge everything that comes within your knowledge respecting the Duca di Urbino.—You stated in your examination that your name is Sanguinario, we are well aware it is but an assumed one, therefore faithfully answer this question, and relate your history progressively."

The Confession of Sanguinario.

"My name is Ambrose Colloredo, I am a native of this city; my parents gave me a good education; and at their death, I should have inherited sufficient to have set me above the scoffs of the world, and to have enabled me to live contented and happy; but as I grew up, I became inclined to every kind of amusement, and at length from having committed a few irregularities, I became vicious: my parents remonstrated against my dissolute life; but the avenues of my heart were closed against the wholesome counsel, they gave me. To satisfy my numerous wants, I became a professed gambler; and as I was sometimes extremely unfortunate, I joined with a party, whose only aim was to rob the unwary. Whenever we played, our dice were unfair; we were at length marked out by all who frequented the public table, and no one would associate with us. My conduct brought sorrow on the declining years of my virtuous parents, and I daily looked forward with anxiety, to the moment when I should become master of their little property. About this time I met with the Duca di Urbino, from whom I won large sums of money—he was unable to pay me, and I held securities, payable on the death of the late Duca. The constant topic of conversation, at this period, at

Venice, was the probability of a speedy alliance between the Duca, and the heiress of the house of Rivarola; but his friend and relation, the Marchese di Lepanto, stepped in, and was preferred; from that moment the Duca di Urbino vowed the most dreadful vengeance on the head of the Marchese, and all his house. After this I became more intimately connected with the Duca, and he made me thoroughly acquainted with his affairs. His father was still a strong healthy man, and bid fair to outlive his son, if he continued in the course of dissipation he had plunged into; but he meditated no less than the murder of his liberal and reverend parent!—My heart, though steeled against all the softer ties of humanity, recoiled with horror, at the mention of the detested crime: but why do I assume a virtuous tone?—Though I was then guilty of enormities, yet my hands, as now, were never polluted with the innocent blood of my fellow creatures. I used every argument I was master of, to draw the Duca from his horrid intention, but still my evil stars pursued me; and one evening the Duca killed a young Signior, while at play, at one of the places of public resort. He immediately left the room—I followed him. I enquired what he intended now to do? —He answered, he intended to leave Venice that night, and try to gain some assistance from his long neglected friend, the Marchese di Lepanto. He then invited me to share his fortunes with him.— Bankrupt as I was, in money, and in friends, I eagerly accepted his offer. I left him at the Castello di Lepanto, and went forward to a small cottage, near the Castello di Urbino. The Duca made but little stay with his relative, the reason, I afterwards learnt, was the ready compliance of the Marchese to grant him a loan, and to whom he had made out a plausible tale of his late rencontre at Venice. I daily met the Duca in the forest, near his father's Castello, as he was fearful of introducing me there.

"I had now become a voluntary outcast from the little remaining society that I kept up; and I found my fortunes entirely depended on the Duca. I one day received a hasty note from him desiring me to meet him at the old place of rendezvous. I was punctual—the Duca was there before me. 'Colloredo,' said he 'wilt thou assist me? —I want thy aid.' 'I have,' answered I, 'been always true to thee, and thou shall not now find me deficient in friendship.' 'Follow me then,' said he. He then led me towards a small postern in the Castello, and taking a key, opened it. We both silently entered—it was near midnight; there was scarcely a sound to be heard in the Castello.—The Duca passed through several passages, and at length we arrived at a small door. 'Now,' said the Duca, 'I want thy utmost aid, and if I find thee for one moment hang aloof, I will plunge my dagger in thy heart!' He then touched a secret spring in the door, and I saw a venerable old man, kneeling before the altar, offering up his prayers to heaven. The relentless, hardened, guilty Urbino rushed forward, and seizing his victim by the throat, dragged him through the library to the vaults beneath; almost faint with the violence that had been used, the old man raised his eyes and closed them quickly—'take this, Colloredo,' said the Duca, giving me his dagger, 'and finish the work I have began;' I took the offered weapon, but at the recollection—even now it curdles in my shrinking veins the lazy blood, and freezes at my heart.—At my unwillingness to perpetrate the damning deed, the Duca taunted me with words that my impatient soul could but ill brook; I, all roused and maddened, plunged the dire steel within the hoary victim's heart; he raised his eyes towards the Duca; 'oh!' exclaimed he, 'I pray thy ravenous thirst of blood is now sated;—oh! most unhappy youth, I should have expected this from any hand but thine!—how canst thou atone to heaven for having shed a father's blood?—whoever thou art, stranger, I do forgive thee.' These were his dying words; at the dire sight my trembling limbs could scarce contain my weight; but the accomplished villain di Urbino smiled at my agitation, and with various jests attempted to raise my drooping spirits—yes, Urbino, even while his father lay at his feet, weltering in his blood, regardless of the crime he had been accessary to, used all the arguments he was master of to sooth my soul. The day after this tragic scene had been enacted, the Duca had his father privately interred; we had that night conveyed him to his bed, a stiffened corpse; and the Duca, who took care to be the first to enter his apartment in the morning, affected that his father must have suddenly died, through the visitation of Divine Providence: however speciously he told the tale, yet many disbelieved it; he therefore thought it necessary to leave Italy, and spend some time in France; and after hastily arranging his affairs, I accompanied him to Paris. There a new field opened to us; the Duca was well provided with money, and I must acknowledge he had the honor, in that instance, to pay me the sums he had lost to me at play. The rich, the handsome Duca di Urbino was every where received; and plunging into a perpetual round of pleasure and dissipation, he forgot the mode by which he had acquired his wealth. Time flew on rapid pinions; and as the Duca was still addicted to gaming, his finances became slender; he had not received any remittances since his arrival at Paris, which was more than two years; he therefore began to think of the expediency of returning to Italy, when a circumstance took place which accelerated his departure.—The Duca had been long acquainted with a young French nobleman, whose name was D'Oranville, and with whom we were inseparable;—I say we, for in whatever society the Duca was introduced, I was always received as his friend. —D'Oranville lived with a female of considerable beauty, who he had seduced, and, with the exception of their not being united by the church, they were in every instance happy. Urbino, like a fiend, sowed the seeds of jealousy in the breast of D'Oranville. Bitterly did Madmoiselle Melidor complain of the neglect her lover evinced towards her: Urbino, using every artifice, gained on her unsuspicious mind, and caused a separation. D'Oranville, hot and impetuous, vowed the most summary vengeance on the despoiler of his peace; but the artful Duca knew well how to hide the baseness of his conduct: by turns he attempted to sooth his friend, then joined in bitter exclamations against the wretch, who had dared to creep in between his domestic peace and him. Thus believing Urbino to be his sincere friend, he opened his heart to him, by which means the villain always averted any scheme that was devised to detect the supposed paramour of Madmoiselle Melidor. The Duca, since the separation, took every opportunity of visiting her in private; he supplied her with money; and at length triumphed over her constancy to D'Oranville. This young nobleman, one evening heated with wine, determined to visit his former mistress: I used every argument to prevent him, knowing the Duca was at that moment locked in her arms; and tried every remonstrance in my power to prevent him from putting his project in execution—headlong he rushed towards the house of Madmoiselle Melidor; I followed with all my speed, but my interposition was too late; for, on my gaining the top of the stairs, I found the unfortunate D'Oranville inanimate and bleeding, and the Duca standing over his body with his drawn sword. In a few words I asked an explanation; the Duca informed me that as he lay asleep, he was awoke by some one attempting to burst the door; he sprang from his bed, and seized his sword; he had only time to place himself in a posture of defence, when the door flew open, and immediately making a pass at the figure of a man, his sword passed through his body, and he fell without a groan. The Duca protested he knew not that it was the injured D'Oranville. We were now aroused to a sense of the danger we ran at remaining any longer at Paris: we disposed of the body as well as we could, by placing it in a hole which we dug in the garden. Every thing was made ready as speedily as possible, and we soon left the towers of Paris far behind us. It was arranged on the road, that Madmoiselle Melidor should take the name of Signiora Benvoglio; I also determined to use the assumed one of Sanguinario. We conducted the Signiora to the Duca's Villa, near Venice, which she has inhabited from that period. The Duca on his entering the Italian States, dispatched his confidential servant to the Marchese di Lepanto, requesting a fresh supply of money; this servant was to meet us at the Villa, but received strict injunctions not to undeceive the Marchese, with respect to the Duca's place of abode, as he had stated in his letter he was still in Paris. At the appointed time the servant arrived; but he brought a positive denial from the Marchese, of advancing any further sums—this refusal paved the way to the death of that unfortunate nobleman. The Duca determined to set forth, for the purpose of trying what influence his presence might have on his relative. Accordingly on the day appointed, we took our leave of the Signiora Benvoglio, for by that name I shall now call her, and proceeded towards the Castello di Lepanto. The Duca had not sent any intelligence to the Marchese of his intended visit, but meant to take him by surprise. When we arrived at the Forest di Lepanto, we dismounted near the Castello, for the purpose of consulting on our future plans. The Marchesa, who the Duca had loved, was even now the object of his utmost wishes; he formed the diabolical design of attempting her honor; and as he was the successor of the vast domains of Lepanto, at the death of the Marchese, and his infant son and daughter, he conceived it would not be difficult to make himself master of these possessions; and by obtaining the hand of the Marchesa, avert the chances of the finger of suspicion pointing at him, and lull every enquiry. I was to remain near the Castello, to be ready the moment I was wanted; we were just going to separate, when our attention was attracted by some one humming a song; we turned towards the spot from whence the sound came, and perceived a female with a child in her arms: the Duca immediately advanced—the woman seemed much terrified; he questioned her as to whose child it was she carried—she ingenuously stated that it was the infant daughter of the Marchesa.—In an instant the Duca snatched it from her arms—the affrighted female struggled to regain her charge; she filled the forest with her cries.— The Duca incapable of freeing himself from her, gave the child to me: nothing could appease this trusty domestic; but the Duca, all frantic to be so pestered with her whining, tied her to one of the trees; and taking her handkerchief, formed it into a gag, and forced it down her throat, we then abandoned her to her fate. Urbino, villain as he was, dared not at that moment appear at the Castello. As soon as we had rode sufficiently far to preclude the probability of being traced, I asked Urbino what he intended to do with the lovely infant? 'Why,' said he, 'we will place it under the care of Signiora Benvoglio—the Marchese, ere long, will fancy her dead, and it will always be in my power to produce her if occasion requires it, or let her remain without the knowledge of her birth, and bring her up under the care of Signiora Benvoglio, and let her pass as her neice.' This being settled, we returned with the babe to the villa, and delivered her over to the charge of the Signiora."

"Then," enquired the secretary, interrupting him, "you acknowledge that Viola, the supposed neice of the Signiora Benvoglio, is the daughter of the Marchese and Marchesa di Lepanto?"

"She is," answered Colloredo, for I shall now use that name, "she is the daughter of Viola di Rivarola and Marchesa di Lepanto: —constantly have I witnessed her opening beauties, and to them I have fallen a victim. The Signiora Benvoglio was desired to preserve a trifling trinket that hung round her neck, with the clothes she then wore."

"This," ejaculated one of the persons, who appeared to be in attendance, "is a most wonderful discovery!"

Messengers were dispatched to compel the Signora to produce

the trinket and clothes, though they did not appear material documents to the establishing of her in her birthright.

Colloredo thus continued, after having rested a little time to recruit his exhausted spirits.—"When the Duca thought that the grief of the Marchese and Marchesa had subsided, he again set forth to the Castello, but as he intended it should appear a visit of condolence, he sent off his servant to announce his coming. The Duca in this visit, so completely wound himself into the good opinion of the Marchese, that he persuaded him to believe that an entire revolution had taken place in his conduct, and he did this with such an air of sincerity, that the Marchese thought him to be a real convert; he artfully drew him in, to again lend him a large sum; this was kept a secret from every one. Urbino then thought it a fit opportunity to declare his unalterable passion to the Marchesa, she spurned him from her with disdain, and threatened to inform the Marchese; he attempted in vain to soothe her, but the only grounds on which she promised to over-look this breach of propriety, was, that he should depart from the Castello; he promised it, and the next morning kept his word; he sought me at a small cottage, where I had remained during his stay at the Castello, and with the most horrid imprecations, vowed to possess the Marchesa, and to over-turn the house of Lepanto. We remained some time plotting and projecting a variety of schemes, all which were no sooner formed than rejected; till at length fortune favoured our utmost wishes; we learnt that the Marchese had gone, attended only by his faithful servant, to see the Marchese Durazzo, who was ill at his Castello; we resolved to watch his return and way-lay him; this we had an opportunity of doing on his returning to his own Castello. Proudly the banners of his house were displayed upon the lofty battlements, and anxiously the Marchesa awaited the arrival of her loved lord; but it was written in the book of fate that he should never again enter his Castello but as an inanimate corpse. We had long waited in our place of concealment, when the sound of their horses advertised us to be on our guard. As soon as they approached near us, the Duca rushed out, while I closely followed, and pierced the noble Marchese to the heart—he fell—uttered a groan—and moved no more: our attention was immediately called—to his servant; we both attacked him, but for a length of time he defended himself with valor, and frequently the contest became doubtful, until my sword pierced his side, and prone he fell; we then took the valuables they had about them, and carrying them far off, buried them, that it might appear the murder had been committed by banditti; the corpse was conveyed to the Castello by some of the foresters who found it, and afterwards magnificently interred. Nothing now stood between the Duca and his most ambitious views, but the infant son of the Marchese. He returned to the Castello, and there proclaimed himself his guardian. The miserable, the wretched Marchesa, lay, the very image of despair; but it was not of a violent kind; a settled gloom seemed to have taken possession of her, and they feared for her senses. Urbino had not yet completed his hellish designs; we therefore concerted to set fire to the apartments of the Castello which the Marchesa inhabited, and in the confusion to bear her off, and to fabricate a tale that she fell a victim to the all-devouring flames; this horrible plan was no sooner formed than it was put into execution; combustibles were provided, and the Castello set on fire; it raged for a long time before it was discovered, and then too late to save any part of the furniture, and this splendid Castello was in a few hours almost level with the ground. The Duca and myself conveyed the Marchesa to the vaults, that run some distance from the Castello, through a private passage. The little Fernando, who was with his nurse, was conveyed far from the conflagration at the first alarm. The Duca cursed his unlucky stars that he had not too fallen a victim—but he was reserved for another fate.

"The Duca exulted at the success of this plan, and felt secure in the possessions of Lepanto and Rivarola. The Marchesa recovered slowly from her illness, but as soon as she was capable of moving out, the Duca visited her, and urged his suit; instead of receiving him as he expected, she treated him with the utmost indignation —upbraided him with the crime of murder! and used every term of contempt she was mistress of.

"The busy tongue of fame began to spread reports injurious to the character of Urbino, he therefore concluded it necessary to withdraw for some time; by this means the Marchesa was left free from his importunities; and for many years he wandered from his native country. Tired of this mode of life, he resolved again to return to his Castello; which he did; he visited the Marchesa in her confinement; he tried by every artifice to make himself master of her person: at length he attempted force, and in the struggle the ill-fated Marchesa received a mortal wound in the breast from a dagger which he wore—in a few hours after she closed her eyes for ever.—The rest of my tale I have already stated."

Colloredo, quite exhausted, sunk on his bed, and it was with difficulty that he was restored to his senses; at this moment the messenger arrived with the trinket and clothes.

"Is this the trinket?" enquired the secretary.

"It is," replied Colloredo, after attentively examining it.

"Let me look at it," said the person who had before spoken. The secretary handed it to him—he took it, and touching a little spring, it flew open. "Heavens be praised!" said he, "it is the trinket the Marchese placed round his daughter's neck; here are the arms of Lepanto and Rivarola; and round the edge, her name and the day of her birth engraved."

"Who art thou," enquired Colloredo, "that art so well acquainted with [the] house of Lepanto?"

The person advanced, and throwing off the cloak he wore, approached the foot of Colloredo's bed.—"Dost thou know me now, thou hardened villain?"

"Take him hence!" exclaimed Colloredo, in an agony. "Forgive me, thou shade of the murdered Rhinaldo—I did indeed pierce thy side, but haunt me not with the recollection of that foul deed!"

"Thine," said the secretary, "is no wandering of the brain, it is the real Rhinaldo, who escaped thy steel."

"Thank heaven!" ejaculated Colloredo, "my hands are free from having committed that guilty deed!"

"Dost thou not remember," said Rhinaldo, "when thou didst lay the bosom of Fernando bare, a certain mark?"

"There was indeed," replied Colloredo, "I do remember it well."

The secretary desired him to state the nature of it.

"The mark," replied Colloredo, "was a dagger; and from the point there seemed to fall two clear drops of blood."

"Thy testimony, Rhinaldo, was never doubted, but this proof sets every thing beyond a doubt."

"Say," exclaimed Colloredo, who lay almost without sensation, and who deluged himself with water to quench the fever that raged within his veins, "say why you asked that last question?"

"It might, perhaps," said the secretary, "bring some consolation to your soul, to know that Fernando, that lovely boy, you so vilely intended to murder, now lives.—Fernando, now Marchese di Lepanto, was rescued from thy assassin grasp by the faithful Rhinaldo —it was he that attacked you in the wood, and stayed the perpetration of that act; he then placed him in the road he knew the Marchese di Durazzo would pass, fearful if he acknowledged the real birth of the young Fernando, it would reach the ears of the Duca di Urbino, and subject him to the hatred and vengeance of that sanguinary nobleman. Every thing succeeded to the wish of Rhinaldo —the Marchese Durazzo took the orphan Fernando to his Castello, and brought him up as his son.—It was this boy who wounded you in the forest, after he parted with you at the cottage of Theresa; and it was Rhinaldo who arrived to succor him.—It was Fernando who you attacked in the streets of Venice, and who again caused thy blood in streams to flow; and again it was Rhinaldo who stretched forth his interposing hand, to save him from thy dire steel. Fernando is now, by right, Marchese di Lepanto, and Condi Rivarola."

Here the secretary ceased; and the impious Colloredo appeared to be silently offering up a prayer: at length he turned, and surveying Rhinaldo, he feebly exclaimed—"Thou art indeed a virtuous faithful servant—how must thy heart exult over the fallen Colloredo—forgive me, Rhinaldo—ask forgiveness for me of the noble, the valiant Fernando—tell him how often I sought his life; but had it been permitted me, I would have raised this now nerveless arm in his defence: but I feel the cold hand of death upon me —my hour is come—the scorpion sting of conscience deprives my latter hours of one consolitary thought.—I quit this world of guilt, to atone before my offended Maker, for my crimes—thy ways, oh, God! are inscrutable."

The villain ceased to speak—his dark spirit had winged its way; and this murderer—this fell destroyer of his species lay an inanimate trunk.

CHAPTER XVII.

RHINALDO, who had been the faithful servant of the Marchese di
Lepanto, during Fernando's visit at Venice, committed the history
of his life to paper, with the avowal of who Fernando was; describ-
ing the wound on his shoulder, and the dagger on his breast; and
dispatched it to the Marchese Durazzo, giving as a reason for
his not personally appearing, that Fernando was surrounded by
danger.

The extraordinary mark spoken of by Rhinaldo, the Marchese
Durazzo recollected to have often seen on the breast of the young
Fernando; and also bore in his memory the cause the Marchesa
attributed it to.—While pregnant, she dreamt that the Duca and the
Marchese had a violent dispute; and that the former drew a poignard, and plunged it in the bosom of the latter; she fancied he then
drew it out, and from the point two drops of blood fell.

As soon as the Marchese had received Rhinaldo's statement, he
thought it necessary to set off for Venice, that the business might be
minutely investigated; but before his arrival, Urbino had succeeded
in carrying off Rosara. Rhinaldo who had constantly watched the
motions of the Duca and his party, saw the villains bear away the
lovely girl; he would have immediately alarmed the domestics, but
he was fearful that before they could be properly equipped for the
pursuit, that the lovely Rosara would be conveyed to some place
of concealment; he therefore resolved to follow at a distance, and
much to his satisfaction, he found they conducted her to the ruined
Castello di Lepanto; he was well acquainted with every secret
avenue, and hoped to be able to render her assistance. However he
found it impracticable to assist her in escaping, as he was not only
unprovided with proper means for that purpose, but she was too
strictly guarded. As he had ascertained the place of her confinement, he determined to return to Venice; but previous to his putting this plan in execution, he had the good fortune to save Rosara
from the murdering arm of Urbino.—In passing through one of
the secret passages, he heard an unusual noise, and loud voices,

as if in contention; he was well aware that it was the apartment Urbino occupied—he gently drew aside a sliding pannel, and to his astonishment, saw the enfuriated Duca in the very act of raising his vengeful steel against the unfortunate girl.—Immediately he stepped in to avert the threatened blow, when the too tenacious memory of the guilty Duca, recognised his figure, and the horrid recollection of the scene that took place in the forest, made him imagine it to be the departed spirit of Rhinaldo. As soon as he had satisfied himself that Urbino was not likely to recover for some time, from the contusions he had received in his fall, he seized the favorable opportunity of going back to Venice; and hoped to reach again the Castello di Lepanto, before the Duca could retire from it with his fair prize. As soon as he arrived at Venice, he repaired to the Palazza of the Condi Vincenti, where he found the Marchese Durazzo: this nobleman recognised Rhinaldo immediately.

The Marchese and the Condi had laid the statement of Rhinaldo before the holy Inquisition, and also bore testimony to many of the facts which it contained. The only thing that appeared necessary to the re-establishment of Fernando in his right, was the presence of Rhinaldo, that he might before the superiors of the court, acknowledge the matter contained in the paper the Marchese had delivered. Rhinaldo briefly mentioned the situation Rosara was in—it was immediately decided that the servants of the Condi, and the followers who had attended the Marchese, should be in readiness to proceed to rescue Rosara from her captivity at the Castello di Lepanto. It was then thought necessary that no time should be lost, and that Rhinaldo should repeat before the superiors of the holy Inquisition, the facts that he had stated: this was directly put in execution, and as the business was of great importance, they soon gained access. Rhinaldo answered with such precision to all the interrogatories that were put to him, that not a vestige of a doubt remained, as to the real birth of Fernando, and his right to the titles and estates of Lepanto and Rivarola.

Directions were issued for the immediate citation of the Duca, to appear before the holy tribunal to answer to the charges preferred against him by Rhinaldo. However on it being made known that Urbino was at the ruined Castello di Lepanto, it was deemed most expedient to seize him, while he thought himself in security. Full powers were then given to Rhinaldo to take the person of the Duca, and to relieve Rosara; he was entrusted with this, as his unshaken fidelity had been proved, and as he was well acquainted with the secret avenues of the Castello. In case Urbino should have left the vaults of the ruins, when Rhinaldo reached it, he was to find out whither he had gone and then return to Venice, if his force was not sufficient to subdue him. The Marchese gave Rhinaldo letters for Fernando, in case he should meet with him, which circumstance appeared to be more than probable: these directed him to attend to the orders that would be given him by the bearer, and if the Duca had fled to his Castello, to proceed immediately and collect the vassals of Durazzo, and lead them forth, to compel Urbino to yield up the lovely Rosara. The meeting between Fernando and Rhinaldo has already been mentioned, and that he arrived too late at the Castello di Lepanto to be of any service; one of the troop had been left almost in the agonies of death, and from him Rhinaldo learnt that the Duca had retired to his Castello, and the banditti, with their leader, Bernardo, had accompanied him. Rhinaldo, after executing his mission, with as much exactness as possible, returned as we have before stated, to Venice in time to hear the confession of Colloredo: it so completely corroborated what he had before deposed, and so thoroughly implicated the Duca, that Fernando and Viola were both acknowledged as the descendants of the late Marchese di Lepanto.

The necessary papers were immediately made out, confirming Fernando Marchese di Lepanto and Condi Rivarola, with all the domains appertaining to these titles. Messengers were sent to the Villa of Signiora Benvoglio; and Viola was removed to the Palazza; the surprise of that amiable girl can be more easily conceived than described. The Marchese embraced her as a long lost daughter, and the Condi received her with every mark of affection. Viola wept and laughed by turns, the change in her situation had been so sudden and unexpected, that she was incapable of moderating the violent transports she experienced; this did not arise from her having been raised to a more elevated rank, but it now placed her in a suitable situation to accept the hand of her adored Alberto; she was even now under the roof of his father; would he interdict his son from following his inclinations, it might happen; then what was wealth and title to her, without Alberto di Vincenti.

It was now necessary for the Marchese Durazzo and the Condi to move forward with the vassals of Vincenti, and those of Rivarola, who had been summoned by Rhinaldo; the whole of the troops being assembled, they set forth to join Fernando on the appointed day, leaving Viola to the care of Signiora Luzia.

Fernando, on his arrival at the Castello di Durazzo, found the vassals already collected, and nothing remained, but to put himself at their head; so anxious was this youth respecting the safety of his beloved Rosara, that he would not take necessary rest, but moved forward immediately. Proudly the banners of Durazzo waved in the air, and the hardy vassals, with shouts of joy, testified their fealty and pleasure, at being led forth by Fernando. 'The loud clarions sound, and the ear piercing fife,' inspired the martial band with generous ardour. At the appointed day Fernando arrived with the vassals at the place of rendezvous. He did not think it necessary to shew his force to the Duca di Urbino, he resolved therefore to remain quietly in the forest until Rhinaldo should come up with the promised succors; he deemed it expedient to post small parties at the different avenues leading to the Castello, for the purpose of gaining intelligence from any of the Duca's vassals that might fall into their hands, this disposition had not been long made, before a trap door was seen gradually raising up, and a man, pallid and haggard, looked cautiously around him; as soon as he conceived himself safe, he came forth, then closing the door, ran towards the wood as fast as his feeble legs would carry him; the men, stationed at that avenue, immediately seized him, and conducted him to Fernando.

"Who, and what art thou?" demanded Fernando of the prisoner.

"I am one," answered he, "who has suffered much on thy account, and who am willing to suffer more; I am a vassal of the Duca's, my name is Hugo; and to my interposition you are indebted for your life. It was I, who under an unseemly garb, conducted you through the private passages of the Castello di Urbino—I have been kept in confinement since that period, and through the assistance of my comrade, who brought me my provisions this morning, I escaped; and by his means, I became acquainted, that the Duca is well informed that you are already here with your vassals, and also, this night, by force, if it be necessary, he intends to lead the lady Rosara to the altar."

"How say you," said Fernando, "does the villain mean this night to force my loved Rosara to his arms?—But it shall not be—this instant will I lead our trusty vassals to the attack, and level the Castello to the earth!"

"I fear," replied Hugo, "that it would be impracticable for thrice thy number to effect so desperate an enterprise; but at the close of the evening, your vassals might with safety pass the secret passage —I will conduct you; and I sincerely hope I might have the glorious opportunity of plunging my sword a thousand times in the bosom of the Duca."

Fernando desired Hugo to be treated with kindness, and every refreshment to be set before him, that his debilitated frame might be in some measure recruited, to bear him through the exertions of the night. Impatiently Fernando waited the arrival of Rhinaldo; he however resolved to risk every thing to rescue his beloved Rosara. Tediously the hours passed, till at length Rhinaldo made his appearance, with a large body of the vassals of Rivarola. This was most welcome to the impetuous Fernando—he quickly made known the intelligence he had received, and the plan he intended to adopt for the release of Rosara; in all this Rhinaldo concurred, and in his turn informed the cavalieros, that the Marchese and Condi would be with them in a few hours.

"I hope," said Alberto, "before that time, to see the banners of Urbino pulled from their standards, and ours triumphantly displayed in their place."

The cavalieros, attended by Rhinaldo, disposed of their men, so as to be ready, whenever it was deemed necessary to commence an attack.

<hr>

Urbino, as soon as he received intelligence from his spies, that Fernando was in the forest with the vassals of Durazzo, found it necessary to see every soldier at his post, and by his own example, to animate them to do their duty with cheerfulness and alacrity. It was the opinion of Urbino, that they should securely wait the attack of the troops that were sent against them.—Bernardo again urged the propriety of attempting to surprise them that night.

"For," said he, "Duca, you know that my troops are used to night work, and I do not doubt but we should cut them off to a man; besides if we remain much longer inactive, our swords will rust in their scabbards—I am tired of being idle."

The Duca, however, overruled this opinion, by pointing out that he would be incapable of reinforcing the Castello immediately; and that it was necessary to be careful not to lose a man wantonly.

"You are to do as you like," said Bernardo, "but fighting is my trade, and if I do not fight to night, I will tomorrow."

The Duca seeing every thing in proper order, determined to try, as a last effort, if he could change the stubborn resolution of Rosara; at all events he resolved that night she should be his: he directed the chapel to be lighted, and the chaplain to be ready in attendance.

The evening had now closed and Rosara sat absorbed in melancholy reflections, little dreaming her loved Fernando was so near, when she heard the voice of the Duca giving particular directions to his attendants, to obey his summons promptly. Rosara had not time to form any conjecture as to the cause of this proceeding, before the Duca threw the door open, violently and unceremoniously.

"This," said Rosara, immediately as he entered, "is like the unmanly conduct of the Duca di Urbino, to break thus suddenly on the retirement of a female—delicacy should have taught him better; but nothing is to be found in the Duca di Urbino but violence and treachery!"

"Still, Rosara," said the Duca, "in that same unbending humour as when I last beheld thee; but Urbino now comes for the last time to invite the lovely Rosara to share his fortune and his titles."

"Fool, that thou art," replied Rosara, "to waste thy time in vain solicitations.—I tell thee, Urbino, I hate thee—despise thee—and sooner than become thy bride, the poignard, at whose sight thy guilty soul shrunk back affrighted, and made thy coward frame to shake, shall open a passage to my heart!—Now do thy worst."

"Hear my firm and last resolve," said the Duca. "Whether thou wilt or not, this night gives thee to Urbino's arms—even now the chaplain awaits our coming, to solemnize the holy rites. Thy loved Fernando with a scanty force, lies in the forest, vainly expecting to subdue the proud majestic turrets of Urbino; but ten times his force would be inadequate to roll one single stone from this massy fabric. —Tomorrow, as my bride, I will lead you forth to view the bands the reptile Fernando has assembled."

"Reptile!" reiterated Rosara, "Fernando is as much superior to thee, as the rays of the all glorious sun are to the moon's pale beams. Thou deceivest thyself, Urbino—no enterprize is too hazardous— no undertaking too arduous for the intrepid courage of Fernando. —He loves me truly, and his approach to the Castello with a force, to wrest me from this vile captivity, but more strongly confirms me in the sincerity of his passion. I will not wed thee Urbino—thou hast heard my final answer."

"Then I will force thee to my wishes," said Urbino, and assuming a fierce look, he called for his attendants; the miscreants readily obeyed the summons, and as soon as they entered, Urbino, with a savage tone of exultation, bade them seize the gentle Rosara, and lead her to the chapel: resistance was vain, and the ruffians rudely grasping her tender arms, dragged her forward to the fatal place.

Rosara did not conceive the Duca would have attempted to put his threats in execution, but on her entrance into the chapel, she beheld it lighted up, and the priest standing at the foot of the altar, robed for the purpose of performing the rites. Her heart died within her, and a cold shivering ran through her veins: my doom, thought she, is irrevocably fixed, and the villain Urbino will by force compel me to suffer his vile embrace.

Urbino took her trembling and reluctant hand, and led her to the steps of the altar. The priest commenced the ceremony; when suddenly the doors were thrown open, and this sacred place was filled with tumult and confusion; Rosara turned to see the cause of it, when she beheld her loved Fernando rushing towards her—she uttered a faint scream, and fell senseless in the arms of one of the villains who had assisted in dragging her to the chapel.

"At length villain," exclaimed Fernando, "thou art within my reach—this time thou shall not evade my vengeance!" and immediately attacked Urbino.

The artful villain stood appalled, and with feeble arm attempted to defend himself against the powerful one of Fernando; fainting and exhausted he sunk upon the ground: the noble youth would have plunged his sword into his bosom, but he stayed his vengeance, in hopes that he might repent of his enormities.

Bernardo met his fate at the hands of Alberto; this villain, courageous to the last, refused to accept of proffered mercy, and died as he lived, a most resolute and determined ruffian. While this was going forward in the chapel, Rhinaldo, guided by Hugo, penetrated to the upper part of the Castello, where they met with but feeble resistance, the vassals being taken completely by surprise. The banditti finding they should have to maintain an unequal contest, plundered what they could, and escaped by the postern.—It was almost the effect of a moment. Fernando now directed the wounded Urbino to be conveyed to one of the apartments, and every aid to be given him, which was immediately done.

Every exertion had been made to restore the senses of Rosara, but, hitherto, all had proved fruitless. Fernando, terrified lest he should lose her at the moment he had rescued her from oppressive power, seized her in his arms, and bore her to her chamber; the motion aroused her from her torpid state, and earnestly fixing her eyes on Fernando, exclaimed "'tis he—'tis my beloved—my faithful Fernando!" and in a violent paroxism, threw her arms around his neck, and sobbed aloud upon his bosom.—At this instant three loud blasts were heard upon the bugle; the terrified girl started and clung more close to Fernando.

"Fear not," said he, "loved Rosara—'tis thy Fernando shields thee in his bosom, and that loud blast that shakes thy nerves with dread, conveys the happy tidings of your father's safe arrival."

"My father say you?—lead me to him—It is a long time since I beheld him, and thee too, my dearest, my noble Fernando.—Where is my brother Alberto?"

"He will be here too, shortly," said Fernando.

At this moment the door was thrown open, and the Condi rushed into the apartment, followed by the Marchese.

"Where," cried the Condi, "is my daughter?—Where is my Rosara?"

"Here," answered the transported girl, and flung herself into his arms. The old man's tears flowed with pleasure at again pressing his lovely daughter to his paternal breast. Alberto now shared in the embraces of his sister. Fernando received the blessing and encomiums of the Marchese di Durazzo, who he always conceived to be, and respected as his father. All was now harmony; but Fernando could not quit the side of his mistress, he took her hand and—

> "Squeez'd it, and worry'd it with ravenous kisses;
> She blush'd, and sigh'd, and smil'd, and blush'd again."

They then took occasion to whisper; and she frankly told him that his constancy should be rewarded.

"I see," said the Marchese di Durazzo, "Condi that the Marchese di Lepanto has already made considerable progress in obtaining the good opinion of Signiora Rosara."

"I am glad to find it," said the Condi, "I have long suspected it, and he shall have my approbation."

Fernando turned pale at this, and holding Rosara more firmly, anxiously enquired into the meaning of what he heard; "for," said he, "I have fondly cherished the hope that Rosara will be one day mine."

"So she shall," said the Marchese, "but still she must consent to accept the Marchese di Lepanto; for I have now to tell thee, my gallant boy, thou art the true noble of that title—these papers will explain all."

Alberto, though hardly able to credit his ears, still most kindly congratulated his friend.

"I have too," said the Condi, "to present you to a sister, who now is at my Palazza."

"A sister!" exclaimed Fernando, "how came these miracles to pass?"

"Read those papers, and you will be fully informed." Fernando retired for that purpose.

Enquiries were sent to know if the Duca's wounds were mortal, the messenger returned to say, the surgeon did not conceive that he could live long.

Rhinaldo now came to inform the Marchese and Condi that every thing was quiet and secure in the Castello. Rosara immediately recognised the countenance of her deliverer in the Vaults of

Lepanto, she thanked in the most bewitching manner, this faithful old servant for his providentially saving her life.

Fernando now burst into the apartment, and taking Alberto by the hand, exclaimed, "I wish thee joy, my friend—Viola, who was the supposed neice of Signiora Benvoglio, is my sister—the villain Sanguinario confessed it, after suffering severely on the rack."

"Good heavens!" said Alberto, "this is joyful intelligence indeed —my beloved Viola, the sister of my friend—and now under the roof of my father?"

"Hast thou," said the Condi, "ever beheld the Signiora Viola?"

"Yes," replied Fernando, "he has, and what is more, he has given his and received her plighted faith, therefore I hope that we shall have a double union in the family." No more was said on the subject. "Thou must be," said Fernando, turning to Rhinaldo, "no other than he, who hast so kindly watched over me from my infancy—to thee I owe my preservation, and shall hereafter make it my pride and boast to acknowledge thee as my friend and protector." Fernando grasped his hand while the big round tear started from his manly eye.

"But tell me," continued Fernando, "the circumstances of your wonderful escape, on that day when my loved sire fell by the barbarous and treacherous steel of the Duca di Urbino."

"It is," replied Rhinaldo, "commanding me to renew those painful moments which I have experienced, and again to open those wounds, which time has in some measure healed. But the mandate of my lord must be obeyed."

"Not so," said Fernando, "for far be it from my wish to cause pain to one who has so tenderly watched over me."

"It will be satisfactory," replied the old man, "to you, to be made acquainted with many circumstances that have lately occured, of which you are still ignorant: if therefore you will pardon an old man's prolixity, I will explain them."

The whole party assented; then drawing round Rhinaldo, he thus began,—

"Some time must have elapsed before I recovered my senses, after I had been left for dead; the blood had flowed copiously from the wound, yet it proved not to be of any serious consequence; as soon as I opened my eyes, the first object I beheld was the bleeding Marchese, lying at some distance from me; the horror I felt at beholding his inanimate corpse, almost again bereft me of my faculties; with difficulty I crept towards him, and found, alas! but too truly, that his spirit had left its mortal tenement. The cruelty of my situation rushed upon my mind, and my imagination painted in gloomy colours, miseries that awaited me. I nearly sank under the mental anguish I endured, and it is not to be wondered at, left as I was, wounded, in a solitary part of the Wood, with the bleeding and lifeless body of the Marchese; and perhaps, myself to languish and expire for the want of necessary assistance. I used every argument within myself to sooth the cruel agitation I experienced. I, in some measure succeeded, and now began to look around me, to form some conjecture as to the part of the forest I was in, and at length joyfully recollected that I was not far from the cottage of Benito. I immediately determined to exert my little remaining strength in attempting to crawl thither, that some of the peasantry might be procured to convey the body of the Marchese to the Castello, and that I might obtain that relief, of which I stood so much in need. With difficulty I reached the humble but hospitable door of Benito: faint and tottering, I nearly dropped at the threshold, but the feeble cry of distress I uttered reached him, and in an instant he flew to succour me. The whole family anxiously crowded around me, and tenderly interrogated me as to the cause of my sudden and extraordinary appearance. My brother, Benito, almost choaked with tears, began to examine my wounds; but the untimely and unhappy fate of the Marchese occupied every thought: I gently declined his proffered attention, and waving my hand to obtain silence, briefly related my sad, sad tale. Instantly Benito sent the blooming Annette, and her constant swain Ludovico, happy then in their mutual love, but too soon, alas! doomed to suffer a bitter reverse, to collect some of the neighbouring cottagers: as soon as a sufficient number were procured, they proceeded to the spot where I directed them, but they learnt from some of the peasantry that the corpse had already been conveyed to the Castello. Silently and dejectedly they returned to the cottage, and deeply mourned the loss of their beloved and noble chieftain.

"It is not in the powers of language to describe the lamentations of the vassalage: in the Marchese they had lost a father and a friend;

but above all, the settled grief that appeared in the Marchesa, would have melted any heart with pity, but that of the relentless ruffian who inflicted the fatal blow; but let me endeavour to forget this eventful epoch of my narrative. A few days before the interment of the Marchese, I heard from Benito that the Duca di Urbino had arrived at the Castello. At length the day came which was to give my lord to the cold and silent tomb: his obsequies were splendid in the extreme; the procession was attended by all the vassalage, whose sorrowful countenances, and tearful eyes, added to the solemnity of the scene; while the mournful dirge, chaunted in full chorus, by the monks of the neighbouring Monastery, induced melancholy, and inspired the mind with religious awe. The Duca di Urbino followed the bier of the Marchese, in all the mockery of woe; for he "could frame his face to all occasions;" he could "smile, and murder while he smiled," "and send the murderous Machiavel to school."

"The funeral meats were hardly cold, before the wily Duca di Urbino declared himself protector to the young Fernando, he being the nearest relative, and the chosen friend of the Marchese: this haughty noble was truly obnoxious to the vassals; Benito had cautiously kept the knowledge of my escape from the hands of the assassins secret, and every one of my friends deplored me as being numbered with the dead. I was fast recovering my strength, and my wound was nearly healed, when I was again plunged into an abyss of despondence, at the information that the greater part of the Castello had been consumed by fire, and particularly the wing which the Marchesa inhabited, of whom there was no tidings, and it was supposed she must have perished in the conflagration. The whole race of Lepanto was now threatened with being extinct: the infant Fernando being the only branch who had fortunately escaped the last disasterous accident, no accounts having been ever heard of the Signiora Viola. The Duca di Urbino gave no directions for clearing the ruins of the Castello, or seeking the body of the hapless Marchesa; but immediately retired to the Castello di Urbino, accompanied by the young Marchese and his nurse. I burnt with impatience to come forward and make known to the world my fortunate escape, with the hopes that I might be placed near the person of my young lord, and if necessary, to shield him from villainy; but the more prudent Benito restrained my ardent wishes. 'Perceive you not,' said this most faithful and worthy of beings, 'that the conduct of the Duca di Urbino is enveloped in a veil of mystery, under the seeming garb of openness and honor? Where are all the tried and firm adherents of Lepanto?—Are they placed round the person of the youthful Fernando?—No, but like a distempered flock, are dispersed and scattered through the vast domains of Lepanto and Rivarola. Where are now the proud and lofty turrets of the Castello?—They lie crumbled into dust, and beneath them buried the remains of the noble Marchesa. Why should not those towers, that once boldly bid defiance to the foe, be again reared? Why should not the minstrel's lay again sound through the majestic halls of Lepanto? Why should not the lofty portals of the Castello again be thrown open and the cheering voice of hospitality echo through the vaulted dome? And why should not the son, under his paternal roof, be taught to emulate the virtues of his sire?—It is because the Duca di Urbino never means that he should enjoy the honors of his forefather. Ah, Rhinaldo! believe me when I say I dread some dark, some bloody tragedy has been enacted; and that the Duca di Urbino wears but the specious mask of friendship to our young lord. We are but vassals, and dare not speak our fears, let them be closely locked within in our bosoms; but my friend, my brother, as the true and liege vassals of our departed lord, it is our duty to watch attentively over the young Marchese, and act as occasion offers.' I acknowledged the propriety of Benito's arguments, and promised to be guided entirely by his superior judgment.

"By this time I had recovered my health; and, except the occasional uneasiness I suffered with respect to my young lord, I began to acquire my usual serenity. Near the cottage of Benito, the door of the subterraneous passage opened, which led to the Castello: it was concealed with the utmost care, and its situation was only known to Benito and myself; the small chamber at the entrance of it was deemed a sufficient place of security for me, at any time it might be prudent to conceal myself more closely than customary, and this gave me a facility of communication with the interior of the Castello.

"No intelligence had for a considerable time been brought to the cottage respecting the young Marchese, and dreading lest some accident might have befallen him, it was resolved that I should proceed to the domains of Urbino, and by lurking in the vicinity of the Castello, perhaps be enabled to hear some tidings, that might efface the disagreeable surmises which had destroyed our repose. Without interruption I arrived at my place of destination; and after various unsuccessful efforts, I was informed that the young Fernando generally took the air in the wood with Jacquelina. I made myself thoroughly acquainted with the path they usually frequented: for several days I concealed myself, in the expectation of beholding my young lord, but without effect. Almost despairing of success, I began seriously to think of making an attempt to gain admittance into the Castello; however, fate decided that it was not to be. One evening I repaired as usual to my place of concealment, when my eyes were gladdened with a sight of Jacquelina carrying my young lord, and Sanguinario with her; they silently approached me, and my heart beat high with pleasing emotions; but judge my surprise when I saw the villain Sanguinario snatch the child from the arms of Jacquelina, and bareing its tender bosom, raised his murderous arm to plunge a dagger in its heart; before the steel could reach its destined victim, my sword was pointed at the breast of the remorseless wretch: more savage than the deceitful hyæna, he grasped his innocent prey, and as undaunted as the lion, sustained my impetuous attack. The spirit of my loved lord hovered over me and protected me.—Heaven approved my conduct, and my arm triumphed. Would that Sanguinario had breathed his last on that memorable day. The moment he fell I caught the infant in my arms, and hastened from the spot, fearful of pursuit; but the moment the hurry of my spirits subsided, and reflection returned, my alarm ceased; for it was evident that I had saved from the assassin's blow the heir of Lepanto; and was it to be supposed that such an outrage could have been committed, as the life of the young Fernando having been aimed at, without the privacy of the Duca di Urbino? And that too by his nearest and dearest intimate, the ruthless villain Sanguinario. I carefully avoided the road that was at all liable to be frequented, and conducted my charge in safety to the cottage of Benito. When the old man saw his young lord, and I informed him of his miraculous escape, the tears flowed in streams down the furrows of his cheeks; he alternately grasped my hand, showering down benedictions on my head, and swearing vengeance against the apostate Sanguinario. His daughter, Annette, busied herself in procuring food for the young Marchese, while Ludovico vainly attempted to hush him to repose; between these two amiable, but unfortunate young cottagers, every thing necessary for his comfort was provided.

"Benito and myself passed several days in gloomy silence, as if each felt anxious that the other should propose some plan for the future security of our charge; but at length Benito, ever fertile in expedients, imparted to me his opinion—'Vain indeed, oh, Rhinaldo! would it be for us much longer to offer our protection to the orphan heir of Lepanto, for soon will it be necessary to instil those precepts in his youthful mind, which will tend to make him a great and virtuous man; but our abilities are inadequate to fulfil the arduous task "of teaching the young idea how to shoot." Born to rank and titles, the Marchese of Lepanto and Rivarola should receive an education suitable to the sphere of life in which he is to figure; this, alas! is not in our province; but lend me attentively your ear.—The Marchese di Durazzo you well know was the intimate, the bosom friend of our lamented lord; none of our nobles are more famed for honor and probity, none rise superior to him in dignity and talents; to him would I entrust the sacred duty of cultivating the mind, and protecting the rights of our young lord. But should we proclaim aloud that the Marchese lives, the wily Duca di Urbino and his satellite Sanguinario, would leave no means untried again to possess his person—this very thought chills the warm current of my blood. However, to obviate any fatal consequences that might occur, I will away on the morrow to the Castello di Durazzo, and by the means of Huberto the castellan, I shall be enabled to obtain information when the Marchese di Durazzo exercises in the forest; my intention is then to place our lord in such a situation, that he cannot escape the sight of the Marchese.—I am well assured his benevolent disposition will induce him to have the utmost care taken of the infant: considered as a foundling, the young Fernando will find a safe asylum within the hospitable walls of Durazzo: though it strikes daggers to my soul, that the child of my loved lord should be reduced to the humiliating state of receiving benefits as the unknown, perhaps the unworthy offspring of some guilty wretch. If the Marchese treats the orphan with that liberality for which he is so justly famed, the secret of his birth shall remain closely locked within my bosom, until he shall have attained the years of manhood; then will I buz abroad the news, and kindle such a flame, that shall be only extinguished with the downfall of the Duca di Urbino. Should, however, the Marchese di Durazzo act contrary to my expectations, I will seek a private interview, and reveal the history of Fernando. Independant of his being thus sure of a safe retreat, the castellan Huberto will have it in his power to give us admission within the Castello, whenever we wish to behold the youth. This, Rhinaldo, is the plan I have laid down, and which I mean to carry into effect.'

"I need only say that the whole of this project succeeded entirely to our most sanguine expectations; for no father could have more tenderly loved, or more carefully instructed an only son, than did the Marchese the little foundling.

"Benito had not long returned from the Castello di Durazzo, after executing his commission, when one day, as we were sitting round the social board, the trampling of horses arrested our attention; I had scarcely time to conceal myself in a corner of the apartment, before the Duca di Urbino entered the cottage with his companion Sanguinario.

"'Well, good Benito,' said the Duca, 'it is some time since we have met.' 'It is Duca,' replied Benito, bowing respectfully, 'and since then I am sorry to say that misfortunes have thickened on the hapless house of Lepanto.' 'Too true it is, Benito,' said the Duca, 'that the young Marchese, ill-fated as his sire, has fallen by the hands of some merciless ruffian; long did Sanguinario maintain a dreadful conflict, risking his own life to save that of the infant Fernando, but without avail.' 'Rumour has then,' replied Benito, 'told the tale too accurately, and all is now confirmed?' 'Alas! poor youth,' said the Duca, 'it was an untimely fate!' and here he affected a degree of sorrow, that was foreign to his flinty heart; or perhaps the genuine tears that rolled down the old man's face, or the deep-drawn sigh that burst from his manly bosom, smote the guilty conscience of the Duca, and caused a momentary contrition, but it could have been only a transitory compunction. Silent and sullen, Sanguinario stood frowning. The Duca now appearing to recover from a reverie, into which he had fallen, proceeded to state to Benito, that as he had succeeded to the domains of Lepanto and Rivarola, in consequence of the entire extinction of the late family, he thought it necessary that the vassals should be made acquainted with these changes, and for this purpose had visited the cottage, to direct that this should be made known. Benito, with marked confusion, replied, 'in this you shall be obeyed.'

"Neither Annette or Ludovico had quitted the cottage, but remained almost transfixed at the sight of the haughty Duca.—Blooming as the rose, sportive as the fawn, and chaste as Diana, the pretty Annette was too conspicuous to escape the lustful eye of Urbino.—'who are those young persons?' enquired he. 'The one,' replied Benito, 'is my daughter, the other a neighbouring cottager.' 'I did not know,' said the Duca, 'that the domains of Lepanto produced so much beauty.' Benito acknowledged the compliment with a slight inclination of the head.

"The Duca thus having ended his visit and his conversation, rode off, to the unspeakable satisfaction of all. As soon as it was thought prudent, I quitted my hiding place, but mirth was entirely banished from our frugal board. The Duca, like an evil spirit, wherever he presented himself, his baneful influence was felt. Benito feared for Annette—alas! but too justly; being an only child, all his hopes, his pride, centered in her. A strict intimacy having subsisted between my brother Benito, and the father of Ludovico, he on his death bed left the infant to his charge: no sooner had his remains been interred, than Ludovico became part of the family.—Brought up from his tenderest years with Annette, it was not to be wondered at that he loved her: before he knew the meaning of the word wife, he had been accustomed to call her by that affectionate name; ere she, that of husband, she would fondly encircle his neck with her little arms, and while caressing him, lisp it on his bosom. Thus did these amiable children grow together like two majestic poplars, promising to afford protection to their parent, when in the vale of years; but as by some rude and sudden storm the tendril of the vine is often blighted, so in an instant were this unhappy pair doomed to suffer by the hand of tyranny and power. Nothing had occured from their infancy to give them pain, or to disturb the pure passion they felt for each other. No swain dared approach the lovely Annette, but as the affianced bride of the fortunate Ludovico. Benito had watched their growing attachment and sanctioned it, and the day was not far distant, which was to have seen them united; but the dispensations of Providence are inscrutable.

"One evening at the hour of rest, we separated as usual, Benito to the cottage, and I to my chamber in the subterraneous passage, where I always slept. During the night I was restless, and a sad presentiment of what was about to happen, took possession of my mind.

"The morning came, but it brought no joys for me; alas! it only served to present to my view a scene of horror and of misery.—Judge of my grief and my despair, when as I approached the cottage, I beheld it laid in ruins, and the breathless bodies of Benito and Ludovico, disfigured and mutilated, stretched on the earth, while the peasants appeared to be attentively searching for something more. This sight was almost too much for me, and I nearly sunk to the earth. I returned to my secret chamber, and having disguised myself, mingled with the crowd, when I learned that the cottage had been burnt during the night, and that my unfortunate brother, with Ludovico, had perished in the flames, but no tidings had been gained of Annette; the peasants conceiving that she must have been buried beneath the ruins, assiduously sought for her body, but it was not to be found; this gave rise to various conjectures, but none were so fortunate as to unravel this mysterious affair.

"Dejected, care-worn, and with a bosom fully charged with woe, I gained my retreat, where I had leisure to ponder on the occurrences of the night, and to feed my melancholy with silent and bitter reflection. It would be needless to relate to you all the pangs I felt at the loss of a brother, and at the cruel destiny of the two lovers. Cut off as I now was from the society of the only persons I held dear to me, I felt a pleasure in wandering over the deserted chambers of the Castello, in fact I spent the greater part of my time there though it had been for a long period inhabited by a fierce banditti, who made it their haunt, soon after it had been quitted by the Duca di Urbino.

"Some months had elapsed, when during one of my excursions through the passages, I heard two men in earnest conversation; I gently opened a sliding pannel, when I plainly distinguished two gaunt figures, the lineaments of whose countenances betrayed their avocation. They stood with the door of one of the cells half open, looking earnestly in. 'Is it all over?' said one of them. 'No,' replied the other, 'she still moves.' 'Well,' said the first who had spoken, 'let us put an end to this farce; why stand we idly here, when in an instant the business might be settled?' 'Peace,' said the second, 'she seems as if she breathed no more; the potion has had its due effect, and the Duca need not fear—come, let us retire.' 'Are you certain that she is gone for ever?' asked the first. 'For should we deceive Bernardo, we shall not easily pacify his anger.' 'She is gone,' rejoined the other, and they quitted the vaults. The moment I conceived every thing safe, I stole into the cell, and by the light of an almost expiring lamp, discerned the emaciated form, and pallid face of the inanimate Annette: her body was still warm, but life had for ever fled. Finding I could render her no assistance, I resolved carefully, by means of the secret avenues of the Castello, to gain the part that communicated with the apartment, which the banditti generally used as a banqueting room, in hopes that I might hear the villains report to their leader Bernardo, the fate of the unfortunate Annette. My expectation was fully answered, for I heard the ruffians relate the story of their having administered to her a poisonous dose, and having seen her breath her last. I heard Bernardo communicate this intelligence to the Duca, and I heard the wretch glory in having first destroyed the father and the lover, then having forcibly triumphed over the virtue of an humble village girl; and lastly, in having secured himself against detection by adding one more murder to the catalogue of his crimes. Disgusted with this barbarous conversation, but happy in being in possession of the above facts, I returned to the cell where the body of Annette lay, and raising it in my arms, I conveyed to my secret chamber, and at a convenient opportunity, placed it in one of the sepulchres in the chapel.

"Tired of leading so desultory a life, I journeyed to the domains of Durazzo; and through the medium of Huberto, unobserved, I had the gratification of beholding my young lord improve in talents, in personal beauty, and to excel in manly exercises. To Huberto I confided the account of the fate of Benito and his family; and after obtaining from him an oath of inviolable secrecy, I imparted to him the rank and history of my young lord. Thus passed many years in my alternately visiting the subterraneous Vaults of Lepanto, and enjoying the friendship of Huberto at the Castello Durazzo.

"The time was rapidly approaching when I thought it necessary to reveal who my young lord really was; when the Condi di Vincenti paid a visit to the Castello di Durazzo, and interrupted my design. I also learnt that the Marchese Fernando was to spend some time at Venice, with the Condi di Vincenti. I returned to the secret vaults to arrange my papers, and the various documents I intended to produce of the Duca di Urbino's guilt; but being detained longer than I expected, the young Marchese had commenced his journey for Venice, and being benighted, accidentally sought refuge in the Castello di Lepanto; however, it afforded me an opportunity of warning him against the danger he incurred, by remaining there. It was Urbino and Bernardo who he heard pacing down the corridor, and utter those mysterious words: they had just concluded upon forming the plan how the Signiora Rosara was to be seized upon, and the mode in which they were to secure the Signior Alberto, who was to have been conveyed to one of the cells of the Castello di Lepanto, where he was to have lingered out a life of misery, or have fallen beneath the ruthless ruffian's poignard, as caprice or whim dictated; and this punishment was to have been indicted in consequence of his interfering respecting his sister Rosara.

"After the Marchese Fernando had left the Castello for some hours, I was astonished at the return of Sanguinario, who urged Bernardo and his associates to take horse, that they might attack two travellers. Fearful lest the Marchese should be the intended victim, I followed at a proper distance, and arrived in time to render him my assistance. I thought it necessary to proceed to Venice, as I was convinced he would be surrounded with danger. Cautiously I watched his every step, and again afforded him assistance, on the night the Signior Alberto was wounded. Being constantly in the habit of walking round the grounds of the Palazza, I discovered men of a suspicious appearance every morning near the alcove. Fearful of treachery, I redoubled my vigilance, and though incapable of offering assistance, I saw the Signiora Rosara rudely torn from her father's protection, and carried off by the banditti. Thinking it would be of consequence to notice where she was conveyed, I traced the steps of the ruffians to the Castello di Lepanto, and by means of the secret pannel, saved the life of Signiora Rosara. Knowing that the Duca lay ill from the terror my appearance caused, I hastened to the Castello di Durazzo, and made known to the Marchese, every circumstance relative to the birth and rank of the young Marchese, and through his exertions, we have been enabled again to see the rightful heir of Lepanto restored to his honors and dignities."

Here the old man ceased, and Fernando was profuse in his acknowledgements; when they were informed that the Duca di Urbino could not long struggle against the violent fever and mortification that had taken place.

The Marchese and Condi, accompanied by Fernando, Alberto, and Rhinaldo, repaired to the room where the Duca lay; as soon as they entered, he loudly called out—

"Yes, the chance is thine, thou reptile!—thou comest I suppose to watch my departing spirit, that thou mayest hug thyself in security—my steel, unfaithful to my wishes missed thy heart!—Would I had power now to plunge my dagger to the haft in thy accursed bosom.—I have heard the tale, that thou art the son of that simple fool, the Marchese of Lepanto—my sword pierced his breast, and would it had been plunged in thine!—thy mother too, suffered by this hand.—What art thou there, thou hoary villain?" pointing to the Condi, "thou dost richly deserve to have fallen a victim to my just revenge!—see hell opens its adamantine gates—would I could seize thee by the locks, and plunge thee into the burning abyss!— hear, hear the stunning sounds of woe!—the din of rattling chains! —of clashing whips!—of piercing shrieks!—of groans!—see, see the streaming fires blaze!—now serpents hiss around my head, and curl in horrid wreaths!—This thou hast done, thou damned wretch!" turning to Fernando; "I would, to avenge my fate, and glut my vengeance on thee, court the fiercest pains!—The deepest remorse I feel, is in not having stabbed thy loved Rosara to the heart! as thou whining silly fool dost call her. That fell monster, Sanguinario, has paid the forfeit of his crimes upon the rack.—The villain Hugo too, turned traitor, would that he might suffer all the torments earth can furnish; would that for his crimes he might be racked and gashed, impaled alive, and then his mangled limbs fixed on high to serve the vultures for a feast!—Oh! there goes the spirit of my departed sire—I see the gaping wounds!—hide me from that stern look!—I care not, come again, and torture me with thy looks, I can bear it all!—The cold hand of death is on me—an icy coldness curdles up my blood!—Damned be thou for having inflicted this wound, and damned——" here the wicked Urbino ceased to speak—his black soul took its flight. He died 'desperate to the last, in every passion furious.'

Directions were given that the body of Urbino should be interred; and as soon as Rosara had sufficiently recovered her strength, the whole party set forward for Venice. After a happy and pleasant journey they arrived at the Palazza. Alberto sprung from his horse, and in an instant was in the arms of his beloved Viola.—The two lovers again renewed their protestations of love.

Fernando was now universally acknowledged not only Marchese di Lepanto and Condi di Rivarola, but, being the next heir, Duca di Urbino. Things being thus arranged, Fernando asked the consent of the Condi to lead the blooming Rosara to the altar; Alberto made the same request with respect to Viola; and every thing being finally settled, the day was fixed, and Fernando made happy in the possession of his loved Rosara, and Alberto at the same time in that of his beloved Viola.

Fernando still permitted the Signiora Benvoglio to reside at the Villa, which now devolved to him, considering the helpless state she had been brought to by the villain Urbino.

THE END.